To Edna in loving memory

The Japanese Connection

Enjoy The Book as much as I
Did Writing iT.

Love

Bill McDonald

The Japanese Connection

Bill McDonald

Writers Club Press

San Jose New York Lincoln Shanghai

The Japanese Connection

All Rights Reserved © 2000 by Bill McDonald

Writers Club Press
an imprint of iUniverse.com, Inc.

For information address:
iUniverse.com, Inc.
620 North 48th Street, Suite 201
Lincoln, NE 68504-3467
www.iuniverse.com

ISBN: 0-595-12986-2

Printed in the United States of America

Dedication

To the forgotten heroes and POWs of the Battle of Java Sea

Epigraph

May you be a week in Heaven before the Devil knows you're dead.

—*Old Irish Saying*

Acknowledgements

Many thanks to my friend Gail Moody for the tireless hours she spent editing this book.

Chapter 1

March 1942

On the bridge Captain Mehler, encircled by his subordinates, hovered over naval charts of the surrounding coastline of Java. Radioman Robert Buenger approached.

"Beg pardon sir, it's a coded message from headquarters."

Mehler, aware the message had to be deciphered immediately, turned to Lieutenant J. J. Schilling and barked out an order. "Find Commander Doll and have him report to my quarters forthwith!"

"Aye, aye, sir!" Schilling replied.

Mehler, a career sailor who graduated from the Academy eighteen years earlier, stood five ten. He was heavy-set in stature and ran a tight ship. His crew surreptitiously referred to him as "Hard-Ass Mehler." At Pearl Harbor, where the top commanders headquartered, he was known as one of the best statisticians in the Pacific.

Quickly returning to his quarters he opened the safe, removed the codebook and deciphered the code. He was concerned about the orders he just received, believing in fighting to the end, not running. The code translated said, "Powerful Japanese invasion force heading for Java supported by the Japanese Navy. Odds too great. All ABDA ships are to return to Brisbane immediately. Break your group up. Advise the four American destroyers to take the Flores Sea route. The *Stuart, Alice Springs,* and the *Helensborough* the Sunda Straits. Notify all ship's captains at today's staff meeting. May God be with you." Signed, Admiral George Carpenter, Royal Australian Navy.

Mehler heard a knock on his cabin door as he stared pensively at the message in his hand. It was his executive officer Commander William

Doll. "Okay to come in, John?" (When alone, the old friends called each other by their first names; otherwise, respect for Navy tradition was the order of the day.)

Mehler opened the door, saying, "I just deciphered a coded message from Brisbane. We're to return to Australia immediately."

Smiling, the sandy-haired executive officer replied, "John, that's the best news I've heard in months."

"I don't like it, Bill. We're letting down the Dutch and telling them to carry the ball alone."

"You're talking from your heart, not your head. It's inevitable Java will be conquered by the Japanese just like all the other countries. John, we're not letting them down, we're going to Australia to have more anti-aircraft guns mounted, pick up some better equipment, and, with the addition of a couple of carriers, when we return it will be our turn to kick ass."

"I know what you're saying makes a lot of sense. Without Naval support the Japs will land at will, but I can't help feeling guilty."

"How did the message read, Skipper?" Doll asked.

"They broke us up into two codes, five and six. Code six is to go by the Flores Sea. At the staff meeting today, during lunch, I'm supposed to inform the ship's captains which route they're taking."

"I hope we weren't given Sunda Strait," Doll said.

"We were, along with the British destroyer, *Helensborough*, and the Aussie frigate, *Alice Springs*."

"I don't get it, John. Why aren't we all going by the Flores Sea? It's the shortest route."

"Command in Brisbane seems to think the entire Japanese fleet is in the Java Sea and has the idea if we break up at least half will get through. My guess is the four tin cans are taking the Flores Sea route because they are out of torpedoes. I noticed the Dutch allowed us all the shells we requested. At the time I thought it was because we would be the lead ship in the ABDA fleet; now I know it's because we're taking the toughest route."

Doll then added, "I was slow to respond to your orders because I was off the ship in the office of the Dutch commander. He told me they were short of fuel, so he was only allowing us enough to fill our tanks half way. I bitched, but it did no good. Now I understand why. No doubt he was taking orders from Brisbane. Hell, we got more than enough to make the Australian port."

The wall clock read eleven bells. Mehler put his arm around his Naval Academy classmate and said, "We better get ready for lunch, Bill. Our guests will be joining us soon."

"Aye, aye, Skipper!" his executive officer answered.

At 1600 hours, the *Stuart*, *Helensborough*, and the *Alice Springs* set sail for Sunda Strait. The *Helensborough* was chosen as the picket ship, being the fastest. Captain Mehler calculated the distance at 450 miles. By going 35 knots, it would take ten to twelve hours to reach the Straits. In a few hours it would be dark, allowing them to sneak through the enemy fleet. The one disadvantage was a full moon.

Hugging the coastline, the big cruiser moved along at her objective speed. The sea was calm with no enemy in sight. As they passed close to the Village of Cirebon, their luck changed. Sitting off the coastline was an enemy destroyer who immediately spotted the three Allied ships, and slipped in behind the *Stuart* while radioing ahead to their flagship, "Three enemy warships approaching the Straits."

At 0500, naval gunfire erupted. The British destroyer had met the enemy. Seconds later, she signaled to the Australian frigate and the *Stuart* that she was under heavy fire.

Mehler ordered the alarm sounded for battle stations. Below deck, four boatswains, Donovan, Alexander, Hughes and Shulmelda jumped down out of their hammocks and headed for the number two eight-inch gun turret.

Mehler knew his ship was under attack. His guns opened fire, damaging the enemy vessel that had launched several torpedoes. The crew managed to zigzag to outmaneuver the torpedoes. They had been in this situation before and were highly skilled in warding off the enemy.

A second destroyer came in for a second run. Once again the *Stuart* scored a hit and once again several torpedoes were launched, all missing but one. She took a direct hit knocking out one of her eight-inch guns. During the third run, she hit two destroyers before taking another hit. Two gun crews had been killed and countless wounded.

Mehler ordered a smoke signal to throw off the enemy and allow for a short break before engaging in battle once more. When the smoke cleared, the enemy cruisers moved in closer and opened fire with their big guns.

The *Stuart* took several hits in her aft, mid, and forward sections, leaving only one of her guns operable. Hitting one of the cruisers with the last of her shells, the *Stuart* was now out of ammunition. Fires were breaking out all over the ship and her gallant crew was attempting to put them out.

Two decks below, the loading crew of the forward eight-inch gun had passed up the last shell. The time was 0528 hours. Unknown to them, the other guns had been knocked out in the battle; the *Stuart* had no firepower left.

The loading crew had worked in a temperature of 120 degrees for the past twenty-eight minutes. Knowing that their ship had been fighting for its life, they passed the heavy shells without a second thought. The steel deck was slippery from their sweat and they were dirty and exhausted, thankful for a moment of relaxation.

The enemy destroyers, knowing she was helpless, made a third run firing at will. Captain Mehler was sickened by the sight of his men lying on deck—most of them dead, but others bleeding to death and crying for help. Reluctantly, he ordered the bugler to blow the call to abandon ship.

Over the loudspeaker in the ammo compartment, the ship's bugler blew out the call; the one every sailor hopes he will never hear. The men looked at each other, some terrified, some stunned, others shocked.

The first swabby to acknowledge the call was young Johnny Hughes, a seventeen-year-old boatswain striker, who hollered out, "Abandon ship! Abandon ship!" No sooner had the words passed the young sailor's lips, the big ship listed, throwing all twelve sailors up against the steel bulkhead. Big Tex Shulmelda, a third class boatswain mate, yelled, "Let's get topside before we're all fish bait!"

Dale Alexander, the team leader and Boatswain Mate First Class, agreed, but added, " First we go up to the next deck and grab ourselves a large mess table, big enough for the four of us to hang onto."

"What for? Ain't we got life jackets?" the Hughes kid asked.

Dennis Donovan, the fourth member of the boatswain team, put his arm around the young striker and answered, "Johnny, for over a year the old man has asked the Navy for new life jackets. The ones we have are old. How the hell do we know how long they will last before they become water-soaked?"

Alexander led his team up one deck, and then headed forward to the mess hall. Two tables remained, indicating others had the same idea. Quickly Shulmelda took one end, Donovan the other, and moved toward the ship's ladder. Alexander and Hughes followed. The *Stuart* began to list, throwing all four of them off the ladder and across the deck. Shulmelda and Donovan once again picked up the table, this time making it topside before she listed for the third and final time.

They were stunned upon their arrival on deck to see what a beating their ship had taken. Bodies were strewn everywhere, some still alive, most dead. Those alive were lying in pools of blood, many with missing limbs, crying out for help. All the gun turrets were knocked out; the only one still operational was the one they had been assigned to. They felt very fortunate indeed their lives had been spared.

Young Johnny Hughes stumbled and looked down to see the body of a dead sailor with half his head blown away. The others were able to control their response to the devastation around them. Not so young Hughes, who promptly proceeded to puke his guts out. Donovan put his arm around the kid's shoulders and asked, "You okay, Johnny?"

"Yeah, Dennis, I'm fine. Can't we do something to help these poor bastards?"

"Kid, we got about a minute, maybe less, to save our own ass. Take off your shoes and tie them around your neck."

"What for?" the kid asked.

"You'll find out when we hit land. Make sure you tie a good knot. If you lose your shoes, you'll be sorry, lad."

The four of them stood together. Another shell hit forward, rocking the big ship. It was time to go over the side. Grabbing the table, they heaved it overboard and jumped into the water.

The full moon worked against them since it lighted up the area like a roman candle. All around they could see silhouettes of men, some on rafts, others grabbing onto anything that floated past. Men were calling out to their shipmates, others hollering not to leave them because they couldn't swim.

Alexander took charge of the group and hollered for them to paddle so that they could get far enough away so that when the big ship went down, they wouldn't be sucked in with it. When he felt they were at a safe distance, he told them to stop. No one said a word as they watched the once mighty *Stuart* stand upward, then take her final plunge. In all their minds was one thought, "God bless the living that are going to their death."

They were fortunate; many of the wounded were too badly hurt to help themselves. Although they could not make out faces, they could hear men talking to each other. Time suddenly became a factor. Seconds became minutes, minutes hours. Where were they? How far from land?

They had no water, no food, and could only hope the current wasn't taking them away from the Island of Java and out to sea.

In the distance a motor was heard. Alexander whispered, "It's probably a Jap motor launch looking for their own survivors. Duck under the table and hold your breath."

The kid didn't agree and said, "Why not let them capture us? I'd rather be a prisoner of war than drowned like a rat."

Tex Shulmelda, the muscleman of the group who resembled Victor McLaughlin, the old-time movie star, answered the kid, "After what happened at Pearl, do you really believe we can trust these bastards?"

The engines from the launch became louder. In the distance they could see a floodlight as they scanned the water. Alexander then gave the word, "Everybody under the water!"

Seconds later the enemy gunboat was on top of them. All her floodlights observed was a large, floating mess table. When they came up for air, the engines began to fade away. Suddenly, they heard machine-gun fire. All they could think was that the gunboat had opened fire on their shipmates. Although no one said a word to young Hughes, he now realized that Shulmelda had given them good advice.

Dawn finally arrived, and they spotted land in the distance. Alexander asked, "Can all of you swim?" They all nodded, yes. "Then I suggest we swim and stay close together. The tide is with us. If anyone gets into trouble, we can help each other."

Donovan shouted, "Then let's swim!" Hughes and Shulmelda hooted in agreement.

Two hours later they reached the beach and fell asleep, exhausted. It was now 0900 hours.

Chapter 2

Island of Java

Donovan was the first to awaken. Lying on his belly he looked over to the end of the beach and saw three Javanese natives with machetes, standing under a palm tree. The Dutch still held the island and he assumed they were friendly, so he shouted to them, "Americans! Friends!"

The natives backed away and disappeared into the brush. His shouting awoke the others. Alexander asked him, "What are you doing?"

"I seen some natives, called to them, and they took off. Must have scared them. At least we know there's a native village nearby."

Although somewhat rested, the sailors were both hungry and thirsty. A short distance from the beach they found a narrow road with a sign on one of the trees that said, "BORGER 70 Miles South, BATAVIA 100 Miles East of Serang."

Shulmelda was the first to give an opinion, saying, "The Jap fleet was off the coast. My guess is they landed troops. If we head for either Batavia or any Serang coast cities, we may walk into an ambush. I say we head inland to the hills."

"You may be right. On the other hand, we have no water or food. Dutch troops are on the island. I say we head for the larger city, Batavia," Alexander said in disagreement.

"Let's take a vote," Shulmelda said.

The vote was three to one to head east to Batavia. The road was narrow. Tall trees lined each side. After walking several miles, Hughes put his arm around Donovan and said, "Thanks for telling me to hang onto my shoes."

Suddenly the four sailors found themselves surrounded by Japanese soldiers. They were small of stature, somewhere between five-three and five-five and looked amazed at the height of the four Americans. They had rifles with fixed bayonets. One had two stripes and appeared to be the leader. He shouted, "Tomare! Tomare!"

Donovan said, "Now I know why those fucking natives took off. They sold us out."

The lead guard hit him on the side of the head with his gun butt, knocking the jovial Irishman to the ground. Tex Shulmelda was about to go after the little man when Alexander grabbed his arm. "No," he whispered, "hold your temper, Tex, those bastards have real bullets in those rifles."

Johnny Hughes helped Donovan up off the ground, handing him a handkerchief to stop the bleeding. Then the two-stripe corporal shouted out orders, "Oguku, oguku, oguku!" Although none of the sailors knew what he was saying, they understood when the other guards pointed their rifles north, that they meant to move.

Marching along the road at a fast pace, the Japs shouted, "Speedo, speedo, speedo!" A word they would never forget, hearing it over and over again for the next three and a half years.

Five miles later, without a word, the Japanese soldiers took out water canteens and took a drink. None was offered to the sailors. In the distance they could see ships in the harbor and dozens of barges coming in carrying equipment while Javanese natives and survivors of the *Stuart*, *Helensborough*, and the *Alice Springs* were unloading others. It was then they realized Java had fallen to the enemy.

They were immediately put to work unloading barges. Ten hours later, exhausted, they were given their first meal, a cup of rice and a can of water. Close to midnight, they began to march again. This time it wasn't in the hot sun, but with no sleep and very little to eat the eight mile hike seemed more like twenty. Entering the village of Borger, they were hustled into a large brick building that had been used by the Dutch for storage.

The building consisted of two floors; both wide open with a small room. This was to become a guardhouse where the Japanese could monitor the POWs. Two bathrooms, each outfitted with two sit-down toilets and two stand-up latrines, were the only luxury. Seven hundred men were jostled together on each floor. There was no room for cots, so each man was supplied with a blanket and slept on concrete. Cooking utensils consisted of a tin cup and tin plate.

To maintain law and order, the two highest-ranking officers were put in charge on each floor. The prisoners were mostly British and Australian soldiers; the only "Yanks" were from the *Stuart*. Lt. Colonel Gordon Cooper, Royal Scots, was in charge of the first floor; Captain John Mehler, the second.

The Japanese only allowed the water spigot to be open for two hours at night. Men had to line up to fill their tin cups. Bathing was out of the question. Once a week they were taken to another building that had rain barrels on the roof to bathe.

They considered the conditions horrendous, but many would soon be transferred to other camps and would longingly remember how it had resembled a country club under Lt. Saito, compared to what they now faced.

Early the next morning, still dead tired from the grueling day before, the prisoners were brought out into an open yard. Lt. Saito and a Japanese sergeant stood on a platform with Cooper and Mehler behind them. The sergeant was tall, standing five ten, and he carried a silver swagger stick under his arm. Saito wore a clean uniform with leggings and high boots. He had a pleasant face and it was later learned he received his college education at UCLA in California. His English was close to flawless.

Talking through a bullhorn, he began, "My name is Lt. Iwate Saito of the Imperial Japanese Army. To my left is my number one sergeant. His name is Oki Tashino. For the next few years you will see a lot of him, since he is in charge in the fields." Pointing to the two Allied officers he continued his speech, "You all know Col. Cooper and Captain Mehler. It will be up to them to restore discipline within your ranks. Our rules are simple. We rise at 6:30, eat at 7:00, and then work in the fields. Here at Borger, we have many fields to harvest. You will work in rice fields, corn, tea and tobacco fields from sunup to sundown. Your meals will consist of rice, fish heads and soup. You will be counted in groups of ten. If one of you even attempts to escape, the Japanese rules are you and one of your brothers will die. So, if you're thinking of escaping, remember, you will have the death of your brothers on your consciences."

Saito paused for a moment, and then continued, "You are prisoners of war. To most Americans the Japanese soldier is an inferior yellow man who can only defeat the Chinese, and is inferior to the white race. I know what I am saying is correct, having lived for several years in your country.

"As for myself, I believe in the Geneva Convention and will allow you such rights. The Convention states that officers are not to work; therefore, they will be your supervisors in the fields. If, however, they fail to perform their duties, we will have no alternative but to put them in the fields alongside you. Our rules are simple. If you obey, you live. Disobey, you will die.

"One last item very important to the Japanese: We bow to our superiors, family elders, and sometimes to each other to show our respect. You will bow at all times to both the Japanese and Korean guards to show them respect. If you should fail to do so, you will be punished. I am now turning you over to Sergeant Oki Tashino."

The Allied soldiers and sailors were surprised to see such low ranking officers in charge of the camp. In reality, both Tashino and Saito were heroes who fought for their emperor in China and had both been severely wounded. Tashino still walked with a limp. Since they were no longer fit for combat, they served as camp overseers.

Like Saito, Tashino also spoke fluent English, having grown up in Hawaii where his parents were servants for the Japanese ambassador. A brutal man with little patience, he often used the steel swagger stick to beat the Japanese and Korean guards when they displeased him. It was not an uncommon practice in the Japanese Army and was accepted as part of the Oriental way of life.

Introduced by his commanding officer, he addressed the POWS "Like the Commandant told you, the order of the day will be handed out each morning. You will be assigned to the field where we need you most. You are not here on holiday. Much of what we harvest is sent to Japan. We work from sunup to sundown, six days a week. If we fall behind production, we will work seven days a week. You are not guests. You are our enemy. Anyone that slacks off will be whipped. You will be shot if you try to escape. Fail to bow to us and you will be clobbered. If you're caught stealing or using a radio transmitter, you will be put in the "hot box," an instrument we use to break your will. I hope I have made myself perfectly clear. Now fall into lines of ten for today's assignment."

Donovan whispered to Alexander, "Sounds to me like this guy is going to be a bastard to work for."

Shulmelda, standing on the other side of Alexander, whispered, "Fucking officers, they always step in shit."

The crew of the *Stuart* found the long day working in the hot sun grueling. They had little time to talk and if they did, the guard clobbered them with the butt of his gun. They all looked forward to working in the rice paddies. Standing in water up to their knees, it was easy to slip and fall to cool off when the sun became unbearable. Also, they had a chance to talk to each other since the guards did not want to wade through the mud.

They were only in camp a few weeks when all hell broke loose. At roll call Johnny Hughes, half asleep, gave one of the Korean guards a half-assed bow. The guard hit him in the back of the head with the butt of his rifle, knocking him unconscious. Tex angrily hit the guard square on the chin knocking him half way across the yard. Tashino, seeing the incident, blew his whistle, bringing attention to a dozen guards. Several of the guards attacked Shulmelda. Ben Ramondi, a gunner's mate along with Donovan and Alexander, went to the aid of the big Texan. Drawing his revolver, the sergeant fired, hitting Ramondi in the head.

Lieutenant Saito was in his quarters when he heard the alarm and came running, arriving about the time Tashino fired the shot. The sailors were fortunate, since Tashino was not a man who believed in a trial. Saito allowed them a hearing in which they were sentenced to the "hot box"—Alexander and Donovan for ten days, Tex Shulmelda and Johnny Hughes for two weeks.

The box was five feet in length and three feet high with only one small window in front covered with wire mesh. To fit, the men had to lie down with their knees up to their chests. Mosquitoes ate them alive at night and during the day the sun boiled them alive. The natives called the box the coffin, since it looked like one and served the same purpose. Chances of survival were fifty-fifty.

The daily ration was a small ball of rice and a half-cup of water. Although Sergeant Tashino wasn't happy that Lieutenant Saito allowed them outside the box for thirty minutes a day, he followed orders, knowing never to question a superior officer.

When they first got out of the box, it took them five minutes just to stand. Saito knew if they stayed in the coffin for any length of time, it was possible they may never walk again.

Thirst was the hardest part of the punishment. Dehydration was imminent. The heat of the day by noon was 110 degrees. They were cooped up like rats in a cage.

Although the four of them survived through the help of a Japanese guard, by the end of the war only three of them would return home.

Chapter 3

Borger, Java—1942

The month of August was coming to an end. They had been imprisoned six months in the POW camp in Borger. They had all been allowed to write one letter, but no mail or Red Cross packages had arrived from home, at least none were delivered to them. This was a violation of the Geneva Convention. Once weekly the officers met with Lieutenant Saito at his headquarters to air out complaints, but when the complaints came up regarding mail he would change the subject.

The POWs were treated poorly, not according to the rules of the Geneva Convention. Each day they were up at dawn. After breakfast they were taken out to the sugar cane fields or the iron ore mines to work, not returning until dusk. It hadn't rained in Borger for the past three months, and working in 120-degree weather, six days a week, or in the hot sticky mines was unbearable.

True, Saito had his good points. They did receive water breaks twice a day and meals were served three times daily, but the same rice, soup, and fish heads became monotonous and the portions were always small.

In a few days the monsoon season would change the dry weather to constant rain and winds. Many of the POWs were looking forward to the rainy season, believing it would slow down the tedious long working day. Others disagreed, believing the rains would cause muddy roads and sickness.

In the evenings with nothing to do, many played dominoes and cards. Others gathered in small groups, talking about their families, love lives, their hometown, or sports. Donovan's bed was next to Walt Eilers, a signalman and walking encyclopedia. As a swabby, Donovan lived for wine, women, and fighting when on shore leave. He never really understood why Japan declared war on the United States. Eilers tried explaining to him the facts about the European war and why the Japanese government declared war. He was amazed with the fact that Japan was only the size of the state of California and had the balls to attack the giant United States of America.

Returning from the day's work detail on August 27th, Sergeant Tashino made an announcement at roll call. The next morning after breakfast everyone was to return to their barracks and pack their belongings. Only articles allowed by the Japanese Imperial Army were to be taken along with them when they departed at 8:00 a.m. sharp. No further details were given as to why they were leaving or where they were going.

Later that evening the rumors began to spread through the barracks. They heard that Barracks One, which was their home, was joining with Barracks Two, under the command of Lieutenant Udea, Japan being the destination.

Whispering softly so the guard wouldn't overhear him, Tex said, "I guess that son of a bitch is going with us."

Several of the men nodded in agreement. Then Tommy Ryan added, "I wonder if we are going to Japan."

Mike Keeley answered him, "Does it matter? By morning someone will start another shithouse rumor that we're going somewhere else."

Laughing in agreement, George Fecke added, "Be nice if one of our mates started a rumor we were going home."

❉   ❉   ❉

The Japanese conquered all of Asia and were contemplating the invasion of Australia and New Zealand. The troops used to guard the 100,000 POWs were by far considered elite soldiers. Most of them were poor combat quality. Added to the group were Korean Army volunteers, who in trying to please their superiors, were usually far more brutal than the Japanese soldiers. The officers were mostly businessmen from good families and knew little about army life. The sergeants were hand picked and many of them had served in the China Campaign where they had brutalized soldiers and civilians of the Republic of China. They would be the key to maintaining the fear between the Japanese and Korean soldiers. In the Japanese Army it was common for an officer or a sergeant to beat a private with his swagger stick if he was displeased with him. In turn, the soldiers of the emperor, when beaten by their superiors, took it out on the POWs.

❉   ❉   ❉

August 28th was another hot day, but thankfully they were marching in the morning. Although still hot, it would feel cool compared to the afternoon boiling sun. Their destination was Batavia, 50 miles from Borger. Sergeant Tashino's group was the first to pull out, followed an hour later by Lieutenant Udea's men. He was on horseback and rode up and down the marching columns of men, shouting, "Oguku! Oguku!" Each time he shouted, the guards would hit some of the men with their bamboo sticks to please their commanding officer. There were two hundred Americans in the march. The other eight hundred were Brits and Aussies. They marched for a little less than four days before arriving at the outskirts of the city, then continued marching through the city and onto a large pier. Two freighters awaited the POWs to board.

The prisoners were lined up on the dock, each man was given a ball of rice and his can was filled with water. It would be the last meal of the day. The POWs stood gazing at the ship called the *Bay of Toymana*. They could not believe it could float. Both its hull and outside frame were a bucket of rust. It had been built in 1927. For the past twenty years it had been used to carry sugar from Java to Japan. It was chosen because of its large cargo hole, which would jam a thousand men into it for the long 1800-mile journey to Thailand. After the war they learned that Barracks Two, consisting of fifty *Stuart* sailors, were sent to Japan to work in the factories.

Boarding was no problem until they reached the cargo hole. Then the Japanese forced them below, resulting in pushing and shoving. Many of the men were separated from their mates. Donovan and Hughes managed to stay together. Alexander found himself circled by a group of Brits. Shulmelda landed with the Aussies.

Dale Alexander, standing alongside a tall, rawboned Brit who resembled the movie star Gary Cooper, nodded, giving a sign of a friendly gesture. The soldier smiled, and then said, "Haven't seen you about, mate. What outfit are you with?"

"US Navy. I'm off the cruiser, *Stuart.*"

"You're one of them Yanks that were on the other side of the barracks. Pleased to meet you, chum. My name is Conrad."

"Mine's Dale. Pleasure's all mine, with the exception of where we are. What's your outfit, Conrad?"

"His Majesty's Imperial Guards."

"I heard of them. They have a hell of a reputation."

"Right so. We gave them a bloody fight, but we never had a chance. They overrun us with men and fighting equipment. What about your ship?"

"Same. We sunk a few of them before we went down fighting half the Japanese Navy."

"Where are you from in the States?"

"Brooklyn, New York."

"Oh, I know all about Brooklyn. My lady and I love the picture shows. We love the way you Yanks know how to make movies."

"So, how do you know all about Brooklyn?"

"We saw 'The Dead End Kids.' Is Brooklyn really like they showed in the pictures?"

Dale laughed to himself to think that this Brit thought that the east side of New York was Brooklyn. No sense in explaining the difference. "No, Conrad. The 'Dead End Kids' were a gang that

Hollywood made up. You know, a gimmick to sell the movie. So, where are you from in England?"

"Liverpool. Have you ever heard of it?"

"Sure. Liverpool's a big city." Changing the subject, Dale asked, "Heard any rumors where we're going? We heard Japan."

"We're going to Thailand, Dale, not Japan."

"I hope you're right. From what I've seen of the Japanese so far, I don't believe Japan is the place to be. Who knows? Both are only shithouse rumors. We could be going anywhere."

"Thailand is not a rumor. It's a fact."

"Where did that information come from?" Dale asked.

"Enough questions, Yank. Let's change the subject."

Unknown to Dale, the Brits and Aussies had a wireless. They were aware help was needed in Thailand and picked up information that thousands of POWs were being shipped there for that purpose. The wireless was kept a secret. If found, the men would be executed immediately. In order to get it into Thailand without being caught it was taken apart and was being carried by over a dozen men, each with a small part.

Before the POWs boarded the freighter, wooden boxes had been lined up alongside the bulkheads on both sides of the ship. Filled with sand, they were to be used as latrines. The Japanese knew it would cause a stench below; however, sanitary conditions were something they did not take into consideration. Packed in like cattle, they had little oxygen below. The cargo hatch was left open to give them the extra oxygen needed. The soldiers above deck were assigned to guard and make certain that anyone attempting to come up on deck would be pushed back down by the butts of their guns. A few with claustrophobia went berserk and were clubbed making the attempt.

The voyage at sea for the first eight days was smooth. The old freighter made the two hundred miles a day that was required. On the morning of the ninth day, shortly after entering the Bay of Siam, the wind began to pick up, followed by rain. Within a half hour the first monsoon of the season had hit them.

Below deck the men were thrown from side to side with the rolling ship, many of them becoming sick and heaving all over themselves and their mates. The stench from the latrines alone was enough to make them sick, not to mention the vomiting; the cargo hole had the odor of a cesspool. Some didn't care if they died, and some did die.

On the twelfth day the freighter docked in Thailand. As they came out of the hatch, the POWs were watered down by a heavy-duty hose to clean them up and take away the heavy, pervasive odor. On the dock they fell in for roll call, to find five had died at sea. Outside of the dock the POWs observed only a small village with no name. The sign on the dock said "Ban Pang" and an arrow pointed north. It had been raining and the ground was a sea of mud.

It was early morning as they marched along the road, dragging their feet in the heavy marsh. Two hours later they entered the village of Ban Pang, which consisted of a few stores surrounded by native huts. The Japanese called a halt and took several of the POWs out of the line to carry supplies and put them onto army trucks waiting to be loaded. Ban Pang was the only village between here and their destination.

The march began once again. The rain changed from a light drizzle into a heavy downpour. Walking in the mud slowed them down and bogged down the trucks. Tashino called a halt and moved all the troops off the road under the elephant trees. Although an occasional raindrop hit, they were oblivious to the downpour and were living in luxury for the first time in two weeks, lying on the ground and resting their bodies. Two hours later the heavy downpour dropped back to a drizzle and they were once again ordered to move out. The heavy rain made the footing tougher than ever. It seemed like they were walking on suction shoes.

Entering the outskirts of the village of Kanchangburi it appeared to look like Ban Pang. The big difference was that this was an enemy post. They observed a tall lookout post with a searchlight on top, then past several barracks occupied by the Japanese and Korean guards. A short distance down the road was about fifteen barracks built of bamboo with palms for roof tiles. As they passed, a few sad-looking soldiers gave them a slow wave of the hands like they were saying "you poor bastards." Once past the village they passed several hundred men, most of them looking like they hadn't bathed or eaten in weeks. They were Brits and Aussies brought from Singapore to build a railroad called by the Japanese the "Siam-Burma." It would be two hundred miles long, and the purpose was to link up with the already established Burma Railroad. The linkup, when completed, would be the gateway for the invasion of India.

The rains subsided shortly past seven in the evening, too late to do any hard labor. Once again ordered off the road to where the trees were, they slept on the ground, to them a luxury, and the second time in one day they were able to relax since leaving Java.

Awakened at dawn, they were told they had work to do. From across the stream over one hundred coolies came to join in with them to build the bamboo barracks. Orders had been given by the Japanese to assist the prisoners to build the barracks they would be living in for the next few months. The natives were rounded up by the Japanese in Java, Cambodia, Thailand, and Indo China to be used as slave laborers. To them the natives were coolie laborers who were considered nomads, and they could care less if they lived or died. Having lived in the jungle all their lives, they had the know-how to build bamboo huts and barracks at a fast pace. By nightfall of day one, five were completed, each to house two hundred men.

The POWs were assigned to do the so-called skilled work on the building of the railroad. Some carried logs to the sawmills and others cut them up to make the rails and the tie rails. Due to the shortage of steel, hardwood from the trees was used. The Japanese engineers were not equipped for the task of building the two hundred mile railroad in one year, the date set by their high command. British, Aussie, New Zealand, and Canadian engineers were asked to help and reluctantly did so.

The coolies paved the way for the railroad by cutting away brush, working through swamps and cutting down the large hardwood trees. Hundreds of them died, being bitten by poisonous water snakes, others by large falling trees, and many by starvation. At day's end, the dead were piled on the side of the road and the natives would dig a large hole to dump the bodies of the coolies, and then cover them with mounds of dirt. Many only half dead, but useless to the enemy, were buried alive. Many lives were lost due to the inconsistency of planning by the Japanese engineers.

The soldiers only knew one word, and throughout the long day screamed it over and over, "Speedo! Speedo!" Telling the POWs to move, move, move. Hitting the prisoners became a way of life. The meals were sparse and so was the water; still, they expected the POWs to perform like they were well-fed workers. As one POW, an engineer from the New Zealand Royal Engineers, put it, "The bloody idiots. They starve us, beat us, work us fourteen to sixteen hours a day, six days a week, give us no bloody medical attention, and shout 'Speedo! Speedo!' at us all day long. If the bloody fools had any brains at all, they would work us a normal day, feed us, look after our sick, and we could build their railroad in three months. The way we're going, we'll be lucky if we finish it in a year."

About a week after the workers were organized into what jobs were expected of them, Tashino visited each barracks and made his speech. Each speech was the same. Although only a sergeant, he was the senior sergeant with a reputation of getting the job done. General Takada was given the undertaking to pick the right men who knew how to get the most out of the prisoners and to put fear into the guards that if they didn't do their jobs properly they would be beaten. Most of the officers were glad to remain in the barracks sitting under a ceiling fan. They were more than happy to let the brutal sergeant do the dirty work.

As Tashino entered the barracks containing a good part of the *Stuart* sailors, the guards called out with a scream words not known to any of the POWs. However, they knew a person important to the guards was entering. The guards bowed, followed by all the POWs. An assistant to Tashino carried a wooden box and placed it in the front of the room. Standing on the box, he could see clearly over the heads of all the men. He played with his steel swagger stick, and then giving his leg a light tap with the stick, began his speech.

"You are no longer in Java. Many of you took advantage of the easy life in Borger and shirked your duties. Our commandant, General Takada, is a soldier who fought in China for the Emperor and was awarded one of Japan's highest medals. His job, given to him by the Emperor, is to finish the two hundred mile railroad in one year. It will be done. Like in Java, our gracious commandant will allow your officers to supervise your labor. If, however, they do not produce, they too will be put on the work force. Some of you may be thinking of escape. To enlighten you, first you would have to bribe the Thai natives who live across the stream. Providing you do, they in turn would sell the information to us, as we have promised them double anything you can offer. Without a machete it would be impossible to hack your way through the jungle. If you did manage to bribe a native for a machete, you would have to fight off wild animals, poisonous snakes, and quicksand. Not knowing the jungle, you would not last twenty-four hours. If you do escape and you are caught, you will be put to death along with an innocent comrade. You are to bow when passing or talking with a guard or one of my sergeants. If you fail to, you will be whipped. We have no 'hot box' here in the jungle. The jungle is the hot box. We have promised the emperor this railroad will be built in one year or less. We will keep that promise. Now, are there any questions?"

Captain Mehler stepped forward, graciously bowed to Tashino, then said, "We are underfed and your guards beat our men for no reason. In many cases the sick bay is lacking medical supplies. We work in the jungle in torrid heat from sunup to sunset six days a week. If you expect my men to work, you will have to see to it they are treated like human beings."

Tashino looked down from his box at the Navy Captain, and then replied, "You are not guests here, Captain. You are prisoners. How dare you question the way the Japanese Imperial Army operates this camp! My men eat the same food as yours. They are out in the hot sun just as long. If your men do their work, we will treat them right. If not, they will die."

Stepping down off his box, his aide picked it up and followed him out of the barracks.

※　　　　　※　　　　　※

Although Tashino didn't forget the incident in Java, because of his duties he could not concentrate on the few men involved in the fight with his men who should have died for what they did, and would have if a weakling like Lieutenant Saito were not the commanding officer. His hate for Americans sometimes caused him to make bad decisions. The railroad had to be built, that was the first priority; nevertheless, he made it a point to inform the sergeants under his command to see to it that the boatswains receive harsh treatment whenever possible.

The long days became unbearable, and the daily death toll continued to rise. The jungle was beginning to take its toll on the POWs with the long days in the hot sun, the bugs biting them during the day and at night, along with the lack of water and the small portions of food served to them. Men began to lose weight, many coming down with malaria, beriberi, tropical ulcers, and a few with the killer disease, cholera. When they did come down with cholera, orders were given to immediately have them incinerated, along with their clothes. As cruel as it sounds, cholera spread so fast that it could easily have wiped out the entire POW camp, along with the Japanese guards. Another form of death was starvation. The Japanese were small people and it was true the diet of

· 23 ·

rice, fish heads, soup and potatoes were enough for them. Still, the POWs received a smaller portion than the guards, yet they were much bigger men who required more food.

※　　　　　　　　※　　　　　　　　※

The first of the boatswains to feel the brunt was Dale Alexander. Every morning at roll call, the sick would report to the British doctors in a large tent. If the POW had a curable disease he was treated, and within a week or so returned to work. If not, he was sent to the hospital where ninety percent of them died because no medical supplies were allotted to the hospital. The ones that lived were men who had good friends or a loyal mucker. In the case of the Yanks it was friends; the British and Aussies called a loyal buddy a "mucker."

Men who came down with malaria were reluctant to report to sick bay in the event the doctors found they had beriberi or tropical ulcers along with the malaria. This would mean the hospital and almost certain death. Dale had come down with malaria and kept it to himself. His work slowed down, giving the sergeant a cause to have him whipped. At dusk Hughes and Tex helped him back to camp.

In the barracks Hughes said, "You're going to sick bay."

"No way," he answered. "I think I have more than just malaria. If I do, it's the hospital, then death."

Tex Shulmelda picked him up bodily and said, "Let's go, Johnny— we're taking this stubborn son of a bitch to see the doc."

Tex and Johnny thought they were doing the right thing. In reality they were. They didn't know that Dale had come down with both tropical ulcers and beriberi. Doc McPherson tried his best to keep any of the POWs from leaving sick bay for the morgue, the name he had given to the hospital, by treating them for malaria which gave them a one to two day rest in the sick bay tent. However, when Tashino visited them and he saw no improvement, he knew that the man was useless to him; and rather than use the medicine, he ordered him to the hospital.

The POW had one great advantage over the coolie who had no rights; he had the Geneva Convention. Although Tashino had no respect for it, he had orders from the high command to follow the lines within limits.

When Tex and Hughes heard Dale had been put in the hospital they were upset and blamed themselves. A meeting was held with Donovan to get Dale out of the hospital and back on his feet. The Japanese did not care what the POWs did after dusk; they were free to roam the area around the barracks and the hospital. If they wanted to visit a sick friend and could help, the Japanese did not interfere, knowing if he did make it back it would be another body on the railroad tracks. With the help of ship's cook, Pat Caputo, and pharmacist mate Barney Epstein, they went to work. Dale needed food and medicine. Plan one was to visit him after work and give him a daily wash down with hot water to clean his body. Caputo worked in the kitchen and supplied the hot water. Epstein was an aid to the doctors and he supplied cotton and bandages. Food and medicine was another matter.

The Japanese did not patrol the complex, it wasn't necessary. On each end of the camp there was a high tower with a light beam, which shone on its side of the camp. In between the movements, for about sixty seconds, there was a dead spot. The Thais lived across the stream and bartered with the POWs. They would trade food and medicine for the POWs' trinkets. Very few POWs had much left. The boatswains were not of that few. They had agreed to hold onto their trinkets—a watch, two rings, pen, charm bracelet, and a ten-dollar bill—for an emergency. In return, they would buy food and medicine for Dale. Johnny Hughes, being the youngest and the fastest, was chosen to make the run. On his first visit, he came back with fresh fruit and medicine that the natives had made out of herbs that they gave to their sick for jungle sicknesses. The medicine by our doctors' standards wasn't acceptable, but managed to do wonders regardless.

✳   ✳   ✳

Starvation was taking its toll, so the first unusual new type of meal tried by the prisoners was roasting grasshoppers, bugs and ants. After a while, the insects became part of their diet. Then it became necessary to eat rodents. Rats came on slow. The first to kill and skin one was an Aussie. He brought it into his barracks, and the odor of fresh meat made him a popular man. Some tried it, others backed off. Those who did said it tasted just like chicken. Within a month, the roof rats that nightly ran up and down keeping them awake had become silent. Catching them by trap in the jungle was the only way. As one Aussie put it, "The natives of Africa and the Aborigines have been eating them for years; we eat chicken, snake, frog legs, so why not rat meat?" Donovan, Hughes and Alexander joined in. Tex was the only one who refused to eat the rodent, stating he would die first.

❉   ❉   ❉

Several more trips were made to the Thai natives. Within a week Dale was out of bed and walking the floor. In two weeks he was walking outside. He knew that without help from his buddies he would have died. Each day he observed the medics putting another body in a bag to be removed to the morgue.

While in the hospital, a British chaplain visited the sick daily. He and Dale became close, and since he was only one of a handful who he was able to have a conversation with, he sighted him out each visit. Most of them just lay in a daze with no hope of making it. One day the minister gave him a Bible to read. Dale had never been a religious man nor was he an atheist, but he read the book every day for hours, and then began asking questions. The minister's name was Art Worthington. Thin like all the rest, he had a long white beard, sea blue eyes, and a reddish face. He had told Dale that before he was captured he had operated a homeless shelter, making Dale think that if he were fat with a red suit he could have passed for Santa Claus. Dale, who at one time thought of making the Navy a career, no longer felt that way. His life had been spared for a reason and when and if he ever returned to civilian life he was sure of where he was going—he would join the ministry.

Donovan seemed to stay the healthiest of the four, learning to live in the jungle with smarts. The railroad was moving along and the end would soon be near. When they moved every three months, a new group of rodents became available. The men learned to catch other jungle species and found they could conquer starvation by doing so. The only one who still refused the rodent was Tex, who had dropped to 130 pounds. Like Dale, he too had come down with malaria and was also afraid to report it. He had more to fear than his mate, knowing Tashino checked out the ones who reported for sickbay to look for fakes. The sergeant once told Tex he would never return home alive. As he lay awake on his hard bamboo bed, he could hear the crickets outside chirping away in unison with the coughing of the men in the barracks.

For the past sixteen months he miraculously avoided illness, not so over the past few weeks. It began with diarrhea. Although he suffered, Donovan had a box of Epsom Salts he stole from the cooks' galley, having once been told by his grandmother it was the best cure. It worked on Tex. The sweat was pouring out of his pores. Maybe if he just hung on eventually it would pass.

❋   ❋   ❋

Shulmelda staggered into sick bay; and upon seeing him, McPherson cried out, "Barney, wrap him in a blanket!" It was obvious Tex had malaria; they had seen thousands of cases.

Seeing that it was the tall American that violated rules and dared to strike one of his guards in Java, Tashino smiled and was pleased to see that this American madman was finally being broken. Smiling sadistically, he walked over to Shulmelda, saying, "I recall an old American saying—the bigger they come, the harder they fall." Then he began to laugh hysterically. Addressing the doctor, he asked, "What's wrong with this man besides malaria?"

Doc McPherson had received a nudge from Epstein, and he knew by Tashino's actions that he had nothing but hate in his heart for this man. "Let me examine him and I'll know better." McPherson checked Shulmelda out thoroughly. Then, turning to Tashino, said, "The man's in good shape except for a bad case of malaria. He needs at least three days."

A disgusted Tashino shouted, "Two days and he goes back to work on the railroad!"

When the sergeant was out of sight Epstein said, "Thanks, Doc. If you said he had anything other than malaria he would have sent him to the hospital. Tashino hates him and has been trying to break him for a year and a half."

"Why?" the doctor asked.

"He knocked down one of his guards in Java."

Touching his chin, and then shaking his head, McPherson said, "I can see why Tashino dislikes the man."

Shulmelda survived his bout with malaria and was back to work in a few days. Doc McPherson was able to give him medicine to help relieve dysentery in case it came back. After the rest, Tex felt like a new man. His hopes were now high that his work on the railroad would be easier for him as the months went by.

Because of rain, accidents, and poor planning by the Japanese engineers, they were behind schedule. When this occurred, they worked seven days a week. The guards continually yelled, "Speedo! Speedo!" trying to make up for lost time. By nighttime they were exhausted and talked very little before falling asleep.

Tex had no relatives, since he was an orphan and never knew who his parents were. Donovan, Alexander and Hughes made a pact—if any one of them survived they would visit each other's families.

Six months after his malarial attack, Tex was stricken again with a tropical sickness, cholera. This time his mates could not help him. Orders were strictly carried out, that the victim and all clothing be immediately burned since the disease spread like wildfire. The three remaining friends took it hard. Their buddy didn't only die, but was cremated and could not be returned to America for a proper burial.

The railroad was finally completed and the Japanese celebrated by giving them extra rice and soup and, more importantly, rest. It didn't last long, though, and within a week Allied planes bombed the tracks and it was back to work repairing the damage. Escape had been impossible, but they were now close to India. Word on the grapevine was that they were to be shipped back to Thailand and then disbursed to other camps that needed workers. Three Australians made a break for it in the middle of the night. Unknown to the other prisoners, they were from the same hut that housed the sailors from the *Stuart*.

"Frog Face" entered the hut with a dozen armed soldiers and began hitting the bunks and demanding all the troops to line up. Johnny Hughes was in the front line, Alexander and Donovan in the rear. Tashino approached carrying his steel swagger stick. One of the guards carried a box with him and placed it on the ground a few feet behind the first line to give Tashino a height advantage over the prisoners.

An army truck backed up and parked a few feet from the "Animal of the Orient." He then began to speak, "When you became our prisoners you were told that if you behaved yourselves and followed the rules, you would be treated like Prisoners of War because we, the Japanese, and our government believe in the Geneva Convention. Disobey and you die. Tonight three foolish soldiers disobeyed the rules. For them we have only one punishment, death. You were told when you came to us if you attempted to escape you would die, along with one of you who shared the same hut. We do this because no one came forward to tell us of the attempted escape."

Tashino then raised his hand and ordered the back of the truck to be opened. Three mutilated bodies were thrown onto the ground. The sight was sickening, to see the extent of the beating they had received. The Aussie soldiers shouted at Tashino, "You fucking animal!" and then moved forward to attack him.

Tashino immediately removed his pistol and shot three of them in the head. There was no doubting the sergeant was an excellent shot. The guards, with fixed bayonets, pushed the prisoners back.

Tashino, using a bullhorn, said, "Three escaped and three died because you failed to notify us. You cannot escape. It is impossible to hack your way through the jungle. For the next week the remainder of you who live in this hut will receive only one meal a day. Now get back to your hut.

Dennis put his arm around Johnny's shoulder and said, "Why, Johnny, why? I'm beginning to lose faith that you and I will ever see home again."

Dale, feeling so differently since his close call with death, spoke out, "Our hope is in prayer. When the Lord calls, we all go. Some sooner, others later. Let's say a prayer for our six brothers we have just lost."

Chapter 4

The "Siam-Burma" Railroad, although started in Thailand, was also built on the Burma side by incarcerated prisoners. When the two finally met, the railroad was completed to the joy of both the POWs and the Japanese. For the tired prisoners, it meant less hours working in the jungle and the hot sun. For the Japanese, it meant pride in the accomplishment of a task set before them by their emperor. Finishing the railroad would lead to the invasion of India.

General Takada, overjoyed at the completion of the railroad, ordered a double portion of rice, fish heads, soup, and threw in the luxury of a boiled potato. Besides the enjoyment of eating more food once again was seeing an old friend, Koki Maehara, who along with a dozen guards was transferred to the Thai side of the "death railroad." No words were spoken, but Maehara knew Alexander, Donovan, and Fecke were glad to see him by the smiles on their faces. Koki was the only Japanese Private the POWs knew by name. The others were only known as guards.

Unfortunately for the Japanese empire, the tide of the war was beginning to change and the Allies were on the offensive. Their celebration only lasted for one week before American bombers began hitting the railroad tracks daily. At the same time, it was announced that five hundred men would remain in Thailand to repair any damage done by enemy planes. The remaining men, amounting to several thousand, would be shipped by rail to the coast of Thailand. The Japanese didn't discuss with the Allied officers where they were going; they didn't have to. They were aware they were boarding ships to be taken to another location where the Japs needed slave labor. The prisoners were also aware, with the help of their hidden wireless, that American submarines were sinking every ship floating in both the Bay of Siam and the China

Sea. Of course they couldn't let their Japanese captors know of the wireless, and any protest to travel would be ignored. The unfortunate result was that several ships carrying POWs who slaved and survived the building of the death railroad died when their ship was torpedoed.

The five hundred men who remained in Thailand were kept busy rebuilding sections destroyed by American aircraft. In order to let the planes know they were POWs, they hung white sheets on the top of the barracks. When the Japanese learned of this, they put a stop to it and moved the prisoners' barracks alongside those of the guards. The warplanes, knowing POWs were in those areas, stayed away from the barracks and concentrated on the railroad.

Although the camp was no bargain, it didn't compare to the days they worked through the jungle putting the railroad together. Food was never enough, but they managed to catch small animals and rodents for supplementation. In 1944 they were given their first Red Cross packages, which consisted of delicacies they hadn't tasted in years. Oddly enough, instead of gorging themselves, they ate a little at a time to make the packages last longer. Finally, they received mail; some with good news about loved ones back home and some with bad news, such as a brother killed in the war or a "Dear John" letter from a wife or girlfriend. The men knew it was only a matter of time before the war ended, but none realized it would end as soon as it did.

✻ ✻ ✻

August 16, 1945—7:30 a.m.

Inside the barracks the men were still asleep. It was unusual for the guards to be late. Each morning they would come running into the barracks shouting "Oguku, oguku!" This morning was different. One of the first to wake was the ship's cook, Caputo, who normally rose at 5:00 a.m. to prepare breakfast. It was light outside, and since he normally left the barracks in darkness he knew something was wrong. As he walked outside, one lone Japanese soldier was standing across the road. Seeing

Caputo, he bowed. Caputo, somewhat shocked, returned the bow. He quickly returned to the barracks and woke up his mates, shouting, "Get up! Get up! Something is wrong!"

The tired POWs all looked questioningly at each other. An Aussie, Leslie MacDonald, was the only man who had a watch. All heads turned to him as he said, "It's 7:35 a.m. The bloody Japs let us sleep in."

Seconds later a dozen Aussies entered the barracks shouting, "It's all over! The Japs surrendered!"

Mike Keeley grabbed one of them by the collar. "Is this a joke?"

"No joke, mate. We heard it come over the wireless. They surrendered sometime yesterday."

For the next five minutes, men hugged each other and cried. Donovan, with his arms around Alexander, spoke as his voice choked with emotion, "We're going home, Dale. We're going home."

"God has watched over us, Dennis. Now I'll have the opportunity to follow Him as one of His servants."

The Japanese still had the guns, but under orders they stayed away from the POWs. That afternoon Commandant General Takada made his last speech. "Yesterday, the fifteenth of August, our Emperor asked us to lay down our arms. We no longer are enemies. Some of you may have thought we were hard on you at times. You must understand we were under orders from our commanding officers in Tokyo to finish the railroad. We will be leaving you shortly. You won't be alone for long, as we have heard American troops are close by." He then bowed his head for a moment. As he raised it, he added, "That's all. You can now return to your barracks."

At noon a lookout who had been watching up the road came running into the camp, shouting, "They're here! They're here!"

All the barracks unloaded to await the American troops. One lone soldier, Tommy Roland, walked into the camp. He had parachuted ahead of the troops with a small detachment to meet with the POWs. Seeing him, they rushed forward and bombarded him with question after question. About ten minutes later, the others arrived one by one. Chocolate bars and cigarettes were handed out to the grateful men. Tears ran down the faces of the paratroopers as they looked at their own Allied men in skin and bones, knowing what they must have been through for three and a half years. Laughing and crying, the blissful POWs were free at last, and in a short time would be seeing their loved ones once again.

Before returning home, the Allied prisoners were given a questionnaire on the treatment they received during their interment over the years. It was obvious to all from their condition and the fact that so many had died that the Japanese government had mistreated the prisoners. The results of the questionnaire were as expected, but the number of names supplied were a disappointment. The POWs knew the names of the officers and sergeants, but few could put a name to any of the guards who were usually addressed by nicknames such as Frog Face, Hard Ass, Weasel Eyes, Mr. Moto, along with a dozen others. Nicknames would be of no help to the War Crimes Committee who would be doing the investigation of the crimes charged against the Japanese soldiers.

After the trials of the Japanese, many were condemned to die by hanging, others received life sentences, scores received prison sentences of five to ten years, and a few committed Hara-kiri, taking their own lives. Many disappeared into the crowd and changed their names and lifestyles to avoid being arrested. One such man was Sergeant Oki Tashino.

After the releases from Thailand, Donovan and Alexander were flown to Brisbane, Australia, for a checkup. A week later they arrived in Honolulu where they stayed at the Royal Hawaiian Hotel to rest. Two weeks later, it was on to St. Albans Hospital in Queens, New York. The tall, formerly husky sailors gained back considerable weight and were beginning to look like themselves again.

Everywhere they went the Press wanted stories about their capture and life in the POW camps. They were treated like heroes. Neither of them could understand why; they lost their ship to the enemy and did nothing to help win the war. Then they were told that they had been guinea pigs and had been fighting off the Japs with no air power, few guns, and poor equipment in order to give the Americans a chance to get the war factories rolling.

St. Albans was home for Johnny Hughes and Dale Alexander; both grew up in the Flatbush section of Brooklyn. Donovan was from Needham, Massachusetts, a city close to Boston. The top military brass told them several times to just ask and, if within reason, it's theirs. Since Tex grew up in Nacogdoches, Texas, as a foster child living with several different families, the trio requested he be honored in his hometown by having a street, American Legion, or VFW Post named after him. After weeks in Naval hospitals, the trio were released and returned to the Fleet.

Donovan remained six years in the Navy. When he returned home to Needham, Massachusetts, he went to work for his dad and brothers in Donovan's Plumbing, starting as an apprentice and eventually becoming a shareholder. Shortly upon his return he was lunching with his brothers at a local restaurant called Keating's. One of the waitresses was the owner's daughter, Mary, who was attending the local college and working part-time for her dad. For Dennis it was love at first sight. She was a tall brunette with sparkling blue Irish eyes and when she smiled, dimples showed in both cheeks. She reminded Dennis of the Big Band singer, Helen O'Connell, except for the fact that Helen was blond. Mary had a dry wit, and sometimes it took Dennis a few minutes to figure if she was serious or just being funny. Although a joke teller and gregarious with the men, it took him all of three months to ask her out. Dennis was ready for marriage within months after their first date, but since Mary wanted to finish her nursing school courses first, they were married after graduation a year later. Today they have three children and numerous grand and great-grandchildren, all residing in the Needham, Massachusetts, area.

When Dale was discharged from the Navy, he worked in the Veterans Administration for a short time. He was heavy into the Bible and joined the local Church of God where he became quite active. Thoughts of the ministry compelled him to discuss the matter with his pastor, who then arranged for him to attend a college in Ft. Worth, Texas. He would read the Bible over and over, and was an inquiring and conscientious student. After graduation he became an assistant pastor to a small Church of God in Trenton, New Jersey. It was there he became acquainted with Carol Polo who, like himself, was very devout. They dated, mostly at church affairs, for two years before Dale asked for her hand in marriage. Later he was chosen to be the minister of a church in upstate New York in the city of Bloomfield. This is where their first two children were born. Several years later when he heard of an opening in Rockville Center, Long Island, where the pastor had died, he requested and was awarded that parish. It was at Rockville Center that his last two children were born. Carol and Dale now have six grandchildren.

Johnny Hughes spent several months in St. Albans Hospital before finally being discharged in late 1946. One weekend he returned to his Flatbush playground where he grew up, and partied with his neighborhood and school friends. All of them were on the 20/20 Club, some waiting to enter college, others enjoying life before finally finding a job. Bob Clairy and Emrick Rockford had just taken the New York City police exam with the hopes of joining New York's finest. Ted McKrell, Tom Kelly, Frank Nolan, Gene Mahan, and Frank Wolfe were going to take advantage of the GI bill and go to college. Johnny hadn't graduated from high school, so after he was discharged from the military, he and another good friend, Billy Hansen, signed up in Colby Academy to get their GED. Johnny found work in construction as a carpenter's helper on the Peter Cooper Housing in Manhattan. All he looked forward to was weekends in Irish Town in the Rockaways or the bars he and his friends frequented in Flatbush. Life was a ball until the night he and Len Conway went stag to a dance where they both ended up falling in love—Johnny with Pam Garner. Double dating soon became a weekend ritual with them. It was Pam who talked Johnny into taking the New York police exam. He was twenty-four. As it turned out, it was a good move. After the Academy, he was assigned to a foot post in the 67th Precinct in his old neighborhood of Flatbush. Moving up the ladder with NYPD was tough, since the Department was a small army of 27,000 men. You had three ways: pass the exams, find a Rabbi, or make an outstanding arrest and be made Detective on the spot. That was how young Johnny Hughes made his mark.

In the Police Academy, Johnny learned how to be a book cop. Once out in the street he was told by the old-timers to throw the book away. To get the gold tin, you would have to be lucky and walk into a holdup or cultivate good informants.

The year was 1950. Johnny's post was along Flatbush Avenue from Church Avenue to Clarendon Road, a lively post on the day tour as well as the four to twelve, dead on the midnight tour. The weatherman said the temperature was ten above with the wind factor ten below. As Johnny walked along Flatbush Avenue, he twirled his nightstick, trying not to look like a rookie cop. He passed O'Shaunessey's Bar where a lone customer sat and "The Irish Soldier Boy" was playing on the jukebox. His hands and feet were numb from the cold, and to get relief from the chill wind he stepped into the covered doorway of a jewelry store. Within minutes he felt warmer without the cold icy wind at his back. He stood protected in the darkness of the doorway about thirty minutes and was just about to leave when he spotted a figure approaching a car parked in front of the jewelry store. The man walked with a limp and was wearing what looked to be a hunting jacket and cap similar to ones the English wear. Johnny saw the man stoop and lower the pillowcase he was carrying to the ground and then proceed to remove the hubcaps, after which he moved to the next car. Johnny thought, "I've got my first collar."

Johnny waited until the thief removed all four hubcaps, then stepped from the darkness of the doorway and walked up behind him. "Your car, mister?"

Seeing the man in blue, the perp froze for a moment. "No, sir," he replied in a scared whisper. Johnny then placed the man's hands up against the car and cuffed him.

The perp, a small-time crook, could see Johnny was a young rookie. He said, "Look, I know a lot of guys you can bust. How about we make a deal? I give you my information and you let me walk."

"You're under arrest, buddy. I don't need any bullshit from you."

The perp begged Johnny not to arrest him, and continued to promise information in exchange. Johnny thought it over. "If I proceed with this collar, it's only a misdemeanor charge. If I take a chance and this guy can supply me with info, it could be my stepping stone."

The young man in question was a loser and a street vagabond. He was called Gimpy O'Douhl and had been in and out of jail several times. The two men, complete opposites, became "business partners" meeting in alleyways and on park benches in a strange relationship for over thirty years—Hughes the cop, O'Douhl the snitch.

Chapter 5

First Weekend in March 1993

During World War II the Japanese prisoners were the Brits, Aussies, Dutch, Canadians, Filipinos, and Americans. In 1952 the victorious countries' politicians signed a pact to release all Japanese prisoners charged with war crimes and to drop all charges against those who changed their names and went underground. It upset the POWs in the victorious countries, since they were tortured, beaten, and starved. The reason behind this move was Russia and the Cold War; Japan was badly needed, as she sat close to Siberia, which was part of Russia.

Billy Ballentine was lieutenant on the *Stuart*. After he was released, he attended the University of Oklahoma and then went into local politics. Upset by the giveaway, he ran for the House of Representatives in 1954 and became a member of Congress, winning hands down. His war background didn't hurt. While in Congress, Billy tried to get a bill through Human Rights, asking the Japanese to pay every POW twenty thousand dollars. The Canadians, Brits, and Aussies likewise were trying to change the attitudes of their governments.

The same year Billy was elected he put together a reunion of the *Stuart* crew in Tulsa. There was one held each year in different cities. They had gone through so much together and were like a family. Billy was always the chairman, but a member living in the city chosen put the yearly affair together. At the end of each reunion they would choose the next year's site, giving the man putting it together a full year in advance.

In the year 1994 Dennis Donovan was the headman and the reunion was held at the Rialto Hotel in Boston. Thirty years ago in 1964 Dennis had been in charge also. The hotel then was brand new. Over the years it went from a five star down to a three, some years even rating only two. However, the food was still great, as was the service. Only the rugs were stained and some of the furniture old. But the nice part for the crew was the price was right. Most all the men were in their seventies and eighties by then and living off a small pension and Social Security.

Mary Donovan still looked good for her years. She managed to keep her figure by working in the garden and taking a mile walk every day. Dennis, however, had lost a lot of weight, was now about 150 pounds. His hair was pure white and he wore glasses. The Donovans lived about a half hour from Boston proper in Needham, Massachusetts. Although retired, Dennis still occasionally helped his son, who had taken over the business.

Dennis had made arrangements to meet Dale and Johnny in the hotel lounge at 2:00 p.m. for cocktails, since the reserved hospitality room would not be open until 4:00. Johnny Hughes lived in Mattituck on the eastern end of Long Island. He arranged to pick up Dale, who lived in Rockville Center in Nassau County.

Dale and Johnny arrived shortly after 2:00, and then checked in at the front desk. While checking in, Dennis and Mary arrived. The six of them did the usual hugs and kisses, and then headed into the lounge where they ordered drinks. Dale raised his soft drink, saying, "To a healthy and happy weekend!"

"Hear, hear!" they all said. Then Dennis raised his glass, clinking it against the others, and said, "My old man, God rest his soul, had a favorite poem. It went like this…

> May the road rise to meet you,
> May the wind always be at your back,
> May the sun shine upon your face,
> The rain fall softly upon your fields,
> And until we meet again,
> May God hold you in the palm of his hand."

"Beautiful," said Pam. "Who was the poet?"

"Nobody knows. It was signed *Unknown*."

"Tell us a clean Pat and Mike joke, Denny," Carol asked.

"Did I tell you about the time Pat and Mike went to Confession?"

"No," Carol replied.

Before Dennis got started, Tommy Ryan approached, saying, "Billy's calling a special meeting forthwith in the hospitality room." He apologized to the ladies, "I'm sorry to be the one to break up good clean fun."

Dale said, "Ladies, hold the fort. We won't be long." As they walked toward the hospitality room, he remarked to the other men, "Must be important. We never had a meeting until 4:00 on Saturday afternoon."

The hospitality room was large but was a tight fit for the 135 ex-sailors. Billy, with George Fecke beside him, sat up front and puffed on his cigar while waiting for all the men to be present. The big guy now was close to three hundred pounds. When all but a few latecomers were in the room, Billy spoke, "I have some unusual news to tell you and it's not good. Tashino is alive and in Los Angeles this very minute as I talk to you."

"What kind of bullshit are you spreading, Billy?" Pat Caputo barked.

"No bullshit, Pat, it's a fact."

"A fact or a rumor?" Walt Eilers asked.

"I have the man sitting next to me that has seen him." Patting George Fecke on the shoulder, he said, "It's all yours, George."

Fecke was a short man and his hair was almost gone. Standing up, he raised a newspaper and spoke to a rapt audience, "It's all in this paper, the *Los Angeles Times*. Two days ago I was reading the business section and his face popped up before my eyes. At first I thought it must just be a look-alike. Then I read the article, and the name he was using was one I would never forget."

"What name was that, George?" Artie Dromerhauser asked.

"One you also will never forget, Artie. He helped save you, Donovan, Hughes, Alexander, Woods, and Fecke. It was Koki Maehara."

"Who the hell is Koki Maehara?" Caputo asked.

"Only those of us who were put in the hot box in Java would know him by name. He was a Korean raised as a Christian who spoke some English but better German. His mother was Korean. They lived in Hiroshima. Artie is German and can tell you more about him."

Artie Dromerhauser was six foot two and kept his build throughout the years. After his release from the military, he went to college in California and majored in physical fitness. He became a high school coach and later an assistant coach in the same college. Both his parents were of German extraction.

"The real Koki's father died when he was young. His mother found work in the rectory of the Catholic Church in Hiroshima. Koki became an altar boy for a German born priest who taught him that language. He understood English, but didn't speak it well. The Japs and Korean guards thought him to be a simpleton, but he was far from being one. He was a guard on the late shift. He knew most of us wouldn't make it without help, so he sneaked us extra water and rice when he had the duty."

"How come none of us knew about this Good Samaritan?" Caputo asked.

"He helped us in Java, and when we were shipped to Thailand he didn't come with us in the beginning. We were in Thailand about a year when he showed up as a guard replacement," Fecke replied.

"So I still don't understand whey he was kept a secret," Eilers said.

Dale Alexander interceded, "If they found out what he did for us in Java he would have been executed. He didn't believe in torture, so he helped us. We were afraid if we told everyone, somebody might possibly slip. So we kept it among ourselves."

Fecke then continued to address the group, "The paper said he was the president of Yoshio Electronics of Tokyo and staying at the Hilton. I was certainly curious, so I went to the Hilton and asked for him. The clerk said he hadn't returned as yet, so I took a seat in the lobby and watched the front door. Two hours later he walked in with another, much younger, Japanese man. He walked with a limp and did not carry himself up straight as the Tashino we knew."

"God, that must have been scary, seeing him after all these years," Tommy Ryan said.

"It was. I followed him into the elevator and stood behind him. Cold sweat ran down my back. I can't tell you how many times I used to wake up screaming, thinking I was back in the hot box. If I had a gun, I think I would have shot him right then and there. When I got back home, I called Billy and told him the facts as you've just heard."

"Do you have a few extra copies of the paper with you?" Alexander asked.

"Brought half a dozen with me," George answered, and then proceeded to read from the newspaper, "It says Mr. Koki Maehara will be visiting electronics plants. His company does business with Freeway in Los Angeles, Big Sky in Chicago, and Fairway in Hauppauge on Long Island. He expects to be in the States about a month."

"I've a question—why didn't he take back his own name when those war criminals were all exonerated? And how did he come up with Maehara?" Walt Eilers asked.

"If you recall, our planes bombed Japanese headquarters nightly. My guess is Koki was killed. Tashino, knowing the war was lost, changed identification with him, feeling that as Tashino he no doubt would be hanged."

"I'll buy that. But in 1952 when we cleared out all he had to do was go back to his real name," Dennis observed.

Dale broke in, saying, "Dennis, he knew that a thousand guys wanted to kill him. He knew he was called the Animal of the Orient. So he kept the name of Maehara; he's no dummy."

Eilers then said, pointing at Ballentine, "So, Billy, how do we handle this situation? We can't let that bastard walk!"

"I'm afraid we have to, Walt. But there's an old saying—the pen is mightier than the sword. Write, write, write to every congressman that's involved in armed forces production. Let the three US companies know that if they don't stop working with "Yoshio" the government and private industries will ban their product. Soon as I return home, I'll get the ball rolling. We will hit Tashino where it hurts the most—in the pocketbook."

This answer seemed to satisfy the group. But not all of them…

⁕   ⁕   ⁕

Ballentine was anxious to get started and kept looking at his watch. Finally, at ten past four all the seats were filled. Rising, he called the meeting to order by rapping his gavel on the hard block on the podium. The room quickly came to order and he intoned, "Ladies and gentlemen, please rise and salute the flag."

Throughout the room you could hear the shuffle as each person stood and put their hands over their hearts, repeating, "I pledge allegiance to the flag of the United States of America." As they continued the pledge, the depth of feeling that permeated the entire room impressed the waiters and waitresses. They could palpably feel these people loved the flag and regarded it as something more than just a piece of cloth. They had almost sacrificed their lives to preserve it.

When it was over Ballentine told them to be seated as he took a drink of water and began his speech.

"It has been fifty-one years since we lost our ship, the mighty *Stuart*, in battle to the Japanese fleet. She didn't go down easily. Our big guns hit a dozen enemy ships before we ran out of ammunition. All of us will never forget that eerie feeling when we heard the bugler blow the call to abandon ship. Those of us above deck were aware of the inevitable. Those below were shocked and stunned knowing our ship had successfully battled the enemy on two previous occasions. But we gave 'em one hell of a fight.

"After the war we discovered that six hundred men died in battle. Another fifty were hacked to death by the Javanese natives who were paid fifty Dutch guilders for every American they killed. Two hundred died in POW camps. Miraculously, some of us survived." He paused, and then took a drink of water before continuing.

"Next year we'll meet in Orlando, Florida. It should be a great reunion, as they all have been. Each one unique in its own way. Always a time of fun and fellowship, plus the inevitable therapy that heals each of us a little more each year as we sort out the past and our individual reaction to it.

"I suggest next year that you take a few days off and visit the local attractions in Orlando. Maybe we can extend the time period for another day or two. Let me know your feelings on the time frame."

Picking up his glass of water he finished it and continued, "Each year we lose a few of our brothers. Let's face it, we're not young men any longer except maybe in our imaginations. I urge you to attend next year if at all possible." Checking his watch, he know from years of experience when to stop a speech. Banging his gavel, he shouted, "Until next year, God bless each of you until we meet again. Now let's eat!"

❉   ❉   ❉

When the ladies retired after dinner to their rooms for the evening, Dale suggested a nightcap in the lounge for a private conversation. When the drinks arrived, Johnny Hughes lifted his glass into the air with a toast. "To the fighting *Stuart!*" Both Dale and Dennis raised their glasses and the trio shouted, "To the *Stuart!*"

(On the way in, Dale had taken Johnny aside to remark on Dennis' lost weight and that he didn't seem his old self.) Dale, the somewhat elder of the trio, put his arm around Dennis and asked, "You're sick, Dennis. What are you trying to hide from us?"

Dennis sat very still and said nothing. Then Hughes said, "We've been through hell together. We lost Tex, and cried together. Tell us, man, what's wrong?"

This time a tear rolled down the once-big man's face and he replied, "I have liver cancer."

"How long have you known?" Dale asked.

"About six months. I tried to keep it from Mary, but when you live with someone as long as we have been together, it don't work that way."

"What about a second opinion?" Johnny asked.

"I've had two already."

"Then let's get a third," Dale interjected.

"Who?" Dennis asked.

"I work a lot with doctors and hospice. Stony Brook has a well-known liver cancer doctor—his name is Jacobson, Marty Jacobson. Come stay with me for a few days and make the trip to Stony Brook Hospital to see him."

"It's worth a try, Dennis," Johnny said.

Donovan looked thoughtful for a moment, and then replied, "I'll have to come alone. Our youngest is expecting and needs Mary close by."

"So come home with me after this weekend, see the doctor, and fly back home in a few days."

"I'm grasping at straws the way it is, so why not? I'll let Mary know in the morning that I'll be staying on Long Island with you and Carol for a few days."

Chapter 6

Monday, March 8, 1993

Returning home from the reunion, the man's first order of business was to call the three companies doing business with Tashino. He found the numbers easily enough by dialing Information.

He called the Los Angeles company first. The switchboard operator was a female, and like so many, is schooled to speak to the public properly and courteously. "Freeway Electronics. Mary Jane speaking. How may I assist your call?"

"My name is Jim Monahan. I represent Cataldo Electronics of Brooklyn, New York. May I speak with someone in public relations, please?"

"That would be Mr. Mike Whalen. Hold on, please."

He waited a short time before a baritone voice answered. "Mike Whalen speaking. How may I help you, sir?"

"Name's Jim Monahan, Mr. Whalen, with Cataldo Electronics of Brooklyn. Is there a chance of speaking with Mr. Maehara before he leaves for Chicago?"

"Mr. Maehara left this morning. Who did you say you represented? Cataldo Electronics of Brooklyn? What's your position?"

"PR department. I'm brand new on the job."

"Sir, I never heard of you. And I really don't know why Cataldo would be calling us in any shape or form regarding Yoshio Electronics. Good day."

As he placed the receiver back on the cradle, he thought, "Good. Now I know he left Los Angeles. Now to call Big Sky." He was about to dial when it hit him, "Why am I calling Los Angeles and Chicago when all I have to do is call Fairway in Hauppauge, Long Island?"

He went through the same calling procedure with Fairway as before with Freeway and got a Bob Hess on the line from their public relations department. "Bob, name's Jim Monahan. I work for Cataldo Electronics over in Brooklyn. We understand Mr. Maehara from Japan will be paying your company a visit soon and my boss would like to know if it's possible to meet with him."

"How long have you been with Cataldo, Jim?"

"New kid on the street, Bob."

"I worked for Don Cataldo three years ago before making the move to Fairway. Is Joe Luciano still in sales?"

"He sure is," he said with fingers crossed.

"He sure had the hots for Betty O'Loughlin, if you know what I mean."

"Let's keep it clean, Bob. A lot of guys are trying to get into Betty's pants."

"I'm surprised old man Cataldo is interested in meeting with Maehara."

"Why?" he asked, acting surprised.

"His kid was killed in the Marines on Okinawa. He was dead set against doing business with them."

"Old Don is up in years and the younger members of the family are the ones interested in meeting with Mr. Maehara."

"I'm afraid I can't help you. Maehara is our man and he can only deal with one company on the east coast. It's something we put in our contract."

"Well, we tried. When's he coming, by the way?"

"He was going to Chicago from Los Angeles; should arrive here around the tenth."

"Does he stay in the City?"

"No, at the new Carlyle Hotel in Hauppauge. Why so many questions, Jim? You writing a book?"

"No, just shop talk."

"Do me a favor, Jim. Is Joe around?"

"No, he's out of the office. What's the favor?"

"Give him my number and ask him to call me. It's been a few years since we've seen each other and I'm rather fond of the old loverboy."

"I'll leave a message in his office as soon as I hang up."

"Thanks, Jim. Sorry I couldn't help you out with a meeting, but rules are rules. And like I said, we're the only company on the east coast that can deal with Yoshio Electronics."

After the man returned the phone to the cradle, he thought how lucky he was. If Bob Hess hadn't previously worked at Cataldo he might have come up with zilch.

Tuesday, March 9, 1993

The man dialed the number of the Carlyle Hotel. He got a male voice on a recording with the usual, "Hello. Thank you for calling the Carlyle Hotel in Hauppauge in Long Island, New York. Press one if you are inquiring about hotel rates, press two if you are a group booking, press three for sales, press four for management, press five for the front desk." He pressed five.

"Carlyle Hotel desk. Can we be of service?"

"Yes, I'm calling from Wilson Florist in Smithtown. We have flowers to deliver to a Mr. Koki Maehara. I believe he's coming in today. Could you give us an idea what time he's due to arrive at the hotel?"

"Hold on a minute, sir. Let me check."

He waited just about a minute. "The Maehara party arrives here about noon tomorrow."

"Thank you kindly." He then hung up the phone.

Chapter 7

Upon arrival at JFK Airport, a limousine sent by Fairfield Electronics of Hauppauge, Long Island, met two Japanese businessmen. It was late in the day and it had been raining off and on for several days. The limo turned off at Exit 57 of the Long Island Expressway, drove a short distance before taking a winding road that led to the entrance of the Carlyle Hotel. The doorman quickly stepped out to open the door. He looked like Lou Costello in a red uniform with gold buttons. His hat displayed more gold braid than Admiral Halsey's in World War II. Stepping quickly out of the limousine was a young Oriental wearing a gray, impeccably tailored suit and carrying a black briefcase. He waved the doorman off and proceeded to help out an older Oriental gentleman. Slowly a cane appeared at the car door and was planted firmly on the ground. Next came a body slowly following the cane, painfully rising out of the car. The younger man allowed him to lean on his shoulder for support. Like the younger man, the older Oriental was dressed in a beautifully tailored gray suit, which gave him a definite look of elegance and affluence.

The hotel was unusual inside with a circular design throughout. The architect had come up with the idea after a night at the Westbury Music Fair, a theater in the round, and had created the design for the hotel lobby from his experience. All the employees wore the same uniforms in red and gold with nametags clearly visible on their lapels.

Upon entering the main lobby, the two Oriental men walked to the receptionist desk and were greeted by a friendly clerk, "How may I be of service to you gentlemen?"

The elder spoke after carefully eyeing the clerk's nametag, "We have reservations. I am Mr. Maehara and this is my assistant, Mr. Miyako."

"One minute, sir, while I check your reservation and get your room card." The clerk then proceeded to check the reservation screen on his computer, issued them two card keys to open their respective rooms, and typed in their time of arrival, 3:20 p.m., March 10th.

✻   ✻   ✻

The perp was aware from his conversation with Don Hess the previous day that Tashino would be leaving the dinner party about eight-thirty or nine. He had checked out the surrounding area of the Carlyle earlier. Sitting below the hotel was a small shopping center containing a dozen stores, the main one being a busy supermarket open twenty-four hours a day. This is where he would park his car so that it would not be noticed. Then he waited until evening.

At 8:00 p.m. he returned to the shopping center and waited about ten minutes for a parking spot close to the supermarket, knowing that later on the car would be too conspicuous if he parked too far away from the market. When the area was clear, he locked up the car. The time was 8:10 p.m. when he began his walk towards the hotel. He didn't want to hang around the hotel too long in case an employee spotted him and later would remember him. He estimated that if Tashino left the dinner party at nine, he would surely return to the hotel sometime between nine and ten. He decided to enter the lobby around eight-thirty, find a seat where he could observe the entrance while pretending to read until Tashino arrived.

Walking up the hill, he kept close to the bushes, stepping behind them if a car passed. Arriving at the hotel, he observed the doorman standing alone. The doorman watched him as he walked toward the front of the hotel. He stopped and pretended he was looking for his wallet, turning his head so the doorman would not be looking directly at him. A car pulled up just then and the doorman transferred his attention to the new arrivals. While he was busy helping them with their luggage, the perp walked in the front door.

He was impressed with the interior. The ceilings were several stories high and several glass-enclosed elevators were busily going up and down. The man sat in a leather chair and pretended to read a newspaper. He was wearing a dark blue suit and a fedora hat. Under his feet was a small black suitcase.

At nine-twenty, two Oriental men walked into the lobby of the hotel. One, an elderly man with a cane. The second was a much younger man. Tashino was described as a man of five feet ten inches, in his seventies, with a pronounced limp.

The man watched them over the top of his newspaper as they approached the front desk to check for messages. As they walked past him, for the first time he got a close look at Tashino. He followed them towards the elevator and stood behind them while they all waited for the door to open. When it did, a tall, slim young employee stepped out and politely greeted them. Both Orientals returned his courtesy by bowing their heads, their way of saying thank you. The third man waiting, a white male, brushed past the young man carrying a black suitcase and entered the elevator, pushed the button for the tenth floor, and stepped to the rear. Both Orientals, seeing he was going to their floor, entered and stood in front of him.

As the door started to close, a voice rang out, "Hold the elevator!" The young Oriental did so, and a young man stepped in. Smiling, he nodded and said, "Thanks." He continued to attempt some small talk, but received no response from the other three passengers. "What a bunch of schmucks," he thought as he got off at the fifth floor.

When the door opened at the tenth, the tall man stood in the rear until the two Orientals stepped out. He walked slowly around the circular hallway to give them a chance to get to their rooms. As he passed them, the younger man was entering room 1003 and his older companion, the room next door, 1004. What a break, he thought. They're not staying in the same room.

Tomorrow would be another tedious day for the Japanese businessman, most of it spent in the conference room. Removing his jacket, he hung it in the closet, and then moved over to the bed. Sitting, he removed his Rolex watch, gold ring, and wallet, placing them on the night table alongside his bed. There was a knock at the door. Assuming it was his secretary, he leaned on his cane and walked over to the door. Opening it, he found the tall white male from the elevator instead of Mr. Miyako.

In a lowered voice, the man asked, "Mr. Maehara?"

"Yes. What is it?"

The stranger then displayed a gun, pointing it directly into Maehara's face and pushing him slowly back into the room. Maehara was stunned. He was aware of the high crime rate in the US, mainly due to drugs. Nevertheless, he was more annoyed than frightened. One of the reasons he chose the Carlyle was their high ranking in hotel security. The company that owned the chain of hotels would hear about this insult. Pointing to the night table, he told the gunman to take whatever he wanted. He told him there was at least six hundred dollars in the wallet.

The gunman smiled, put down his suitcase, opened it, and removed a swagger stick identical to the one Tashino carried during the war. The gunman stood up and removed his wig, displaying a full head of gray hair.

The Oriental's face turned ashen. He had no idea who the stranger was, only that he must have been a prisoner of war under his command during World War II. His mind flashed back fifty years to the camps in Java and Thailand where he had been stationed. It was a part of Tashino's life he had forgotten long ago. He knew, however, he had only a few seconds to live, so he swung his cane, hitting the intruder on the side of his head, drawing blood.

Tashino leaned forward and grabbed him by the hair. The perp realized then that he wasn't as agile as he had been a few years back. He fired two shots. The first was wild; the second hit the Oriental below the eye. Maehara's body jerked violently, having taken the equivalent of fourteen hundred pounds against his face. Dazed, he fell backward. The man fired a third time at point blank range into the forehead. This time the whole body slumped, eyes staring but not seeing. The man grabbed Tashino's wrist and felt for a pulse. There was no doubt in his mind that Tashino was dead.

The perp then quickly locked the door, dropped on his hands and knees to look for blood or any other incriminating evidence the police identification team might locate. Finding none, he picked up the three spent cartridge shells. He went into the bathroom and removed his handkerchief from his pocket to wipe off the blood that had coagulated where Tashino had hit him on the head. Then he remembered the cane and brought it into the bathroom, thoroughly washing off his own blood. It would be a simple procedure to type the blood of the shooter if the slightest trace was found in the room.

When he was satisfied he had covered every base, from the black suitcase he had brought with him he removed a maroon jacket, beige slacks and shoes, a maroon shirt, and a dirty blond wig. He then took off the clothes he was wearing and stuffed them away in the suitcase. When his transformation was complete, he was pleased as he surveyed himself in the full-length mirror of the bathroom door. Surely no one would connect him with the man in the dark suit.

He gave the room another once-over, cleaned the bathroom sink again with his handkerchief, and then put it with the rest of his previous disguise. He had worn gloves except while washing his hands, and knew there were no fingerprints left behind to tie him to the murder.

Before leaving the room, he stood over the dead body, talking to it as though it still had the breath of life, "Like a friend of mine recently said to me, 'Only the good die young,' and you lived a long time, you bastard.

I believe a higher power led me to you. Now you're out of this world. May your soul rot in Hell!"

Opening the door a crack, he saw there was no one in the hallway. He listened for a few seconds, and then heard a door close just around the circular hall. He moved quickly and headed at a fast pace for the stairwell. He slowly descended the ten flights of stairs, with the adrenaline pumping through his body. Using the stairs gave him a secure feeling, since hotel guest would not likely be using them.

Reaching the first floor, he carefully peered out into the lobby before proceeding. The area was clear, with the exception of the doorman. The rest of the staff was in the area of the desk. He would have to wait. After five minutes that felt like an eternity, he saw a taxicab pull up in front of the hotel. Just the break he needed. He quickly opened the door and casually strolled out through the lobby. Once he was out of sight down the street he quickly picked up his pace until he reached the shopping center.

The doorman, DeMarco, a Damon Runyon-type character, had the eyes of a fly, seeing in all directions. He noticed the tall white male leaving in a hurry carrying a small black suitcase, heading west. He sensed something was wrong, since the parking area was to the east of the hotel. The employees had recently gone through days of tedious training by local burglary detectives and were stridently quizzed on what to look for, what constituted questionable behavior. He felt this to be one of those instances; then it hit him. He remembered the guy in the dark suit earlier who had the same walk and had carried a similar suitcase. "That son of a bitch is probably a hotel cat burglar," he whispered to himself. Removing a small pad and pen from the pocket of his coat, he wrote down the time, 10:10 p.m., and a description of the man and the clothing he had been wearing on both occasions.

After twenty years in the business, the doorman knew his hunch was probably right on. As a young man with no high school diploma, he had taken a job as doorman of a large Manhattan apartment building.

It was supposed to be temporary until he could find something better, but he never did. Although the money sucked, tips and whatever else he could hustle made up for the low pay. Once he learned the business along with all the tricks of the trade, he made the job a career. He caught on quickly that the big bucks for a doorman is at a large hotel. His record was clean and he was able to move up to better and better jobs. Calling cabs, carrying luggage, and occasionally tipping off a guest where to have a good time, paid handsomely. Another way to make a buck was to alert Security when he spotted what he thought looked like a con artist or burglar. By keeping his eyes and ears open, he made himself an easy dollar.

At midnight when the other doorman came on duty, he searched out the hotel security guard on duty, Joe George, but he was nowhere to be found. He had him paged from the main desk, and when he still failed to show up, he left a note describing his man in both sets of clothing with Mel Kreim who was still manning the front desk.

"Mel, mind putting this note in Joe George's box?"

Kreim took the folded note from DeMarco and said, "Going home so soon? Working just a half day, fatso?" That statement was truer than he thought. DeMarco had indeed just worked a half-day, a twelve-hour shift, to be exact.

"Up yours," DeMarco responded under his breath.

He hadn't given the information to Security because he was a loyal employee, but out of habit. If the guy did turn out to be a cat burglar, DeMarco would make himself a few bucks, and why not? If he gave them a lead, why shouldn't he get a piece of the action?

C h a p t e r 8

Thursday, March 11, 1993

Yozo Miyako knocked on the door of his employer, Mr. Koki Maehara. The time was 7:59 a.m. Today was the first meeting between Yoshio Electronics of Tokyo, Japan, and subcontractor Fairfield Electronics of Hauppauge, New York. The meeting was to begin at 9:30 sharp in the conference room at the Hauppauge office. Before retiring the night before, Mr. Maehara emphasized they were to go down for breakfast at 8:00 a.m. Once the business meeting got underway, the Japanese businessmen, knowing it would be a long day, wanted to have a good breakfast before the tedious day began.

The secretary knocked several times, receiving no answer. He knocked again, this time harder—still no answer. Strange, he thought to himself, Mr. Maehara San is always prompt.

Returning to his room, he tried calling his employer on the phone. After ten rings, he hung the phone back on the cradle. "Is it possible he went down to breakfast without me?" the secretary thought. Picking up the phone once again, he called the coffee shop on the main floor. It rang twice before a soft female voice said, "Carlyle Coffee Shop, Maria speaking. Can I help you?"

"Yes, please. My name is Mr. Miyako. I'm a hotel guest. I'm trying to locate my business and traveling companion, a Mr. Koki Maehara. Can you check, please, and see if he's having breakfast in the restaurant?"

"Both your names sound Japanese. Is Mr. Maehara a Japanese gentleman?"

"Yes, please, he's an elderly Japanese man in his seventies and walks with a cane."

"I myself have not seen him, sir. However, it's possible he is in the restaurant and I missed him. Hold on, please—I'll check with the waitress." He waited a short time before she returned, and then her voice came over the airwaves once again. "Mr. Miyako, I checked with all the girls. None have served him. Leave your room number with me, and if he should come in I'll call you right back."

"Thank you kindly," Yozo replied, "It won't be necessary. I'm on my way down to look for him."

The secretary was worried, knowing his employer was a diabetic, along with a heart problem. Reaching the main floor, he headed straight over to the desk. The clerk on duty was a blond female. Her tag read T.C. Murphy.

Seeing the hotel guest approach the desk, she put on her best smile and said, "Can I be of some help, sir?"

"Could you kindly check Mr. Maehara's box, he's in Room 1004, and see if he left a message for a Mr. Miyako?"

The young lady stepped back and checked the box. Finding no messages, she returned to the front desk, addressing the young Oriental, "No message, sir."

"Please, may I speak with your Manager?"

A minute or so elapsed before the Manager appeared. He was a slim man about five-ten, and his suit fit like a glove. Over his vest pocket was a plate that read Manager, Mr. Robert Bauman. Smiling, he approached the guest. "Good morning, sir. How can I help you?"

"My name is Yozo Miyako. Both my employer and myself have rooms on the tenth floor. This morning I knocked on Mr. Maehara San's door and he did not answer."

"So what you are telling me is that you cannot locate Mr. Maehara?" Bauman asked.

"Yes, sir," Miyako answered.

"How do you spell his last name, Mr. Miyako?"

"His first name is K-O-K-I. His last M-A-E-H-A-R-A."

Bauman called to his clerk, T.C. Murphy, on the other side of the desk. Then he wrote out the name of the missing employer on a blank piece of paper, handed it to her and said, "T.C., have this name paged throughout the hotel and ask him to come to the main desk, please." She did as requested.

Yozo waited about ten minutes before he approached Mr. Bauman a second time. The young secretary then asked, "Is it possible for you to open Mr. Maehara's room, please?"

"Why, you said yourself he's not in the room."

"Mr. Maehara is not a well man. He is diabetic and has had a heart bypass operation. It is possible he may have had an attack and could not get to the phone."

"You should have mentioned that he's a sick man. I'll call Mr. Hart and have him meet you in front of Mr. Maehara's room."

Bowing his head slightly, Yozo said, "I am most grateful for your assistance, Mr. Bauman. If I failed to mention the room number Mr. Maehara occupies, it is one-zero-zero-four on the tenth floor."

The secretary returned to the tenth floor to await Mr. Hart. While waiting, he once again knocked hard several times on his employer's door. Still no one answered.

The elevator door opened. A tall, heavy-set man with a red nose emerged with a large cigar in his mouth. He was wearing a fedora hat. To Yozo, he resembled the detectives he had seen in American movies. The big man walked over to the complainant and extended a large hand. Smiling, he removed the cigar from his mouth and introduced himself, "Bob Hart, Hotel Security."

Yozo, who at five-seven and one hundred thirty pounds was dwarfed by the house detective, shook the big man's hand and replied, "Mr. Yozo Miyako."

"What seems to be the problem, Mr. Miyako?"

"I am employed by Yoshio Electronics. We are located in Tokyo, Japan, and are here to do business with Fairfield Electronics of Hauppauge.

This morning we were to have our first meeting with them at 9:30. It is my job as Mr. Maehara's secretary to knock on his door at 8:00 a.m. Since it was to be a long day, we were going to have breakfast in the hotel before leaving for our meeting. I have knocked several times, had him paged, and checked the restaurant. He is nowhere to be found."

The big house dick took a puff on his cigar, blew out smoke, and asked, "This employer you're talking about, what position does he hold down?"

"Mr. Maehara San is the President and main stock holder."

"You said you checked the restaurant. Maybe your boss just took a walk."

"Very unlikely, sir. He is a sick man. His heart is not good, and he depends on his cane in order to walk, as one leg is shorter than the other."

Hart took a card key from his pocket. Talking with the cigar in his mouth, he said, "Let's have a look inside."

Hart fumbled with the card key, then finally placed it in the door slot. Looking down at his small complainant, he said, "Keep your fingers crossed."

Yozo had mixed feelings as to what the detective would find when the door was opened. He was hoping Mr. Maehara would not be in the room. If he was, there was no doubt in his mind that he would be unconscious. Hart, a retired NYPD homicide detective who spent most of his career in the borough of Brooklyn, over the years had seen it all. He had the uneasy feeling they would find the Japanese businessman DOA (in police jargon, dead on arrival).

Turning the knob, Hart opened the door slightly and immediately saw the body on the floor. He pushed Yozo back, saying, "Wait here; I'm going in alone." He closed the door and walked over to the body. He knew immediately it was a case for Homicide. The victim was lying on his back with his eyes open, dried blood was on his face, and a few feet away was his cane. His guess was the deceased man had been that way for several hours. A pro, he touched nothing, then returned outside where Yozo was waiting in the hallway. "Mr. Miyako, what room are you in?"

"Next door, in one-zero-zero-three."

"Your boss is dead. I need to use your phone."

"Heart attack?" the secretary asked.

"No, he's been murdered."

Hart called the County Police. A female voice answered, "Suffolk County Police."

"My name is Bob Hart. I'm head of security at the new Carlyle Hotel on Meadows Lane, off exit fifty-seven. Could you have a uniform car respond regarding a theft? Tell them to ask for the house detective at the main desk."

Hanging up, he turned to the young Japanese secretary and said, "Your boss was shot several times about the face. I touched nothing, so I don't want anyone to go into the room until the police give it a good going-over. I want you to stay in this room. You're to tell no one about the murder."

Miyako was puzzled as to why Mr. Hart told police headquarters he was calling about a theft. Why didn't he tell them Mr. Maehara was dead?

Hart, unlike Miyako, knew if hotel management was informed a homicide occurred, all hell would break loose and the media would be swarming all over the crime scene. This he learned from years of experience when called to the scene of a homicide. He had one thought in mind—keep the crime scene clean.

The murder occurred in Hauppauge, Long Island, somewhat of a bedroom community of New York City, located in Suffolk County. The police department was a county force and employed some 3500 people, which included both police and civilian personnel. Their jurisdiction consisted of the five western towns in Suffolk: Babylon, Islip, Huntington, Smithtown, and Brookhaven. All the towns past Riverhead had their own town police and state troopers. As of the last census, the population was one million, three hundred fifty thousand, located in an area of nine hundred square miles.

Police headquarters was located in Yaphank, a Brookhaven township, along with all of the county office buildings. It was in a large two-story building a block long that housed the police commissioner along with all the top brass of the department. The complex also housed all the special service detectives and main office detectives, including Homicide, Communications, Supplies, and Records. The main work force was located within the six precincts, however—three on the north shore, three on the south shore.

Each precinct had a commanding officer with the rank of Deputy Inspector and a general service squad of detectives under the command of a Detective/Lieutenant. To the uniform sector car operator, the general service men were known as "precinct dicks." When a felony was called in to headquarters, a sector car from whatever precinct the crime occurred was dispatched to the scene. If a detective was needed, the uniform man called the squad and a detective responded. If the investigation belonged to a specialized unit from the main office, the general service detective made out a supplementary report on what he did, then turned it over to them.

In the case of the "Carlyle Caper," the murder occurred in the township of Smithtown where the Fourth Precinct was located.

Munching on rolls and coffee, Police Officers Roy Russell and Jim Wild were enjoying breakfast when the call came over the air, "Headquarters to Car 404."

Russell picked up the mike and answered, "404 here."

"A ten-two. See complainant, a Mr. Robert Hart at the Carlyle Hotel off exit fifty-seven. The complainant is head of hotel security. He's waiting for you at the front desk. Time of call, 8:15 a.m."

"Ten-four, we're on our way!"

Russell continued eating his roll and with a mouthful said, "It's only a larceny. Let's finish our breakfast first."

At 8:45 a.m. the phone in the back room rang. The first detective to pick up was Barry Falk. "Detective Falk, Fourth Squad."

"Barry, it's Roy Russell. I got a heavy for you."

"I'm listening."

"I'm over at the Carlyle Hotel off exit fifty-seven, the new one on the hill. They've only been in business about ten days, and it appears they have their first homicide."

"A hotel homicide? What happened, some guy find his wife shacked up with his best friend?" Falk replied with his usual dry humor.

"I'm afraid it's not that simple. When you turn this one over to Homicide, they're gonna earn their money."

"Sounds interesting. What's the score, Ray?"

"Headquarters gave it to my partner, Jim Wild, and myself as a ten-two. Since it was a routine call, we took our time getting over to the hotel. When we did get there we headed for the main desk and were sent up to the tenth floor to see a guy named Hart who heads their security.

"At first I was pissed, thinking this guy got a pair of balls and should have been looking for us on the ground floor. As we got off on the tenth, he was waiting for us by the elevator. With him was a Japanese man in his twenties he introduced as Mr. Miyako, the secretary of the victim. I said, 'What victim!?' Then he took us to the room where an old Oriental guy was lying on his back with his eyes wide open with dried blood on his face."

"How come the call came over as a ten-two larceny?" Falk asked.

"The head of security, Hart is a retired dick out of Brooklyn Homicide. He knew if he called it in as a murder, the media would pick it up and probably be at the scene before the cops."

"What a break for Homicide. Am I to understand that the hotel management isn't aware of the facts?"

"Hart told them he was investigating a hotel burglary and asked them not to notify top management. When he finishes his investigation, he'll call them himself."

"So Homicide will have a clean room to check out," Falk replied.

"Yeah, them primadonna homicide dicks won't have anything to bitch about. Nothing's been touched. He's lying on his back with dried blood on his face—where the shooter hit him."

"You can't blame them, Ray. Put yourself in their shoes. You'd probably be the same way," Falk observed. "How long has he been a stiff?"

"Rigor mortis is about to set in. The air conditioner was shut off, so it's hard to tell at this point."

"I'll let your desk know you and Wild will be tied up for a while. Stand by the scene until Identification responds. I'll call the duty officer and have him notify Identification and the medical examiner. Then I'll call Homicide, since they have a long haul from Yaphank. My partner and myself will be over to set the scene for Homicide."

After notifying the duty officer, whose job it was to notify the duty detectives working Identification, and the medical examiner on call, Falk dialed the Homicide Bureau. It was answered on the second ring, "Detective Rubin, Homicide."

"Joe, it's Barry from the Fourth. I'm responding to a homicide at the Carlyle off exit fifty-seven in Hauppauge. How long before your guys can respond?"

"You'll have to talk to Sergeant Gore about that. Hold on, I'll switch you over to him."

"Wait! Before you switch, since you work steady days, how come you didn't make the meeting at the temple Monday night?"

"I had to go to a PTA meeting. Sorry about that, I won't miss the April meeting. I'm switching you over to Gore."

Seconds later a voice answered, "Sergeant Gore."

"Sarge, I'm on my way to the new Carlyle Hotel in Hauppauge. The security guard found a stiff on the tenth floor apparently shot in the face."

"Who's calling, please?"

"I'm sorry, Sarge. Detective Falk, Fourth Squad."

"Are you calling from the scene?"

"No, I'm on my way over after my call to you. I know it's my duty to check out the call first before calling you guys. The reason I'm calling ahead is the stiff's a foreign Japanese businessman."

"Give me the details."

"Police Officer Russell informed me by phone that the victim was lying on his back and appeared to have taken the hit in the face."

"Where did the shooting take place?" Gore asked.

"In the victim's room on the tenth floor of the new Carlyle Hotel, in Hauppauge."

"Anyone standing by the crime scene?"

"Yes, sir, Officer Russell and his partner. They have the door secured and know that no one is to enter except police officials."

"Good, you made the right move calling us before you responded. I have one man that hasn't checked in as yet. When he does, we'll be on our way. Take care until we arrive."

After Falk hung up, Gore then dialed the DA Office. The phone call was picked up on the second ring, "Investigator Kip Alden, DA Squad. Can I help you?"

"Kip, Sergeant Gore of Homicide. Put me into the ADA. Office."

"You got it, Sergeant," Alden replied, then switched him to the ADA.

"Assistant District Attorney, Dick Purcell."

"Dick, it's Gore of Homicide. Your head man in yet?"

"He's out of town. Anything I can help you with, Jerry?"

"We got a possible homicide over at the Carlyle. I need an ADA to respond."

"Sounds interesting; I'll respond. You calling from your office?"

"That's right," Gore answered.

"Then I'll meet you at the hotel in about a half hour or so."

"Thanks, Dick." He then hung his phone back on the cradle.

The Fourth Precinct is the smallest of all the six precincts in the county. Along with size, it also has the least amount of people. It's a middle to high-income area and is not considered a high crime area. Most of the felony calls are for burglary, car theft, and assault.

Falk, like Russell, was a fourteen-year veteran. Both had known each other many years, having graduated from the Police Academy together. His brother officers considered Barry Falk as the serious type that sometimes overwhelmed his teammates with an occasional comeback of dry humor. Divorced, he had two children, both living with his former wife. Well-liked by his co-workers, he was considered a thorough investigator by his boss, Jake Wimmer. A health nut, he maintained his weight at 160 pounds. At five-nine, he stayed in top shape playing handball, tennis, and racquetball. A non-smoker, he also was a light drinker. When he did, it was usually a glass of wine with the meal.

At 9:22 a.m., Falk arrived at the hotel with his partner, Tim Rochester. Tim resembled the old-time movie actor, Broderick Crawford, who once played a cop on the TV series, "Highway Patrol." Approaching Room 1004, they found Russell still standing in front of the door.

"Where's your partner?" Barry asked when he did not see Jim Wild.

"The Loo called us on the walkie, wanting to know how long we would be tied up. When we told him, most of the morning, he told Jim to take the car and call back into service and for me to stand by until the detectives responded."

"Does he know it's a homicide you responded to?"

"Yeah, Wild called him on the phone in the victim's secretary's room. We knew not to put it over the air."

Entering the scene of the murder, he found four men already in the room and working. Detective Tommy Tuiet was dusting for prints, along with his partner, Joe Callahan, both from Identification. The third man was Doc Alchermes of the Medical Examiner's Office, and also Detective Cuomo of the Lab, who had arrived only a few minutes before Falk and Rochester.

Doc was an old-timer in his sixties and considered by Homicide to be the best in the business. Both Fourth Squad detectives walked over to the body and stood over Doc as he gave the cadaver a preliminary going-over wearing rubber gloves. Looking up at the two detectives, he said, "He took two hits in the face, one below the eye and one in the forehead. He most likely died instantly."

"Can you make a rough guess about the time he died?" Falk asked.

"It will be a rough one at this point. Give or take an hour or so, he died last night sometime between eight o'clock and ten o'clock. Unlike the TV homicide detectives, we can't give you the exact time."

Putting his hand on the shoulder of the Medical Examiner, Falk said, "Thanks, Doc."

Addressing his partner, Falk suggested, "Tim, why don't you knock on a few doors. Who knows, maybe you'll get lucky and find a witness that may have heard the shots."

"Where are you going," Rochester asked.

"While we're waiting for Homicide, I'd like to talk to the house detective and the victim's secretary; they're in the room next door."

As Falk and Rochester were leaving the room, Callahan was taking a video of the crime scene. Tuiet was taking the victim's fingerprints. When finished, he would take a still picture with a Polaroid camera.

Falk went next door to question Hart and Miyako. Seeing the big house detective, Falk introduced himself, "Detective Falk, Fourth Squad."

Hart, shaking Falk's hand, said, "Bob Hart, Hotel Security."

"I understand you found the body," Barry asked.

"You got that right. I opened the door at the request of Mr. Miyako here, and there he was staring at me eyeball to eyeball."

"I'm told you're retired from NYPD."

"Brooklyn Homicide," the big guy answered.

"Figures. You made a smart move when you didn't put the homicide call over the airwaves."

"Who knows better? I put in thirty-five years on the job, my final twelve in Homicide. I've seen how the media can destroy evidence, so I told Management we had a burglary and I had a suspect, to stay clear of the tenth floor until I cleared the way."

"All I can say is we lucked out having you as the house detective," Falk said. "So all you can really tell me, Mr. Hart, is you were notified by Mr. Miyako to check Room 1004, opened the door, and there he was."

"That's about it," the big guy replied.

Falk then turned to the Japanese businessman, "Mr. Miyako, mind if I ask you a few questions?"

"I'm at your service, sir," the Oriental replied.

Falk then put his hand on Hart's shoulder and said, "Do you mind making your rounds? I'd like to talk to him alone."

"Hell, no, it's your case. I'll be out in the hallway waiting around until your Homicide team arrives. If you need me, you know where to get me."

As Hart left, Falk turned to the Japanese businessman, "Let's have a seat, Mr. Miyako, and make ourselves comfortable."

Being there was only one table in the room, they found two chairs and made use of it. Falk opened his briefcase, took out a pad, and asked, "Mr. Miyako, do you mind giving me a short statement?"

The Japanese businessman bowed slightly to the American detective, and then said, "It would be my pleasure to assist in any way I can be helpful in apprehending the killer of Mr. Maehara San."

"Good, then let's get started. Your name, please?"

"Yozo Miyako."

"What is the name of the company you work for?"

"Yoshio Electronics of Tokyo, Japan."

"What position did the victim, Mr. Maehara, hold with the company?"

"He was the president."

"Your position?"

"Mr. Maehara's secretary."

"What exactly are your duties?"

"I take all the company notes in shorthand and use a tape recorder as backup. I am also required to know the sales background of any company we are dealing with, where they stand on the stock market, and their yearly profits."

"Have you always been his secretary?"

"No, just the past three years. Before that, I was the company's leading salaryman."

"What does the term *salaryman* mean? Is that what we here call our paycheck?"

"To be more specific, I was the company's leading salesman. In Japan, the working man is called a salaryman, regardless of what trade or business."

"How long have you worked for Yoshio?"

"Seven years. It was my first employment after I graduated from college."

"Why did you choose Yoshio Electronics?"

"I didn't, they chose me. You see, I was in the top five percent of my class in a university considered to be number one, somewhat like your Harvard. I had my choice of a dozen companies. I chose Yoshio because they offered the best benefits along with large bonuses if you produce. There never was a doubt in my mind I wouldn't be at the top within a few years."

"If you were tops in sales, why did you take the job as secretary?"

To be secretary to the president of the firm is an honor. If I wasn't the top salesman in the Yoshio organization, Mr. Maehara San would never have chosen me."

"Strange country you come from," Falk replied, "Here in the States, if you're making big bucks as a salesman, that alone would be satisfaction."

"In Japan we have a different culture. We also have different methods of selling and producing our products. A worker in Japan puts his job above his family. He works long hours with few breaks and is proud of his accomplishments. In sales we choose the personnel accordingly. I speak German, Italian, French, and English. When I travel abroad I can sit in with the board of directors and talk their language. That, besides my knowledge of selling, is why Mr. Maehara chose me as his traveling secretary."

"In the three years you have traveled abroad with Mr. Maehara, has he stepped on the toes of any of the companies you dealt with in the States, or Europe?"

"What do you mean when you say stepped on toes?"

"Did anyone ever threaten him with words like, I'll get you, I'll kill you?"

"No, Mr. Maehara was a gentleman and was highly thought of by all the companies he did business with all over the world."

"How about you? Did you have a good relationship with your boss?"

"We respected each other, if that is what you mean."

"When was the last time you saw your boss?"

"Last night, about nine-thirty in the evening."

"Prior to nine-thirty, where did you and your employer spend the evening?"

"We were guests of Mr. Eugene Myers, the president of Fairfield Electronics, in Hauppauge."

"Where does Mr. Myers live?"

"Not far from here in a place called Fort Salongo."

"Your pronunciation is a bit off. You mean Fort Salonga."

"Yes, that's how it is pronounced."

"How many people were at the dinner party?"

"There were twelve of us. Except for Mr. Maehara and myself, all the others were from Fairfield Electronics."

"How long did the dinner party last?"

"Mr. Maehara is an early riser. Knowing the importance of the meeting the next day, we left about 9:00 p.m."

"How did you get back to the hotel, by cab?"

"No, sir, we had a limousine at our disposal. All three American companies always provide us with one."

"How is your company's relationship with Fairfield?"

"Excellent. They have shown us a nice profit over the past three years."

"How about the other companies your company deals with in the other cities?"

"We have two others, Freeway Electronics in Los Angeles and Big Sky in Chicago. Like Fairfield, they also showed a profit."

"When you arrived back at the hotel, did you notice any strangers? Maybe a guy watching you in, let's say, an unusual manner?"

"No, sir, not that I'm aware of."

"Did you go straight up to your room?"

"No, we checked at the main desk for messages."

"Did you see anyone at the desk or nearby, other than employees?"

"No, sir."

"After checking for your messages, what then?"

"We went directly up to our rooms."

"Were you two alone in the elevator?"

"There was a man in a blue suit; he got on the elevator the same time we did."

"Anyone else you can think of, Mr. Miyako?"

"As the door of the elevator was about to close, a man called out to hold the elevator door, and I did so."

"Were both men white?"

"Yes, sir."

"So there were two men in the elevator with you and Mr. Maehara?"

"Yes, sir," Yozo replied.

"Did you see any other person besides the two males in or around the elevator before it went up to the tenth floor?"

Yozo thought for a moment, then raising his forefinger in the air, said, "Yes, when the door opened, before we got in, there was a tall hotel employee in the elevator. As he left, he said hello to us."

"When you say tall, how tall? Six foot or taller?"

"He was over six feet."

"Describe the first man to me, the one in the blue suit."

"He was over six feet in height, slim, wore a fedora hat, tinted glasses, and carried a small, black suitcase."

"How about jewelry?"

"If he wore a watch or ring, I couldn't have seen them. He kept his arms folded."

"Describe the second man to me."

"About the same height as Mr. Maehara, five-ten, stocky build, beige suit with shoes to match, and wore a lot of jewelry—a gold chain around his neck and several gold rings."

"No baggage?"

"Only his briefcase," Yozo replied.

"Did you talk to him or the other man?"

"The tall man stood in the rear and said nothing. The stocky one said thanks for holding the elevator door for him and good evening when he got off the elevator."

"What floor was that?"

"The fifth."

"And how about the tall one?"

"The same floor we did, the tenth."

"Did you see him enter a room?"

"No, he was behind us when we left the elevator, and passed us in the hallway, disappearing around the bend."

"You're a very observing witness, Mr. Miyako. Your memory of the two men in the elevator astonishes me. You gave me a very vivid description of both men. Considering they were strangers to you, I'm impressed."

"It is all part of the way I've been trained. I'm a speed-reader and born with a photographic mind. My memory is far above the average person and my IQ is above normal. You're asking yourself if I'm above suspicion. I can assure you, I am."

"Don't try to read my mind, Mr. Miyako. Let's get back to the two men. How old would you say they were?"

"The one wearing the jewelry was about my age, close to thirty. The tall man was much older than he was pretending to be."

The last statement took Falk aback. "Tell me what you mean when you say he was pretending."

"In Japan we look upon our elders for wisdom, understanding, and we respect them. In America, being young seems to be very important. Some of your elders hide their age by having face-lifts, wearing wigs, using numerous skin products to make themselves look young. Americans are afraid of aging. The tall one was doing just that or he was pretending to look younger than his years."

"An interesting concept. What did the tall man wear that put you wise to him?" Falk asked in a sarcastic manner.

"He had crow's feet under his eyes, his skin was sallow, and his hair was dyed or he was wearing a wig."

"How old would you say he was?" Falk asked.

"I'm no magician. I got a good look at him for the first time when we reached the tenth floor. It's only a guess, but I'd say he was in his late fifties."

"Did he speak at all?" Falk asked.

"He spoke no words. Like I said before, he passed us and disappeared around the circular hallway."

Falk's mind began to race. Could the tall man in the blue suit be the killer? Could the Japanese businessman be right about his being older and wearing a wig? Finished with his statement, he said to Yozo, "Your English is very good. Did you study with an American English teacher?"

"As a matter of fact, Detective Falk, I did. He came to our university from California. He was an American, but his nationality was Japanese."

"I guess it doesn't hurt to know more than one language," Falk interjected.

"In our business it's a must for those of who travel, as I told you before. Learning English is the most important, since we do so much business with your country."

Russell popped his head into the room and hollered to Falk, "Homicide just got off the elevator!"

Falk handed the statement to the Japanese businessman and said, "Please read the statement. If it's okay, sign your name on the bottom."

Yozo was satisfied with the statement taken by the American detective. Finding no mistakes, he signed it. Falk then picked it up and said, "Thank you for your cooperation, Mr. Miyako, you've been very helpful."

"If you're finished with me for the present, I will have to cancel the meeting with Fairfield today."

Falk then asked, "Where is the meeting supposed to be held?"

"In the meeting room of Fairways."

"I suggest you take Mr. Hart with you, to make sure you don't tell them that your boss has been murdered."

"If you insist, I will ask Mr. Hart to accompany me. However, I know the investigation is the job of the police, and I would not interfere or hinder in any way."

"Thank you, Mr. Miyako," Falk said with relief.

Chapter 9

Falk met the homicide team out in the hallway. He wasn't surprised to see four of them, as he was aware of a heavy investigation. They did so to garner all information possible in the early stage of the investigation. This, no doubt, would be considered a heavy by the fact that the victim was a prominent visiting Japanese businessman.

Sergeant Jerry Gore led the homicide team. With him were the members of his team, Detectives Joe Sanchez, Danny Wolfe, and Frank Arena. Bob Hart had met them in the lobby and brought them up to the tenth floor.

Before leaving headquarters, Gore asked his boss, Lieutenant Jim Kelly, for additional bodies for the initial investigation. Kelly called Jake Wimmer at the Fourth Squad and was given permission for Gore to use his two Fourth Squad detectives. Homicide worked on evidence; it was known throughout major police departments that the first seventy-two hours were the most important for putting facts together.

Falk approached the tall, six-foot three blonde sergeant and handed him the statement he had taken from Mr. Miyako, then added, "I'll give you a supplementary report on what Detective Rochester and myself have accomplished, then bug out."

"You're not going anywhere. I got permission from your boss to use both you and your partner today and tomorrow."

Falk liked what he heard. His ambition was to become part of the Homicide team. He was aware the Fourth was not a heavy, or a busy, precinct. To make Homicide, having a "rabbi" was still the best way. A phone call to the right ear could do the job. The only connection he had with a rabbi was his Jewish heritage. As for a hook, he had none. In the next two days, he had his chance to impress Gore, and hoped the tall sergeant would become his "rabbi."

Gore finished reading the statement Falk had taken and was impressed. Addressing him, he said, "Nice job, Barry. Neat, precise, and to the point."

Falk was pleased at Gore's remarks, then added his own opinion, "I think you might want to talk to Mr. Miyako. He's a sharp piece of work. As you can see from his statement, he believes the man that got off on the same floor as they did either dyed his hair or was wearing a wig. His thought was the man was trying to look younger than his true age. There's an outside chance he could be the perp, Sarge."

Gore nodded, "Thanks Barry, I'll keep that in mind."

Detective Rochester approached the team leader and handed him a statement he had taken.

"Who gave you this?" Gore asked.

"I took it from a James Lamberson who has the adjoining room to the victim. He and his wife went out to dinner and returned to the hotel about nine o'clock last night."

"Did you check his background?" Gore asked.

"Yeah, he and the bride are from Brockton, Massachusetts. They spent their honeymoon out on Montauk Point and are flying back home from MacArthur Airport in the morning."

Putting his hand on Rochester's shoulder, with a straight face, Gore said, "I got news for you, Rochester. If I was on my honeymoon and a cannon went off, I wouldn't have heard it."

The remarks drew laughs from both Rochester and Falk.

Doc Alchermes came out the room carrying his bag. Seeing Gore, he approached him, saying, "Sergeant, the wagon is on its way to pick up the body. I'm heading back to the morgue to do an autopsy. Who's the lead detective watching the autopsy?"

"I haven't assigned one as yet. I'll witness it myself. Give me about an hour, okay?"

"See you at the morgue," the doctor replied upon leaving.

Sergeant Gore, along with his team, went into Room 1004 and reviewed the body. Addressing Detective Callahan, he said, "Joe, as soon as you can, when you get back to your office, I want you to put a package together. We need a set of the victim's prints, along with a picture, to send to the Tokyo police. Detective Arena will pick it up this afternoon."

Answering the homicide sergeant's request, Callahan said, "We've already taken his prints, Sarge."

Gore then asked, "Did you lift any good prints?"

"Plenty. My guess is they all belong to former guests or the house cleaning crew. There's no doubt in my mind this dude used gloves. We did pick up two sets of dried blood found by the laser flashlight. One was on the rug, close to the body; the other on his walking cane. Besides the dried blood, we found several strands of gray hair. It's possible the victim got off a blow before going down for the count."

Gore was pleased by the finds Identification picked up. The ID detectives and the Lab were always in the background, receiving little recognition on the clearance of a major crime.

Gore then commented, "I have a strong feeling both the blood and hair the laser flashlight picked up belong to the shooter." Then he added, "I'm heading over to the Medical Examiner's to witness the autopsy. When I'm finished there, I'll head for the lab and pick up the report myself."

The county police department was a large one and had all their facilities at headquarters, including a topnotch lab, unlike many small departments that have to send out forensic evidence to their state capitals where the FBI labs usually do the work. This advantage saves the county many hours and often helps seal a case within the first seventy-two hours.

Returning to the hallway, Gore addressed his team, "We need a room to talk and go over what we have."

Hart, standing close by and overhearing, called over to Gore, "Room 1010 is available, Sarge. You're welcome to use it."

"Thanks, Mr. Hart. We'll only need it for about an hour."

"Stay as long as you need," Hart replied.

Just as they were about to head toward the room, the elevator door opened. Out stepped a smiling Dick Purcell. Seeing Gore with his team, he walked over to him and said, "Sorry I'm late. I had a last minute call on a case I'm taking to trial tomorrow. The call took longer than I anticipated."

"Knowing you, Dick, I'll take that line with a grain of salt," Gore commented.

The young assistant district attorney was always telling jokes and war stories about his cases. It was hard to know when he was kidding or telling the truth. A dapper dresser, the five-six Purcell wore stacked heels to give a taller appearance. He had a pleasant face with a ruddy complexion that accentuated his bright blue eyes.

Pointing to his team, Gore said, "You know Sanchez, Arena, Wolfe. Meet Barry Falk and Tim Rochester, Fourth Squad."

"I know both of them," Purcell said. Then with a wave of his hand, added, "Have no fear, men, Dick is here." With that, they all laughed.

Room 1010 had only two chairs, so Hart supplied the rest. After all were seated, he addressed Falk and Rochester, saying, "When you guys in the squad have a case you do the investigation, make the arrest, then hand your paperwork over to an assistant district attorney. We, in Homicide, have to call him right off the bat. Since it's a major crime, he comes to the scene, checks over the cadaver, talks to the specialist detective, like ID Lab, and usually the man in charge. We do the investigating; hopefully we make the arrest, and then turn the case over to him to prosecute. Any questions on that?" Having none, the sergeant continued, "This case is a major investigation. Why? Two reasons: one, politics; two, it's a homicide. Up to this point, hotel management is not aware that a murder was committed on the premises. All they know is that some kind of a crime took place on the tenth floor. Shortly, I will go down and notify them before the meat wagon arrives on the scene and they start screaming."

Gore coughed, and then continued talking, "From the looks of what we have learned so far, it appears to me we're not going to solve this one within the first seventy-two hours. Whether we do or not, one thing is for sure—we're gonna put a hell of a dent into the case.

"As all of you are aware, homicides are not solved by a superman detective like on TV and the movies. That type of detective does not exist. The name of the game is teamwork. We follow the book, no primadonnas. All agreed?"

All nodded in agreement, then the boss continued, "On a heavy like this one, we need bodies. Since two of our detectives are out, Andy Laurencelle who's sick and Joe Gentile who's on vacation, I have borrowed two Fourth Squad detectives temporarily. As for who our lead detective will be, I haven't given it a thought and probably won't until I see how much we accomplish today and tomorrow. So, let the games begin."

Gore paused for a moment, and then gave out assignments. "Danny, cover the floor. Rochester has done Rooms 3 and 5, so skip them. If no one's in, leave your calling card. Try and find out if anyone heard a scuffle or possible gunfire, or saw any suspicious people in the hallway last night."

Wolfe raised his hand and asked, "How many shots were fired?"

"Three," Gore replied.

"It's my guess, since no one in the adjoining rooms heard anything the shooter used a silencer."

"You're probably right, Dan," said Gore. "Still, we have to cover our ass and follow the book."

Gore then addressed Falk, "Barry, get the address and phone number of the doorman. Call him. Then head over to his house and get a statement. It's been my experience in the past that doormen are like clergy, they see and hear a lot." He then turned to Sanchez, "Joe, take Rochester down to the main floor with you."

Handing Sanchez the statement Falk had taken from the victim's secretary, Gore continued, "Have the manager make you two copies and give one to Rochester. It describes a possible suspect. Ask all the hotel personnel about him. It's very possible someone saw him in the lobby. Get a list of the night personnel and call them from the manager's office."

Addressing Rochester directly, he said, "Tim, hit the shops on the main floor, the restaurant and lounge. Find out if the Japanese businessmen purchased anything from them. The Japs are great for shopping and picture taking. Describe the tall man in the dark blue suit. It's possible he may have been shadowing them and came into the store the same time they did. Do the same at the restaurant and lounge."

Sanchez then interjected, "You want me to see the manager and ask him for a list of the employees who were on the night shift last night. What am I supposed to tell him when he asks me what's going on up on the tenth floor?"

"We'll go down together. I'll fill him in on what happened last night. Then I'll apologize for the inconvenience we caused, disrupting the daily activities of the hotel, and tell him how important it is not to talk to the media."

Looking across the room in the direction of Arena, Gore said, "Frank, return to headquarters. Call Big Sky in Chicago and Freeway in Los Angeles. See the victim's secretary next door for the names and phone numbers of the headmen to call. Give them the facts and try to find out anything we should know, like did they receive any phone calls for Maehara.

"Then call the Fourth Precinct desk, get the names of the sector car operators that covered the Carlyle last night. Ask them if they checked the shopping center, how many times, and describe the tall man to them. It's a shot in the dark, but who knows? Anything is possible.

"In the afternoon, see Callahan. He has a package for you, a set of the victim's fingerprints and his photo. Fax them to the Tokyo police along with a statement giving them all the facts and requesting his background. Who knows how clean this guy really is? And if he's dirty, he very well could have made a lot of enemies. Any questions, Frank?"

"Just one. This morning we passed a small shopping center. I noticed a supermarket and a half dozen stores. Is that the one?"

Gore replied, "That's the one. It's a good thing it's small. If it was a large one, it probably wouldn't be worth looking into."

Dick Purcell then entered the conversation, saying, "While you were talking, Jerry, I read the secretary's statement. What's his room number? I'd like to have a talk with him."

"He's next door in Room 1003. I'm stopping by to see him before going down to the main floor. I want him to come to headquarters and meet with our police artist in Identification. His description of the tall man in the elevator could be the key to solving this case."

Before returning to headquarters, Gore stopped at the morgue in Hauppauge to watch Doc Alchermes perform the autopsy. The medical examiner is one of the most important men in a homicide investigation. If needed, he can tell you what the victim ate before death and the time he had the meal. In a rape case he can, by examining the vagina, tell if forced penetration was made; if so, the rapist's semen becomes an important part of the investigation. In the case of Koki Maehara, all that was needed was the time of death, what type of bullets was used, and the angle the bullets entered. This often tells if a right or left-handed person killed the victim.

Gore witnessed the spent bullets being removed, then with the use of forceps, being placed in an evidence bag. From the angle the bullets struck, it appeared to the detective that the shooter was left-handed. However, he would let ballistics decide on that one. The casing of the spent bullets was scratched. Gore had seen this before. His guess was the perp had taken his weapon to a gun expert and had a silencer hole bored into the inside of the weapon. Again, this was something he had learned from a specialist in ballistics, since that was not his field of expertise. On the stand, an expert would be the only one qualified to express an opinion.

In the meantime, Frank Arena returned to the Homicide office and sat down at his desk. His first call was to the Fourth Precinct desk. The phone rang twice before being answered, "Officer Karczewski, Fourth Precinct."

"'Ski, this is Arena from Homicide. I need a favor."

"Name it."

"Who were the sector car operators who covered the Carlyle Hotel on the four to midnight last night?"

"Hold on a minute, I'll check the log book."

The Homicide detective waited about forty seconds before the desk officer returned and responded to his question, "Joe Banasiak and Rudy Schopp."

"They on tonight?"

"Last night for both."

"When they come on duty, could you have one of them call me at Homicide?"

"I'll see to your request myself, Arena. Any suspects on the Carlyle murder?" Karczewski asked.

"I never mentioned a murder, 'Ski."

"You didn't have to. When a Homicide dick calls asking to speak to last night's operator that covered the hotel, I just put two and two together. Why else would Homicide want to know who worked the four to twelve shift covering the Carlyle?"

Arena answered the desk officer by saying, "Then you'll have to read about it in *Newsday*. They usually have all the information first. I appreciate your help, Ski. I'll expect a call sometime after four."

After his conversation with Karczewski, Arena dialed the number of Freeway Electronics in Los Angeles and asked to speak with the manager, Mike Whalen, after identifying himself as a police detective from Long Island.

"Mike Whalen here. What's this all about?"

"Mr. Whalen, I'm sorry to tell you that a Mr. Maehara, who I understand is a business associate with your firm, was murdered last night in his hotel room in Hauppauge, Long Island."

"Oh, my God, I can't believe it. He was here just a week ago. What happened, Detective?"

"He was shot twice in the head sometime about ten o'clock last night."

"Robbery?"

"No, nothing was taken. As of now, we have no motive."

"Is there anything I can do to assist you in your investigation?" Whalen asked.

"Yes, that's why I'm calling. Think back, did anyone contact your office asking for information about Mr. Maehara? What I'm getting at is we believe the man who murdered Mr. Maehara was keeping tabs on him and possibly knew when he was arriving at the Carlyle. We have the description of a possible suspect: a gray-haired man, possibly six-two, slim, and although I know it sounds ridiculous, a senior citizen. It's only a guess, but he very well may have known Maehara. Since your company was working with his firm, can you shed some light on why he was murdered?"

"I've known Mr. Maehara for a number of years. He has always been quiet, polite, and a gentleman. We had the utmost respect for him here in Los Angeles. I really have no knowledge of anyone who might have been his enemy, unless..." The phone went quiet for a moment.

Arena, unable to control his excitement at a possible lead, asked, "Unless? Unless what?"

"We had a call the morning Mr. Maehara left for Chicago from a man who called himself Jim Monahan, claiming he was with an outfit called Cataldo of Brooklyn. He wanted to talk to Mr. Maehara regarding his company. I took him for a phony and hung up on him."

"Why did you think he was a phony?" Arena asked.

"Several reasons. One, I knew Maehara was very happy with Fairfield in the New York area. And two, I have a good deal of respect for Cataldo. They have integrity and would never hire a salesman who would try to undercut."

"Jim Monahan. I'll check him out. Thank you, Mr. Whalen. If you think of anything else, call me." He gave his phone number and hung up. Then he called Big Sky in Chicago.

The call was answered on the second ring. "Big Sky Electronics. Hold, please." Good thing the department's paying, Frank thought, since these are long distance calls.

"Go ahead, please," a fast-talking operator shot back.

"Detective Arena, Homicide, Suffolk County Police Department. It's important that I talk with your general manager."

"That would be Mr. Earl Huminek," the fast-talking operator said. "Hold, please. I'll connect you."

Shortly a male voice answered, "Huminek here. What's this all about?"

"Sir, my name is Detective Frank Arena. I'm investigating a homicide that occurred in our area. Last night, Mr. Maehara, a Japanese citizen, was murdered in his hotel room, sometime about ten o'clock."

"Mr. Maehara dead? I don't believe it."

"He's dead, all right. The reason I'm calling is we believe the killer followed his path from Los Angeles to New York."

"I can't believe it, Mr. Maehara dead," Huminek repeated once again.

"Believe it, sir. Can you tell me something about Mr. Maehara?"

"All I can say is he was a perfect gentleman."

"Did anyone call your company asking questions about him?"

"Not that I'm aware of."

"How about a man who calls himself Jim Monahan, representing Cataldo Electronics?"

"I'm familiar with Cataldo Electronics. They have a good reputation. But I've never heard of a Jim Monahan."

"Sir, take down my number here in Long Island. Call if you think or hear of anything that might shed some light on our investigation. Ask for Detective Arena."

"I'll call you immediately if I do, Detective," Huminek said, and then once again repeated, "I can't believe Mr. Maehara was murdered."

Arena gave Huminek his phone number and sat back. The time now was after 3:00 p.m. Leaving his desk, Arena walked around the hall to Identification and picked up the fingerprints and photo. As he walked back to his desk, he noticed Sergeant Gore had returned from the morgue and was in Lieutenant Kelly's office reviewing the case.

He glanced at the wall clock, which showed three-fifty. Most all sector car officers were relieved at a quarter to the hour. So, no doubt the man he wanted was in the car and reading the daily activity report; he should be calling soon. Mental telepathy then took over and the phone rang. Picking it up, he answered, "Arena here."

"Detective Arena, this is Joe Banasiak. What can I do for you?"

"I'm sure by now you know a murder occurred last night at the Carlyle."

"That's what the man I relieved told me. How can I help?"

"How often do you check the shopping center at the foot of the hill below the Carlyle?"

"Depends on how busy our tour is. Thursday nights are usually slow. I believe we checked it two, maybe three times. Who you looking for?"

"We're grasping at straws. The victim's secretary gave the description of a man who went to the tenth floor with them. He's tall, six-two, slim, wearing a fedora hat and dark blue suit. So far, we don't know if he was a hotel guest or the possible perp. Did you see anyone fitting that description coming or going? Oh, one thing more, he was carrying a small black bag or suitcase."

"I myself saw no such person. Hold on, I'll ask my partner." Returning a short time later, he said, "He saw no one fitting that description, either."

"Calling you was a shot in the dark. Thanks anyway, Banasiak."

"Good luck on your case, Arena." Then he hung up

❈   ❈   ❈

It was 5:15 p.m. when Barry Falk walked into the Homicide headquarters in Yaphank. He was the last of the team to finish his assignment. Gore, realizing his team would bump heads with the night crew coming on duty, made arrangements with the commanding officer of Homicide, Detective Lieutenant Jim Kelly, to use his office. Gore sat down, facing his detectives who were sitting in a circle on the other side of Kelly's desk.

After reading Falk's supplementary he was ready to begin to put the pieces of the puzzle together. Looking over the desk in the direction of his team, he said, "Before we go over each individual report, let's review our case from the beginning. Our victim was a man, seventy-seven years of age. He, along with his secretary, a Mr. Yozo Miyako, were here on business and knew no one, with the exception of a few of the personnel from Fairfield Electronics, a local company in Hauppauge that does subcontracting work for the victim's firm."

The blond sergeant continued to address his team, going over the day's investigation so that each member would know what was accomplished. Gore believed in working as a team, holding back nothing from his men. By working together they would piece the puzzle together.

Leaning on the desk with both elbows he continued, "Last night sometime between 9:30 and close to 10:00 p.m. an unknown perp enters the victim's room and shoots him twice in the head. Rooms on both sides are occupied, his secretary on the east, a young couple on the west. All of them are young and no doubt their hearing is good. Still, neither heard a gun go off or heard a struggle. We have to presume at this point the shooter used a silencer.

"On his night table laying out in plain sight was his wallet containing about six hundred dollars, a very valuable gold ring, and a Rolex watch. Strangely enough nothing was taken, which leads me to believe he may know the person and that's the reason he opened the door. If it was a crack addict, he would have been cleaned out. Since nothing was taken, we're temporarily ruling out robbery as the motive.

"So, let's see what we learned today, beginning with Dan."

The sandy-haired, former jughead was the senior investigator on Gore's team. Standing five-ten, he was built like a johnny pump with large hands and biceps. He reminded Gore of Brian Dennehy of the movies, both in looks and mannerisms. Often told he was a look-alike by friends, he would answer with, the only thing we have in common is we both graduated from Chaminade High School in Mineola.

Speaking up and answering his sergeant, he said, "I found very few of the guests in their rooms, so I left my calling card under the doors. The few I did speak with didn't see anything out of the ordinary coming or going to their rooms. I caught one that was in his room last night. He heard no shots. That's all I have to report."

Gore then called on Rochester, "What about you, Tim?"

"My job was to check all the shops on the main floor, the lounge, and the coffee shop. Unlike most visiting Japanese who like to shop, these two spent no time in any of the shops. I described the tall man in the elevator and found no one who saw him.

"As for the lounge, it was closed for renovations. The girl in the coffee shop said the secretary called her on the phone, but she never saw either one of them. Again, no one in the restaurant saw anyone that fits the description of the tall man in the elevator. That's about it, Sarge."

"Thanks, Tim." Then Gore pointed toward Sanchez, "What about you, Joe?"

The five-nine Latin was a muscular man, somewhat like Wolfe. But unlike Dan, whose build was genetically gifted, Sanchez kept in shape working out several days a week in the gym at Headquarters. His tight-fitting suits were made for him to show off his muscular body and his black mustache gave him the macho look. In the bottom of his desk he kept a shaving kit, toilet articles, and hair spray. A natty dresser, he always appeared as if he just stepped off the runway of a fashion show. The fact was, he was the team's swordsman, a term used by the metropolitan police in New York, meaning he was a ladies' man. He was also outspoken and gregarious. His mannerisms were a constant annoyance to Gore. Often during a serious briefing he would tell a joke, bringing laughter throughout the room and breaking up the sergeant's thoughts. In spite of his comical attitude, he was a good cop and always came through when Gore needed him.

Addressing his sergeant, Sanchez said, "You cleared the way for me, Sarge, when you filled the manager in on what happened the night before. I might add you did a nice con job on him, letting him know if he called the media before the police released the story, he could hamper our investigation. Bauman took me into his office, gave me all the privacy I needed and the use of his phone, along with a list of the night crew's addresses and phone numbers.

"My first call was to Joe Sacca, the night manager. His wife answered and told me he was sleeping. When I told here a murder happened last night while her husband was on duty, she woke him up. It took him a minute or so to come to the phone. I thought for sure he'd be pissed being woke up out of a deep sleep. Much to my surprise he was a cheerful guy. When he asked about the murder, I gave him all the facts I had.

"Then, when I told him the victim was Japanese, he asked if it was the older one or the younger one and if it was robbery. I explained why it wasn't robbery and that we have no witness or motive or any idea who killed him. As it turned out, he was no help to us at all. Seems he spent most of the night in his office making up the payroll. He suggested calling the night clerks who had been on duty and was about to tell me who they were when I told him I was calling from Bauman's office and had their home addresses and phone numbers.

"The next call I made was to a clerk named Mel Kreim. This guy is a heavy sleeper. He let it ring eight times before answering the phone. I gotta say, if someone called me and let the phone ring eight times I'd be pissed. At first he was annoyed, but when I told him who I was he calmed down. Kreim remembered giving Maehara his card key, and thought it was about 9:15 or so. I then asked him if a man about six-two wearing a dark blue suit registered last night, and he said that no one of that description checked in while he was on duty. He suggested I call the other clerks.

"On the third call, I struck gold. According to the records, the clerk I called, Len Conway, is a student by day at Stony Brook University and works at the Carlyle at night. He described himself as a professional gofer, part-time clerk, part-time bellhop, whatever and wherever he was needed. When I told him that Maehara was murdered while he was on duty last night, he said, 'No shit, who killed him!?' 'That's why I'm calling you, kid. We have no idea and we're trying to put our facts together. We know Maehara came back to the hotel about 9:22 last night. Were you working with Kreim behind the desk at that time?' The kid paused for a minute, then took the wind out of me when he said, 'I think I can shed some light on your case, Detective.' He told me that last night at 9:10 a couple named Brown from Columbus, Ohio, checked into the hotel. The bellhops were busy, so he took their luggage up to their room. Returning in the elevator to the main floor, the doors opened and there were three people waiting to get on. Two were Japanese, the third a white male. I asked the kid how tall the white male was and he replied, 'Same height as myself.'"

"How tall is the Conway kid?" Gore asked.

"I haven't seen the kid in person, but he described himself to me as an underweight, six-foot-two stringbean."

"Did he describe the man?"

"His description fits the one Miyako gave to Falk. Tall, wearing a blue suit, tinted glasses, fedora hat, and a small black suitcase."

"Could the kid ID him in a lineup?"

"I asked him that question, Sarge. His answer was, 'maybe yes, maybe no. The man's hat covered part of his face, and the tinted glasses covered his eyes.'"

"How about the second white male that we know entered the elevator? Did he hear him holler for it?"

"He said the guy ran right past him, and the kid knew him because he was on duty when he checked into the hotel. Name's Allan Dent, a jewelry salesman from Cleveland. I asked Bauman, the manager, about Dent. Seems he's here for a jewelry seminar and is usually back in the hotel between 4:00 and 5:00, except for one day when they ran late.

"So I decided to wait around since it was already three o'clock. When he didn't arrive at three-thirty, I decided to wait a little longer. At four-ten he walks in. From behind the desk Bauman gives me the eye, so I approached Dent. The guy is a walking target for a hit man—gold dripping around his neck and several gold rings. Nice guy, though, and gave me his full cooperation.

"He said the tall man stood in the back of the elevator with his arms folded. He wore a fedora hat and large, dark tinted glasses. He figured he was a new hotel guest because he had a small black bag between his legs. He didn't pay much attention to him."

"Could he recognize him if he saw him again?" asked Gore.

"His answer was the same as the Conway kid, maybe yes, maybe no."

"Did you take a statement from him, Joe?"

"No, didn't think it was necessary. I taped him, and we have his address in Cleveland if we should need him."

"Nice piece of work, Joe," Gore said reluctantly. Then, calling on Falk, he asked, "How did your investigation go, Barry?"

"Very good, Sarge. My assignment was the doorman, a guy named Pat DeMarco. Like the others, he was sleeping when I called. He was cheerful enough, and when I told him I wanted to talk to him regarding a crime that occurred last evening at the Carlyle, he perked right up and seemed anxious to hear what happened. Then he invited me to come over to his house.

"He's no Harvard grad, but a guy with a lot of street sense and will make a hell of a witness for the district attorney. He's in his fifties, a bachelor, no roommates, lives alone. It was apparent from the inside of his home he never used a cleaning lady, or for that matter, no one could ever call him Mr. Clean."

"Get to the point, Barry. We don't need to know his personal history," Gore interjected.

"He saw the tall man in the dark suit, he believes on two occasions. The first time DeMarco spotted him the guy was walking towards the entrance carrying a small black bag. When DeMarco eyeballed him the tall man seemed to be looking for something in his wallet. Then a car approached and he lost track of him. He looked at his watch, a habit he says he has learned over the years. The time was 8:30 p.m."

"Could he identify this man if he saw him again?" the sergeant asked.

"He was about twenty feet away, but claims he could ID him again," Falk replied.

"You said he was wearing a blue suit. How about the fedora and the tinted glasses?"

"He was wearing both."

"Very good, Barry. Very good," a please Gore responded.

"There's more, Sarge." Falk then continued, "A couple of hours later he was helping a new guest with his bags when he sees a man carrying a small black suitcase walking in a fast pace down the hill in an easterly direction. He thought, why didn't that guy call a cab? Then it hit him that he was the same size and build as the guy he had seen earlier in the blue suit. Both had been carrying a small black bag."

"If he was suspicious, why didn't he confront the man and ask him for identification?" Gore asked.

"He was sure he was a cat burglar and could be packing. If they were dressed the same, he would have called the police. Since they weren't, he thought they would think he was crazy, so he did the next best thing and wrote down the guy's description and the time he left, which was 10:10 p.m."

"You said the 'second' man was dressed different."

Falk continued, "The 'first' man wore a blue suit and a hat. The second man wore a maroon jacket and had dirty blond hair."

"This DeMarco, is he psychic? He never saw the second man's face, yet he says he is the same man he saw earlier dressed different? Is it possible the doorman is one of these guys who fantasizes and is making the whole thing up?"

"My opinion of DeMarco is he has good street sense and he's telling it just the way he saw it. We know there was a man in a blue suit. We never told him, still he told us. For what it's worth, Sarge, it's possible he saw the perp coming and going. The best part is he eyeballed him the first time, and most likely can give the police artist a hell of a facial description."

"Did you tell him a murder was committed?"

"No, he seemed to think he spotted a cat burglar, so I let it go at that."

"What did he do with the information he wrote down?"

"After he was relieved at midnight he went inside and looked for the house detective. Unable to find him, he left the info in Security's night bin."

"Strange," thought Gore, "Hart never mentioned a note." Then, pointing to the last man to be heard, Gore said, "Frank, fill us in on what you found out."

The five-ten detective, known by his teammates as The Quiet Man, maintained his one hundred sixty pound frame by watching his diet. On occasion he would eat up a storm, usually when he visited his father or a relative. He had to be given a lot of credit for controlling his will power, considering cooking was his hobby. Growing up in Corona, a heavily populated Italian section located in the borough of Queens, on Saturday afternoons when all his friends were playing ball, young Frank could be found in the kitchen of his father's restaurant watching his dad, Antonio, preparing the meals. His father grew up in Siracusa, Sicily, where his father before him was also a chef. Along with his brother, Francis, they learned the art of cooking in a fine gourmet restaurant. The brothers immigrated to the States, both becoming chefs in small Italian restaurants. Saving their pennies, nickels, and dimes, they finally had enough to open their own Italian restaurant in Corona, naming it *Enrico's* after their father.

Checking his notes, Arena addressed his team, saying, "The Sarge gave me the job of sending a fax to the Tokyo police, giving them the details of the homicide regarding one of their citizens. I came back to Headquarters and asked Detective Callahan for a photograph of Mr. Maehara, along with his fingerprints. Then I faxed them to the Tokyo police. I'm still waiting to hear from them.

"I also contacted Freeway Electronics in Los Angeles by phone. The victim's secretary, Miyako, supplied the name of the general manager, a Mr. Mike Whalen, as the man to talk to. I found out from Whalen that about ten days ago he received a call from a Jim Monahan claiming to represent Cataldo Electronics of Brooklyn and asking to speak with Mr. Maehara. Whalen asked why and the guy gave him a cock and bull story that Maehara was interested in doing business with his firm. He was lying, of course, so he hung up on him."

"Why," Gore asked, "would Whalen think the man was giving him a cock and bull story?"

"He gave two reasons; first, Cataldo is a firm with integrity and wouldn't hire a man like Monahan; second, when he left Los Angeles, Maehara told Whalen he was more than happy with the three firms he did business with in the States. That, of course, included Fairfield."

"My next call was to Big Sky in Chicago. The man I was told to speak with was a Mr. Earl Huminek, the headman. All this guy kept saying was, 'I can't believe he's dead.' He was no help at all. Apparently Monahan never called him.

"My guess is Monahan called Los Angeles, and when Whalen told him Maehara had just left for Chicago, Monahan skipped calling Big Sky and instead made a call to Fairfield."

"Did you check out Cataldo and Jim Monahan?" Gore asked.

"Yes, Cataldo is for real. They are an electronics firm out of Brooklyn. As for Jim Monahan, their personnel department has no record of any employee by that name."

"As you can see, the case gets more interesting hour by hour," said Gore. "Now, let me tell you what I have learned from the medical examiner, lab, and identification department. Doc Alchermes removed two bullets from the victim's head. One hit was below the eye, the second right smack in the forehead. Both bullets had pointed heads. This occurs when a silencer is used. It has something to do with the boring when the silencer is screwed into the weapon. From the size of the bullets, he no doubt used a thirty-eight special. Doc believes from the way the bullets entered the victim, our shooter may be left-handed. Doc's not an expert, and you can be sure I'll check it out with Ballistics, but the Doc is rarely wrong.

"After the autopsy I went to see Callahan in Identification and he had some good news. The laser flashlight showed a few strands of gray hair and dried blood. He sent it over to the lab along with the walking cane he found it on. Apparently, the old man may have hit the shooter before he was killed. Callahan also found a few specks of dried blood on the rug alongside the victim. He cut the piece out and sent it to the lab to Detective Cuomo.

"As for fingerprints, he found plenty. Tonight the night team will print the employees at the Carlyle who worked last night. Tomorrow, Identification will do the same with the cleaning crew. Like Callahan said, the job has to be done, but our shooter no doubt wore gloves. Any questions?"

"I have one," Wolfe said. "Was the blood on the cane and the rug the same type?"

"Yes, Dan. Both the blood on the carpet and on the victim's cane came back O-negative."

"Who's to say the blood belonged to the shooter? Maybe the victim also has O-negative."

"We checked that out, Dan. He has A-negative blood. Any more questions?" No one responded, so Gore summed up the day's work.

"This morning we had a dead cadaver, age seventy-seven, found with two bullet holes in his head. We now know both bullets came from a number thirty-eight and the shooter used a silencer. That's why neither his secretary nor the honeymoon couple heard a gun go off. The victim's wallet containing over six hundred dollars, his gold ring, and Rolex watch sat only a few feet away from where he fell, yet our shooter took nothing. We know he has been following Mr. Maehara, at least by phone, using an alias, Jim Monahan, from California to New York. Why?

"We have a possible suspect about six-two, slim, and who has gray hair. Most likely he's a senior citizen. Witnesses say he wore a dark blue suit, a fedora hat, tinted glasses, and carried a small black bag. One witness, the doorman, claims he may have changed clothes. He could have been carrying a change of clothing in the black bag. He apparently did not use a car to get to the hotel. My guess is he parked close by and walked.

"We've accomplished a good bit, but we still have a long way to go. We've done all we can today. Tomorrow is another day, so go home and get a good night's sleep and report back here at 9:00 a.m. sharp, full of piss and vinegar."

Gore then finished up with, "I know I don't really have to tell any of you—but no quotes to the media at all. We have to be careful how much we tell them, and that's my job. See you in the morning."

✤ ✤ ✤

The night supervisor, Kevin Fagan, was in the Sergeant's office when Gore entered. Looking up from his sitting position, he said, "Heard you picked up a heavy. Any leads?"

"Description, no names," Gore answered. Handing Fagan a press release, he said, "Kelly wants you to give this to the media when they make their late calls. Since the victim was a prominent businessman, you will no doubt get calls from all the New York media and maybe some from the surrounding areas."

Detective Stan Mullins stood in the hall and waved to Gore through the glass partition in the upper part of the office door. "You have something for me, Stan?"

"There's a visitor downstairs. Says he has an appointment with you. His name sounds Japanese."

"Shit, I forgot all about him. Stan, do me a favor. Call the desk and have them issue him a pass and directions to Identification on the second floor. I'll meet him there."

Mullins asked, "Is he your witness?"

"One of them. He's the secretary of the victim, and hopefully got a good enough look at our perp to give the police artist a good look-alike sketch."

Outside in the parking lot, Sanchez walked side by side with Wolfe. It's early, Danny, how about stopping for a cold one?"

"Not tonight, amigo. Marsha's holding supper for me. Besides, I got a promise."

"All you married guys are alike, no balls," said Sanchez. Then he spotted Falk and Rochester walking behind him. "Any of you guys interested in stopping for a cold one?"

"I'll take a rain check," Falk blurted out.

Rochester, on the other hand, said, "Why not? I got no one to go home to."

Putting his arms around the shoulders of the big detective, Sanchez smiled, "You single, Tim?"

"You bet your ass. Tried it once and that was enough for me."

As they walked away from Wolfe and Falk, Sanchez could be heard saying, "After we have a few brews, we can stop at my place for a shower, then grab a bite to eat before we hit the Siren Wails Disco. Tonight's ladies' night and the best meat rack in town. If we fail to score there, I know two sisters that give the best head in town."

＊　　　　　　＊　　　　　　＊

Shortly after Arena sent out his fax, the Tokyo Police Communications Bureau picked it up. Immediately the report was sent to the office of Chief Inspector Mitsuo Mauri and stamped, "READ IMMEDIATELY." The chief of the detective division had read about the death of Maehara and was aware he was the victim of a murder in America. He was pleased that the American police had sent him the report requesting his assistance.

Mitsuo Mauri was one of Japan's new breed, far removed from the old society. At the university he studied criminal justice and linguistics. Japan was now somewhat of a democracy initiated by the United States after World War II under the reign of General Douglas MacArthur. When Mauri joined the police department he was aware of two things. One, to master the English language. And two, to attend all the upper as well as middle class functions. No better way to get ahead. Since he rose to the rank of Chief Inspector he had been invited to most of the wealthy and socially prominent Japanese parties. And although he had met many of the leading businessmen, he had never had the pleasure of meeting Koki Maehara, the city's leading electronics giant. An ambitious man, Inspector Mauri looked forward to the day he would be number one in the Tokyo Police Department.

Before turning the case over to one of his subordinates he pulled out the case file on the mighty and wealthy businessman. Unlike the other leading industrial giants of the business world, the report showed Mr. Maehara led a quiet life, belonging to no local clubs. The report stated he was the president of the Yoshio Electronics organization, a high-tech firm. The company began its first small factory in northern Japan and went unnoticed for many years. In the mid-seventies the company stock began to rise, and overnight Yoshio became well known. The records further showed that Maehara had an apartment in Tokyo and a large home in northern Japan.

Sitting at his desk, he read the fax report once again. He thought it strange that the killer took nothing from the hotel room. Reaching across his desk, he pressed a buzzer. A few minutes later there was a knock on the door. The Inspector spoke, saying, "Come in."

A short, thin, bespectacled man entered the room and said, "You sent for me, sir?"

"Yes, come in. I have a special case I want you to investigate."

Inspector Kase Nomura was a twenty-eight year old inspector who had moved up the ranks faster than many of his older fellow police officers. Like his superior, he too majored in criminal justice in college and studied English knowing that it could enhance his advancement with the department. Nomura bowed, and the chief inspector with a wave of his hand motioned for him to sit in the chair next to his desk. Mauri handed him the fax report and said, "Read, please."

Nomura did so. When finished, he handed the report back to his superior and said, "I have read about the tragic death of Maehara San in the newspapers and have seen it on the television news. It is sad that such an honorable gentleman died such a brutal death so far from home."

The chief inspector nodded his head in agreement, then said, "The Americans have asked for our assistance. I myself know little of Maehara San. He was a very private person who shunned parties and avoided newspaper interviews. Until the New York police faxed his photo to us, I had never seen a picture of him."

Agreeing with his boss and shaking his head, the young inspector said, "It is true that most businessmen belong to a club. Like yourself, I too have never seen a photograph in the newspapers of Maehara San, although I have read about him often in the newspapers."

The chief then addressed his subordinate and said, "I have chosen you to follow up the request of the New York police, because your work is thorough and I consider you one of my better investigators."

Bowing his head, Nomura rose half way and said, "I am deeply honored, Chief Inspector."

"The Americans are asking for a background check on Mr. Maehara. This, of course, we know is routine but nevertheless has to be done.

During the war all the service files were taken to a safe place in northern Japan. After the war they were brought back to Tokyo. Since Maehara San is a man of seventy-seven years of age, he most likely served in either the Army or Navy. I suggest you check his prints with the prints on file by our government."

"As you implied, Chief Inspector, it is a routine matter. Do you believe the Americans are looking for something they may not have indicated to us in the fax report?"

"They are police investigators like we are. Police officers are always suspicious, especially in a murder case. I am sure they have their reasons. Our job is to cooperate with them at this time."

Inspector Nomura rose and bowed. "It is my pleasure that you have chosen me for this important assignment. You have my word that your request shall be done." He then backed out of the room with his head bowed in a graceful manner.

Chapter 10

Friday, March 12, 1993

Sergeant Jerry Gore was born and raised in Fayetteville, North Carolina, the son of a Baptist minister. His parents were of average size, mom five-six and dad five-ten. They were somewhat shocked when young Gore continued to grow, finally stopping at six-foot three inches tall. In the local high school, he was a three-letter man in sports. Since basketball was his best game for a scholarship opportunity, he dropped football and baseball in his senior year, concentrating on the round ball. As luck would have it, his team made the sectional finals, which gave him a lot of exposure to college scouts. Offered a dozen scholarships, he accepted St. Johns in New York, for two reasons: one, he had never been out of the state of North Carolina and two, the Johnnies were a national ranked team. In his four years with St. Johns he never did make the starting lineup. Nevertheless, as the seventh man, managed to get in a good amount of playing time.

It was on a blind date in his sophomore year that Jerry met Linda Gomez. They say opposites attract; in this case, they collided—both falling in love at first sight. They were married and Jerry continued to go to school. Although it was not planned, halfway through Jerry's junior year Linda became pregnant. Her parents lived in Bayshore in Suffolk County. To make ends meet, and for lack of cash they moved in with the Gomez family. Jerry was going into his senior year. In order to maintain his scholarship, he had to play basketball, as he was not able to pay the tuition without it. Off-season he worked part-time for Linda's dad's construction company, trying to pay off the medical bills he owed and the loan he borrowed to pay the doctors.

One of his teammates, also married, confided that he was going to take the New York City Police Department exam. His reason was good pay and benefits, and with a college education, he should be able to advance in rank. Although he never thought of becoming a cop himself, Jerry's teammate's reasons for joining the force seemed viable, and therefore a seed was planted.

A few weeks later he read in Newsday that a new Suffolk County Police test was upcoming. He was surprised to see that the Suffolk County Police were of the highest paid in the United States. But what really impressed him were the benefits. Linda recently learned she was pregnant again and without a job, paying the bills would be a struggle. Sitting down together and going over their finances convinced both of them it was worth a try. A few days before the written examination, he was shocked when he read in the newspaper the large number of men and women that were taking the test.

Entering the junior high school the morning of the test, Jerry was nervous. He slipped into the last available seat in the room. The instructor was walking up and down the aisles handing each candidate a booklet and telling them that at 9:00 a.m. they were to open the booklet and start answering the questions. The time allotted was three and a half hours.

At 9:00 a.m. Jerry opened the booklet and glanced over the pages. He was delighted to see that about half of the one hundred fifty questions were on reading interpretation and grammar. English was his best subject both in high school and at St. Johns. At the conclusion of the exam, he was confident he scored well and wasn't surprised when he was informed of that several weeks later and asked to go through another battery of tests and interviews. At the end of six months, he entered the police academy. That was sixteen years ago…

Sipping a hot cup of coffee, Linda sat alone in their colonial home in the East Patchogue section of Suffolk County staring at the headlines of Newsday, Long Island's leading newspaper. The Carlyle murder took up the full front page. Turning to page two, she read the details of the murder of a Japanese businessman killed in his hotel room by an unknown intruder. A Mr. Hart, head of hotel security, found the body at 8:25 yesterday morning. The newspaper went on to quote her husband, describing him as the detective in charge of the investigation. As usual, his quote was short and to the point, 'The perpetrator or perpetrators entered the victim's room last night sometime between 9:30 and 10:00 p.m., shooting him twice in the face—once below the eye and once in the forehead, using an automatic weapon. At this point in time we have no motive or suspects...'

Sweet Jerry, she thought, how he hated to be interviewed by the press for fear he would be misquoted. The paper went on to say that the police were looking to question two men seen at the hotel. One of the two men was seen entering the lobby about 8:30 p.m. and was described as a slim, white male over six feet tall, wearing a fedora, tinted glasses and a dark blue suit, carrying a small black suitcase. The second man was about the same height and build with dirty blond hair. He was seen leaving the hotel some time after 10:00 p.m. wearing a maroon jacket, beige pants, and also carrying a small black suitcase. Anyone at the hotel the night of March 10th who may have observed either of these men were to call Sergeant Gore at the Suffolk County Police Department. All information would be kept confidential.

A third article quoted the president of Fairfield Electronics, Mr. Eugene Myers, who said, 'We of Fairfield Electronics are appalled by the senseless killing of a business associate all of us admired. The Fairfield company is offering a reward of ten thousand dollars for information leading to the arrest of the killer or killers.'

A sleepy-eyed Jerry Gore entered the kitchen and kissed Linda on the forehead, saying, "You're up early."

"Early? It's after eight o'clock. Who do you think gets the kids up, feeds them, and gets them off to school?"

"Just kidding, just kidding. I forget how easy it is to arouse your Latin temper, especially early in the morning."

Handing him the newspaper, she said only one word, "Coffee?"

"That would be nice, and I'd like an English muffin, too, if it's not too much trouble."

Putting the muffin into the toaster, she then poured his coffee and set it on the kitchen table in front of him. She poured herself a second cup and joined him. "I see you made the headlines. Did you know Fairfield Electronics is offering a ten thousand dollar reward for information leading to the arrest? That Japanese businessman must have been a well-liked man."

Jerry drank some of his coffee and said, "Linda, there's an old saying, 'It takes money to make money.' Fairfield does several million dollars in business with the Japanese company Mr. Maehara was the president of. So by posting a large reward, they are showing the main office in Japan that they are concerned about the death of their leader and are assisting the police in the apprehension of the killer."

As Linda buttered the English muffin, she said, "That makes sense." Then, handing it to Jerry, she added, "The papers also said the police have no suspects, is that true?"

"I'm sorry to say it is. We have a good description of a possible perp, but that's all. This, my dear, won't be an easy one to solve."

"I've heard that song before. You say it every time you have a murder with no suspects. Then, bingo, you make an arrest and it's all over."

Jerry gulped down the rest of his coffee, grabbed the English muffin, and kissed Linda again on the forehead, "Gotta get going. The boss wants to see me in his office before he has to go to the staff meeting."

❄   ❄   ❄

Before he hit the hay the night before, Kelly had called and said he wanted to see him early in the morning before the regular schedule got under way. Although Gore had gathered no new information since he had left a copy of the case jacket on Kelly's desk, the commanding officer of Homicide wanted to make sure he had all the facts before reporting to the Chief of Detectives.

At the staff meeting Lieutenant Kelly would be answering all the questions regarding the Carlyle homicide. Most questions would come from the police commissioner. As the commanding officer of the Homicide Bureau, Jim Kelly's hours were supposedly nine to five with weekends off. Nevertheless, he rarely got out of the office working an eight-hour day. Jerry Gore was also considered a supervisor in command of Team Two under Kelly, who was in command of three teams. Kelly was well aware that if his teams did not produce he could be replaced. One way to have a successful squad was to be sure the detective sergeant was a strong leader.

When Jerry arrived at his boss' office he was greeted warmly by the six foot one, heavyset, bespectacled Irishman, "Have a seat, Jerry, we have a lot to discuss."

"Mind if I help myself to a cup of java?"

"Help yourself," Kelly answered.

Gore then asked, "Have you read the case jacket I left for you?"

"I did, but since I have to face questions from the P.C. and the Chief at the staff meeting, I want to be damn well sure I have all the answers."

Gore shifted in his seat, clasped his fingers together, and then replied, "Let's take it right from the start. Our victim was known as Koki Maehara, the president of Yoshio Electronics of Tokyo, Japan. He subs his work abroad. In the States he works with three companies—one in LA, one in Chicago, and the other in our jurisdiction. The outfit here he deals with is in Hauppauge and the company name is Fairfield Electronics.

"He arrived here in the morning day before yesterday, along with his secretary, a Mr. Yozo Miyako. They were given adjoining rooms on the tenth floor. That night an unknown perp enters Maehara's room between nine-thirty and ten, approximately. And in spite of the fact that his secretary was occupying a room on one side and a honeymoon couple the other, Maehara takes two shots in the face with an automatic weapon and no one hears anything. How am I doing so far, Loo?"

"That's the way the crime happened. Now continue. I've read your report, but it's possible you missed something."

"Okay. Neither the victim nor his secretary has any relatives or friends on the Island, with the exception of the upper echelon of Fairfield Electronics. As a matter of fact, they both had dinner with the boss, a Mr. Eugene Myers, the night Maehara was killed."

Gore took a sip of his coffee, and then continued. "The doorman, a man named Pat DeMarco, observed a tall, slim man over six foot, carrying a small black suitcase, dressed in a dark blue suit, wearing a fedora and tinted glasses, enter the lobby sometime around eight-thirty in the evening. The secretary and another hotel guest from Ohio observed the same man going up with them in the elevator and get off at the tenth floor where the victim was staying. Later we found a clerk named Len Conway who had seen the same tall man entering the elevator as he got off at the main floor. Here we lucked out. Conway was able to tell us the exact height of the man in the blue suit, since he walked right past him. Both he and the mystery man were the same height.

"At ten after ten, the doorman saw a man leaving who was about six feet two inches and slim, also carrying a small black suitcase, only this dude was dressed different. He was wearing a maroon jacket, beige pants, and had dirty blond hair."

"So, we're looking for a shooter who's six-two, slim, and according to your written report, possibly a senior citizen."

Nodding in agreement, the sergeant continued, "Slightly more, Loo. We know his blood type is O-negative, his hair is gray, he used a silencer, and he made phone calls to Los Angeles and Chicago inquiring about Maehara and when and where he would arrive in New York."

"Then it appears the shooter very well may have known Maehara," Kelly said.

"We feel that way. It wasn't robbery. He left six hundred dollars in cash in his wallet, an expensive gold ring, and a Rolex watch in plain sight. I can't figure out why the perp didn't try to make it look robbery, unless for some reason he wanted us to know the shooting was personal. But why?"

"I also see in your report that Mr. Miyako was at Identification last night and a drawing was done by Officer Snyder."

"He was, and drove Maureen crazy. He changed the nose three times, and the ears, chin, eyes a half-dozen times. She finally finished sketching an hour and a half later, one with the hat and shades and one without."

"Does the secretary think this sketch is a good look-alike?" Kelly asked.

"He claims the sketch is a dead ringer for the shooter. We have to remember, though, the fedora and shades covered half his face."

"Do you feel he's reliable?"

"More than reliable. If Miyako said that's what the shooter looked like, I believe him. He has made it a lot easier for us."

"Your supplementary report says a thirty-eight was used. Have you checked with Ballistics?"

"Not yet. I'm doing that this morning."

"It also states that Identification found blood and gray hair by using the laser gun. It seems the victim was able to get off a blow with his cane before the shooter got him. He must have been an agile old man."

"Or the perp himself is up in years and not very agile," Gore added.

"We got a break on the case with the hotel house detective being a former New York City Homicide man."

"You can say that again, Loo. Having Hart on the scene could very well ice this case for us."

"You talked about a second man leaving sometime after ten. He appeared to be the same height and build and also carried a black suitcase. I presume inside the suitcase was a change of clothing."

"That would be my thoughts, providing he was the man in the blue suit."

"I see you had one of your men fax the victim's fingerprints and photo to the Tokyo Police. What do you expect to find?"

"Who knows? Maybe dirty linen, maybe nothing."

"You certainly have given me enough ammo to knock the wind out of Chief Francis. I'll show the sketch to staff this morning." Then he paused thoughtfully, and asked, "How many fliers have you made of the sketch?"

"More than enough, Loo."

Walking over to where his sergeant was sitting, Kelly put his hand on his subordinate's shoulder and said, "It's very important you keep me up to date on all that goes down. This being an international case could very well get as much publicity as the Amityville Horror case, one we had back when I was a rookie."

"Like I said, Loo, before I leave you'll have a full report of the day's activities." Gore stood up and the two supervisors shook hands. Standing alongside each other, Kelly was dwarfed by Gore. In reality he was only two inches shorter, but their builds were entirely different. Gore neither drank nor smoked, a throwback from his youth in the Bible Belt. A physical fitness buff, he jogged, worked out in the gym, and watched his diet. The big Irishman, on the other hand, was forty pounds over the one hundred eighty he weighed when he entered the Academy twenty-four years ago. Every time he had a conversation with Gore, he vowed silently to start getting in shape. That lasted until their next meeting when he vowed all over again.

Arriving at headquarters, he found his team all present with the exception of Sanchez. Like most cops, the first order of business after he signed in was to head for the coffee pot. Pouring himself a cup, Gore looked at the wall clock, the time was 8:55 a.m. Hollering across the room to his team, he called out, "Okay, guys, finish your coffee, then head into my office."

At 8:58 a.m. a puffing Sanchez joined the team. Addressing him, Gore said, "See you made it on time, Joe. Heavy date last night?"

The Latin smiled, "Estaba con una chica anouch que me iso sentir fantastico."

Gore grimaced, "I don't know what you said, nor do I care, so let's get started with the business on hand. By now all of you have read the newspapers and are aware Fairfield is offering a ten thousand dollar reward for information leasing to the arrest of the killer."

It was the first Sanchez heard of it. He was too busy the night before to watch television, listen to the radio, or read a newspaper. "Man, could I put that ten G's to good use!"

"Forget about the money, Joe," said Danny Wolfe. "When it comes to a reward we get zilch."

Gore waited patiently for the air to clear, then continued, "Last night I met with Mr. Miyako. We went to Identification and met with our sketch artist, Maureen Snyder. It took over an hour with Miyako making many changes until he was satisfied the final drawing was a good likeness of the perp. Forty copies have been distributed to all the commands and here are some for all of you."

Sanchez looked at the drawing and shouted, "This joker is a double for my brother-in-law! I never did trust that scumbag that married my sister."

Gore shot a dirty look in Sanchez' direction, then said, "Let's cut out the horsing around, Joe." Addressing the rest of the team, he gave out the orders of the day. "Our work is sometimes repetitious, so today instead of talking to the same witnesses, I'll let you try another direction. Unlike yesterday, we have an ace in the hole—the artist sketch. I'll be in the office all day, so if any of you come across any vital information, call me. Like yesterday, when you're finished I want all of you to head right back to the office." He looked pointedly at Sanchez before continuing.

Addressing Barry Falk, he said, "I want you to return to the hotel. Talk to both Bauman and Hart. At least today we have the drawing. Show it all over the hotel, and when you talk to Hart ask him why he never told us about the note the doorman left in Security's bin.

Pointing to Wolfe, he said, "Danny, take Sanchez with you and head over to Fairfield Electronics. Call first; most large firms have morning meetings. The man you want to talk to is Gene Myers, the president. If he's not available, then find out who's minding the store and interview him. We received a fax from Los Angeles regarding a man that called himself Jim Monahan. See if they know anything about him. I'm not trying to tell you how to conduct your investigation, just mentioning a few important facts."

Then addressing the big detective from the Fourth Squad, Gore said, "Rochester, call the Conway kid. If he's in school, go there. Show him the sketch and get his reaction. If it's different, bring him in and we'll have the artist draw from his description."

Gore paused for a moment, and then looked over at Arena. "Frank, call DeMarco. Tell him we want him to look at the artist's drawing. If he can't make it to headquarters, go to his home and show him the sketch. If he agrees with Miyako, that's the sketch we'll use. If not, he'll also have to meet with Maureen so she can draw his look-alike."

"It's been my experience that no two people ever agree on what the perp looks like," Arena replied.

"You've got a point, Frank, but I was impressed with Miyako. So before we call in Conway and DeMarco, let's show them the sketch."

Arena followed orders and called the doorman. The phone rang a dozen times before a groggy voice answered, "Who's this?"

"Good morning, Mr. DeMarco. How are you this fine morning, sir? It's Detective Arena of the Homicide Bureau." Arena was deliberately cheerful; arousing another fellow human from his warm bed was particularly satisfying when he himself was wide awake and looking forward to a grueling workday.

"What time is it?"

"Nine-thirty."

"For Christ's sake, are you guys crazy? It's the middle of the night for me. And I already told Detective Falk all I know."

"That's not the reason for the call, sir. We have an artist's sketch of the suspect. We'd like you to look at it and see if you agree with the description. Could you come down to the headquarters in Yaphank?"

"I'm sorry, I can't. I have no wheels. A few nights ago I was on my way home from work when some smart-ass kid jumped a stop sign and broadsided me. If the son of a bitch had hit me on the driver's side, you wouldn't be talking to me now. I'd be six feet under."

"Well, how about I come over and pick you up?"

"If it's okay with you, Detective, can we make it another day? There's a problem at work. The afternoon doorman called in sick, so I've got to work a double shift today starting at one-thirty. The hotel airport car is picking me up at one o'clock."

Arena looked at his watch. He had more than enough time to get over to DeMarco's place with the sketch himself. "Stand by, Mr. DeMarco. I'm leaving headquarters in a few minutes. I'll bring the sketch to you." Hanging up, he put the sketch in his briefcase, took a set of car keys off the board, signed out, and was on his way to Lake Ronkonkoma.

DeMarco lived on Hill Street, a well-known area to Arena. As a boy in his early teems, his family rented a bungalow on the lake for six weeks to get away from Corona. His dad and uncle closed the restaurant for two weeks in July and the rest of the family enjoyed all six weeks in what was then known as the country. One of his family's favorite hangouts was Monaco's Candy Store on Hill Street by the railroad station. He, along with his brother and two cousins, went for the five-cent eggnog, which was seltzer and milk, and the Hooton chocolate candy bars.

As he drove by MacArthur Airport, a large commercial jet flew overhead. Thirty-five years ago it was a small airport that housed planes flown by the weekend airdales. Arriving at the railroad station, he lost his bearings. The Long Island Station had doubled in size with several new shops in the area. When he finally located what had been Monaco's Candy Store, the sign above the door read Sal's Pizza Parlor. The changing of time, he thought sadly. At last he knew he was on target when he saw a street sign that read Hill Street.

All the summer bungalows were gone, most of them transformed into year-round homes, others torn down and replaced with new, bigger residences. It was a dead-end street with about seven homes on each side of the road. He was impressed with the cleanliness of the entire block and the well-maintained houses; that is, until he reached the end of the street.

The last house was backed up against a large fence that covered a small shopping mall on the other side. The sign on the mailbox read DeMarco. The lawn was mostly dirt and the house was badly in need of a new paint job. It was apparent DeMarco was a bachelor and just used the house as a place to eat and sleep.

Pulling into the driveway, Arena honked the horn twice. DeMarco came out wearing a New York Mets baseball jacket and matching cap. He walked over to the car and asked, "So where's this sketch?" Arena handed it to him and waited for his reaction.

DeMarco looked at the sketch steadily for over a minute, and asked off-handedly, "Who did you say gave this description to your artist?"

"I didn't say, but since you're asking, it was Maehara's secretary, Mr. Miyako."

DeMarco, with a typical old-style Italian gesture of shaking and raising his hands in the air, exclaimed, "Madrone! Let me tell you something, Detective. You don't need me to go see your police artist. This here drawing is about as close a facial description you're gonna get, because this is just the way I saw him, wearing shades and the fedora."

❄   ❄   ❄

While the Homicide team was on the road investigating the murder of Koki Maehara, Commissioner William Reichart addressed his staff one by one. When it came to the Detective Division, he called on Chief of Detectives Charlie Francis. "Chief, what's the latest on your investigation regarding the murder of the Japanese businessman?"

"Progress, sir," Francis answered. "We have a possible suspect, no name at this time, just a good description, along with his blood type. We believe he may be a senior citizen."

"Was the motive robbery?" the police commissioner asked.

"No, sir. The shooter left a large sum of cash and some obviously expensive jewelry on the dresser."

"He could have been scared off," observed the commissioner.

"Unlikely, sir. We believe he used a silencer and may have been an acquaintance of Mr. Maehara. We also believe he made phone calls to firms in Los Angeles and Chicago that were business connections of Maehara. Both times he misrepresented himself. Apparently the purpose of the calls was to track the victim."

"Interesting," was the only comment from the commissioner. He then went on to other, more routine matters, beginning with the Traffic Division.

Thirty minutes later on their way out of the staff meeting, Chief Francis told Jim Kelly to accompany him to his office. Once inside, Francis indicated a chair to the side of his desk, "Have a seat, Jim." Then he handed Kelly a pink message slip and said, "I have a heavy schedule. Can you take care of this for me?"

Accepting the paper with the name and phone number of the man to be contacted at the Japanese Embassy, Kelly said, "Sure, Chief. It will be done forthwith." When Kelly returned to his own office, he in turn called Sergeant Gore to his office and handed the paper to him in typical chain of command fashion. "Jerry, take care of this phone call when you return to your desk."

"Who is Hiroshi Seki?" Gore asked.

"He's an aide with the Japanese Embassy in Washington. Seems the Maehara murder is big news in Japan. Call him and tell him we're investigating the case and have a dozen men working it."

"Why me, Loo? I'm only a sergeant. Seems to me a ranking officer should be making this call."

"You're answering the call, because you're the Investigating Officer, and let him know so."

Gore knew he had been had, but being the lowest ranking supervisor on the case, he had no one to whom he could pass the buck. He returned to his desk and dutifully dialed the number. A soft feminine voice directed his call in only a matter of minutes.

"Thank you for returning my call so promptly, Sergeant," said Mr. Seki. "Are you the officer in charge of the investigation regarding the death of Mr. Maehara San?"

"Yes, sir, I'm in charge of a twelve-man investigating team. My men are out in the field following up leads as I speak with you." Gore bit his lip and crossed his fingers as he spoke. Exaggeration was not natural to him.

"Do you have a suspect, Sergeant?"

"None whatsoever," Gore replied.

"I presume the motive was robbery," Seki ventured.

"We don't believe so, Mr. Seki, for several reasons. Right now we're up a dead-end street. When we do learn the motive, hopefully that will help lead us to an arrest."

"Sergeant, anything you tell me will be kept confidential."

"Sir, with all due respect, in reality you are a stranger to me, and I'm not at liberty to disclose our investigation over the phone. I can assure you when we do make an arrest, you will be notified."

"Sergeant, please don't misunderstand my reason for asking you questions. In Japan when the police are investigating an important case, our government does not interfere. In the case of Mr. Maehara San, try and put yourself in my shoes. He is one of Japan's leading industrial giants. It is my job to learn all the important facts when a Japanese citizen is killed on foreign soil."

"I understand. And, as I said before, if anything important comes up you will be notified. I promise I will personally call you."

Gore hated being pressured by politicians, especially those from a foreign country. Leaving his office, he headed for the coffee pot, mumbling under his breath. Meanwhile, Arena had returned from his meeting with DeMarco, and had just finished reading the fax from Tokyo when Gore passed his desk. The Quiet Man followed Gore over to the coffee area and said with a smile, "What'cha mumbling about, Sarge?"

"I just finished talking to a politician from the Japanese Embassy. He wanted to know all the facts about the Maehara case. I don't blame him; he was just doing his job. What pisses me of is, the brass, instead of telling him it's a confidential investigation, they drop the ball in my lap."

"Calm down, Sarge. I got some good news for you."

"DeMarco recognize the sketch?" Gore blurted out.

"Better news than that, I received this today from Tokyo." As he handed the fax to Gore, he added, "Now we have a motive."

Gore sat down and read:

POLICE DEPARTMENT, TOKYO, JAPAN, TO DETECTIVE FRANK ARENA, COUNTY OF SUFFOLK, NEW YORK.

Sorry for the delay in answering your letter. We had several calls to make, one being to Kyushu where government records are stored underground to preserve them during the war since most of our major cities were under heavy bombing attacks.

We checked with the United States Provost Marshall and discovered the records of Japanese servicemen were brought back to Tokyo. These records included fingerprints of all servicemen. Since Mr. Koki Maehara was in his seventies, we presumed he was in the service. After the surrender many committed suicide or hara-kiri. Our country was in a terrible state of affairs and many of the families did not know if their loved ones would ever return.

We were fortunate in the case of Mr. Maehara San. When we checked the fingerprints, much to our surprise they belonged to Sergeant Oki Tashino. Records showed he had been killed in Thailand. Sergeant Tashino's records also showed that he was to appear before the War Crimes Commission on brutality charges. Since he was presumed killed, no one ever looked for him. The war crime charges were brought by men off the Navy ship *Stuart*.

Mr. Maehara's records showed that he came from the city of Nagasaki, a city destroyed in World War II. We attempted to locate any relatives, but found none.

As for Sergeant Tashino, he came from Morioka in northern Japan. We again failed to find any relatives. Sergeant Tashino's records showed that he was born in Hawaii. He served with the Japanese army in China, receiving a severe wound to his leg in Manchuria. At the start of the war he was sent to Java, then Thailand, as a guard in the prisoner of war camps.

Apparently Sergeant Tashino took the identification from Private Koki Maehara, who served under him in Java and Thailand. Mr. Maehara's body was never found, and is listed as missing.

I hope we have answered a few questions for you. We are always available to assist any police department throughout the world.

Detective Arena, are you a baseball fan? If you are, maybe you have heard of Mr. Sadaharu Oh, the greatest home run hitter to come out of Japan. He beat both the Hank Aaron and Babe Ruth records, having hit over 800 in his playing days. My favorite American ball player is Mr. Howard Johnson of the New York Mets.

If you ever visit Tokyo, please contact me before you arrive. I will show you my city through the eyes of a Japanese citizen. It will also be my pleasure to take you to see my favorite team. In Japan, baseball is called 'beisuboru.'

Sincerely,
Chief Inspector Mitsuo Mauri

Gore was more than pleased with this information. He was also impressed with the fine job of investigation by the Tokyo Police. On paper it was only two pages. In reality, a lot of effort was expended in that background check. He looked up at Arena and smiled, "I'd say we have a motive."

"Revenge!" said Arena, nodding in agreement.

They were both in Arena's office when Sergeant Lauriguet from the Third Squad called and asked for Gore. "Jerry, we got a doubleheader for you."

"Where?"

"At 1141 Merrywell Street. Family speaks very little English."

"You got an interpreter at the scene?"

"I sent Bernheim and Quinlan to the scene along with a plainclothes cop named Collardo who speaks Spanish."

"Have you notified Identification and the medical examiner?" Gore asked.

"You know better than that, Jerry. I'm not a hotshot Homicide dick, but I do know procedure."

"Give me the details," Gore requested.

"It's a husband and wife affair. The guy that was knocked off was rooming with them. He worked days, the husband nights. When the husband was working, the roomer was taping mommo. Anyway, the husband must have suspected something, because he didn't go in to work, but waited outside for a few hours, then walked in on them, putting both of them to sleep."

"Do we have the weapon the shooter used?"

"Yeah, he dropped it at the scene, then took off. Neighbors heard the shots, and then saw him running from the house. The weapon was a thirty-eight Colt special, and no doubt we'll find his prints all over the gun."

"I'm sending Detectives Probst and Rubin, my two day men, over. They should be there in about thirty minutes. I'll respond shortly after them. I have a few details to clean up first."

Gore called to the two day men who had just returned from a grounder in north Babylon. "Joe, Bob, get over to 1141 Merrywell Street in Brentwood. We got two DOA. Get started with your neighborhood canvas. As soon as Wolfe and Sanchez return, I'll have them relieve you."

"Who'll be the lead detective, Sarge?" Probst asked.

"Sanchez. He speaks Spanish."

Gore looked at his watch. The time was 3:00 p.m. Sanchez, Falk, Rochester, and Wolfe were still on the road. As long as he had the day men standing by, he knew the crime scene would be protected. Both Rubin and Probst had been in Homicide a long time and knew what had to be done. They had earned their battle scars over the years.

Arena was somewhat stunned as to why the boss wasn't sending him instead of waiting for Wolfe and Sanchez to respond. Arena thought, I don't get it—I'm supposed to be part of the team. "Why don't you and I respond instead of the day men, Sarge?"

"I got other plans for you, Frank. Come on in to my office. I got a case I'd like to discuss with you."

Arena followed his sergeant into his office and took a seat alongside the desk. Gore than handed him the case jacket that read: CC-138954 VICTIM: Mr. Koki Maehara. Then he said, "As of this moment it's your squell."

Arena still did not quite understand what he was getting at, and said, "Who's working the case with me?"

Answering, Gore replied, "Nobody. Take this case jacket home, read it over, and study every little detail. You're the Lead Detective on the Maehara, alias Tashino, Squell."

"Why alone?" Arena asked.

"For a week or so you'll be on your own. See me tomorrow morning as soon as you sign in. We'll go over the game plan."

"Why me?" Arena asked. Before Gore could answer, the rest of the team began to stream into his office.

Rochester and Falk had posted the police artist sketch at the Carlyle Hotel in the employee lunchrooms. They also posted a sketch on the bulletin board of the supermarket that was located in the small shopping mall near the Carlyle. No one they showed the police drawing to at the hotel or shopping center could identify the sketch. They also questioned Hart as to why he never mentioned the note left in the

Security bin by the doorman. His answer was, 'I found out that the night security guard, Joe George, was a lush and spent more time at the bar in the shopping center than on duty at the hotel, so I fired him. He most likely took the note with him.'

Sanchez and Wolfe learned that the personnel manager at Fairfield received a phone call from Jim Monahan asking the whereabouts of Mr. Maehara the day of his murder. Hearing that, Gore was convinced more than ever the shooter was once a POW under Tashino's jurisdiction—and for the first time he realized that this case would be opening a real can of worms.

Gathering his team, he addressed Falk and Rochester first, saying, "I want to thank both of you men for your assistance, and I'll be sure to let your boss know about it on paper." Reaching out, he shook hands with both men.

Then, returning to Sanchez and Wolfe, he glanced at his watch. The time was 4:10 p.m. "We got a doubleheader in Brentwood. The Third Precinct has a Spanish-speaking cop on the scene, so we know it's most likely Latino. I sent Rubin and Probst over to handle the case until we get there. Joe, since you speak the language, I'm making you the Lead Detective on this one."

Sanchez grumbled under his breath, "Shit, there goes my date. Couldn't have been one body, it had to be a fucking doubleheader."

Five minutes later, the three Homicide dicks were on their way to another major homicide.

On his way home Arena tried to understand why Gore made him the leading detective on the Tashino case, as it would now probably be called. All he could figure was that he was the junior man on the team, and since Gore now knew that whoever murdered Tashino was probably an ex-serviceman who hated the guy, he could be living anywhere in the United States. Suddenly the case looked like one they would never solve. 'Sometimes being the junior man hurts,' he thought. 'Maybe I should've stayed in the First Squad.'

Chapter 11

Saturday, March 13, 1993

When Frank Arena arrived at work the following morning, he noted all the team, including Gore, had signed in, but the only detective in the squad room was Bob Probst, one of the two steady day men. Probst was leaning back in his chair while reading Newsday and enjoying his morning coffee. Seeing Arena, he said, "Fresh coffee in the back room, Frank. Just made it a little while ago."

Taking Probst's advice, he headed to the back and poured himself a hot cup of java, then returned to the squad room. Probst was still absorbed in the newspaper. "Bob, where are all the troops?"

"Rubin's working a suicide in Central Islip. Sanchez and Wolfe are canvassing the Brentwood crime scene and interviewing relatives and neighbors."

Looking over at Gore's office, the top half of the door being glass, Arena noticed it was empty. "Where's the sergeant?"

"In with Kelly. They want you to join them regarding the case you're working."

"Why didn't you tell me when I came in?"

"Relax," Probst replied. "It's not nine yet. Enjoy your coffee."

"I'll take the coffee with me."

As Arena entered the lieutenant's office, Kelly was sitting in a relaxed manner behind his desk, chatting with Gore who was seated to his right. The chair alongside the sergeant was empty. Kelly greeted him heartily, "Have a seat, Frank. We were just talking about you. I'm pleased Gore made you the lead man. You're a top investigator. If anyone can get the information we need, you're the man that can do it."

"Thanks, Loo, for having confidence in me."

Gore then addressed his lead man, saying, "We have to learn all about the men that served on the *Stuart*—where they live, how often they meet for reunions, who their leader is, and so on. We may be going down a dead-end street, but it's all we have right now. We're aware of the description of the shooter. We know he's a senior citizen, his height, his build, his blood type, and hair color. So, although it's not going to be easy, it's very possible we will find him."

Kelly interjected, "You were in the service, weren't you, Frank?"

"Yes, sir, US Army."

"Do you have any idea where you'll begin?" Gore asked.

Arena nodded, "Yes. First I need a list of the men of the *Stuart* still living. I'm a vet and receive both the American Legion and VFW magazines. They have a list of outfits having a yearly reunion, with the name of the man in charge. They also have a 900 number to call in the event you want to contact the men running those affairs."

Kelly interjected, "You've done your homework, Frank. As a VFW member myself, that was a suggestion I was going to make."

Arena continued, "I could call the naval personnel in St. Louis, but by the time I go through the red tape, we could lose three or four days. So, after I leave your office, I'll call the Legion's 900 number."

Gore then said, "The sooner we get started, the better."

Arena rose in agreement and headed for his desk. He dialed the 900 number and spoke with a helpful young clerk who gave him the name and phone number of a Mr. John Niebsch living in Brockton, Massachusetts. When he dialed the Brockton number, it was answered immediately.

"Mr. Niebsch?" Arena asked.

"Speaking. Who's this?"

"Sir, my name is Detective Frank Arena. I'm with the Homicide Bureau of the Suffolk County Police located on Long Island."

"Good heavens, that's quite a mouthful, young man. How can I help you?"

"I'm trying to get a list of the remaining members that served on the *Stuart* in World War II."

"Are you aware there were two *Stuarts*?" Niebsch asked.

"The one I'm interested in was sunk in the early part of the war."

"Okay, that's the one I was on. How did you get my name, Detective?"

"I called the 900 number in the service magazine. I believe you were the host of the reunion you had two weeks ago?"

"Yes, myself and Dennis Donovan," he replied. "You mentioned the Homicide Bureau—who was killed?"

"A Japanese sergeant, or I should say former sergeant, now a civilian visiting our area from Tokyo. Seems during the war he was assigned to a POW camp where several of the *Stuart* crew were held as prisoners. His real name was Oki Tashino. He was using the name Koki Maehara."

"Who could forget Sergeant Tashino? Yes, I remember him. Before I was sent to Japan, I was in Thailand while he was there," said Niebsch. "He was a sick, mean, sadist. The man you need to speak with is our chairman, William Ballentine. We call him Billy. He was a former congressman in his state and lives in Broken Arrow, Oklahoma. Do you have a pen?"

"Yes," Arena replied.

Niebsch then gave him the phone number in Oklahoma, not even having to look it up. Then he asked, "What has the crew of the *Stuart* to do with a Japanese visitor killed in your jurisdiction?"

Arena chose his words carefully, "Probably nothing. However, I'm trying to find out some background of the men who were in the camp where our victim was a sergeant. Maybe some of them can shed some light on my investigation."

"I'm sorry I can't give you any help. However, Billy has the entire list. And since he is our chairman, it's best you go through him."

"I will, sir," Arena responded.

Niebsch then asked, "Do you know much about the battle which sunk the *Stuart*?"

"To be honest, sir, I don't."

"She was a helluva ship and one Americans can be proud of. It took half the Jap navy to sink her."

"I intend to read up on her, sir. Thanks a mil for your assistance." He placed the receiver quietly back on the cradle.

At 10:25 a.m. Arena dialed the Ballentine residence in Oklahoma and introduced himself when a female voice answered. "Good morning, ma'am. I'm calling from New York. My name is Detective Frank Arena. It's important I speak with Mr. Ballentine."

"Did you say you were a detective?"

"Yes, ma'am."

"My husband went downtown earlier to have his car serviced, but he could walk in any minute now. Give me your number and I'll have him call you back."

"It's long distance, Mrs. Ballentine. It's ten-thirty now. I'll call him, say, eleven."

"It's eight-thirty here, Detective. How about calling him at eleven-thirty your time? Can I tell him what this is about?"

"I need some information regarding the cruiser *Stuart*. I was told he's the man that has a list of the crew."

"If your call is in regards to the *Stuart* I'll have him call you. He has an open account when it comes to giving information about the *Stuart*."

"Good," said Arena. Then he gave her his telephone number. "Tell him to ask for Detective Arena."

He didn't have to wait long. Fifteen minutes later his phone rang. He picked it up on the first ring, "Detective Arena, Homicide."

"Howdy, pardner. Billy Ballentine here. What can I do for you, Detective?"

"I'll make it short, sir. We had a visiting Japanese businessman in our county who was murdered. He called himself Koki Maehara. However, through the magic of fingerprinting, we now know him to have been one Oki Tashino. Does this name ring a bell?"

"Holy cow! Then what we heard at the reunion was true. Our reunion this year was in Boston on the sixth of March. I'm the chairman of our retired organization, and George Fecke, one of our guys, called me to let me know that Oki Tashino, the guard we all knew as the 'animal of the orient,' was alive and president of a large electronics company and now traveling on business in the States. He saw Tashino's picture in a newspaper article, but he went to his hotel to get a look at him and make sure. After that, I informed the men at the reunion in Boston."

"You say he was positive the man was Tashino, Mr. Ballentine?"

"Yes. Why is all this so important, Detective? Ballentine gave out a belly laugh, and said, "You don't think one of the old men of the *Stuart* had anything to do with the killing, do you, Detective?"

"We have no suspects, sir. I'm just calling for information."

"What kind of information?"

"I would like you to fax me a list of the remaining crew. As I said, we have no suspects. I'd like to learn more about Tashino. I thought by talking to some of the men who were POWs under his command, I might understand something of the man."

"Sounds reasonable," Ballentine responded. "From what I've been told, he was a sadist. I, myself, was only with him a short time before I was shipped over to Japan where I stayed as a POW throughout the war. If you think talking to some of the men would help your investigation, I'd be glad to fax you the list of the crew. I'll do better than that. I'll list their backgrounds and addresses, too."

"Thank you, Mr. Ballentine." Arena gave him his address and fax number and asked how many names would be on the list.

"As of now we have 131 still with us. How much do you know about the *Stuart*, Detective?"

"To be honest, not a damn thing."

"Let me give you a little background. We were a proud crew of eleven hundred men. After I graduated from Texas A&M, I joined the Navy and received a commission as an ensign where I was assigned to the

Stuart. I might add, she was my first and only ship. We went through a lot, and she was probably one of the few fighting ships equipped to take on the Japs. We were in three engagements—two with enemy planes, the third was a naval engagement where we lost a lot of our crew. We were trying to get back to Australia, along with two smaller ships, when we ran smack into the Japanese fleet. Most of the crew died in battle. Although about four hundred or so survived, we lost another one hundred in the POW camps and others through attrition."

As Ballentine spoke, Arena detected a sadness in his voice. He no longer had the jolly laugh of just a few minutes before.

"Let me say this to relieve your mind, Mr. Ballentine. It's unlikely the man who murdered Mr. Tashino is off the *Stuart.* However, we have to follow all the leads given to us."

"May I make a suggestion, Detective?"

"I'm listening."

"Before you interview any of the sailors, go to your public library and read about the Battle of Java Sea. Then and only then will you be able to get into their minds. They all hated Tashino. Most will cheer when they hear he's dead, and if they for one minute think you're trying to put the finger on a shipmate, you won't learn a damn thing. And if you have the time, look for the Time-Life book on POWs. The pictures alone will tell you a lot and help you understand the men a little better."

"That's good advice, sir. Tomorrow's my day off. I'll spend some of it at the library."

"Were you aware Tashino was to appear before the War Crimes Commission?" Ballentine asked.

"Yes, sir, I was. I sent a fax to the Japanese police in Tokyo and they informed us he had been using the name of another soldier who had been stationed at the camp where he was a sergeant. So, as far as our government knew, Tashino was a victim of the war."

"How did the Tokyo police ever figure that one out? All this happened half a century back," Ballentine remarked.

"Prints don't change. I can only presume they did their homework. Seeing the fingerprints didn't belong to Maehara, the police must have checked them against the other men stationed at the camp and came up with Tashino."

"Clever, those Japs," Ballentine said wryly, then added, "How far is the city of Rockville Center from you?"

"It's in our sister county, a little over an hour away from our headquarters."

"When you receive my list of the *Stuart* sailors, look up Dale Alexander. He's a minister and his church is located in Rockville Center. Ask him about Tashino and Maehara. He knew them both quite well."

"I'll do that, sir. Thanks for the tip, along with the information and cooperation you've given me."

※　　　　　　　※　　　　　　　※

Sitting around the dinner table that night, Frank's wife, Eleanor, said, "It's great you have the weekend off, Frank. We've been invited to Norm and Marilyn Scull's house for dinner tomorrow night."

"Sounds good to me," Frank replied. Then addressing his son, he said, "Frankie, we've got a lot of yard work, so I'll need your help tomorrow. You cut the lawn and I'll do the weeding and trimming."

"I've got baseball practice in the morning at the high school field. Coach is making the final cut tomorrow. Can it wait until the afternoon?"

"Sure. I have to go to the library tomorrow. I'll go in the morning and drop you off at the ball field on the way. Be ready at eight-thirty."

The next morning the tall, gangly youth jumped into the front seat with a doughnut in each hand and an apple dangling from his mouth. They rode in silence as his son devoured his food. Pulling up to the baseball field, Frank said, "What time do you think practice will be over?"

"About twelve," he answered.

"I'll be across the road in the North Babylon library. Come over and meet me when you're done with practice. Don't hang around talking to your friends. Mom and I are going out tonight and I want to see the lawn cut, understand?"

"The lawn won't take me long, Dad. Last time I did it I was finished in an hour."

"I know. Take a little longer this time."

It was 8:55 a.m. when the detective pulled into the parking lot of the library. It was nice being early as it wasn't crowded. He and a few high school kids were the only ones waiting for the door to open at nine o'clock.

As he approached the front desk a tall rawboned woman in her fifties said, "You look like a man who needs help."

Smiling, he answered, "Yes. I'm looking for two books. One on the Battle of Java Sea and Time-Life book on POWs. Any other books you may have on POWs that were imprisoned in Asia would also be helpful."

Stepping from behind the counter, she motioned for him to follow. On the other side of the desk was a large cabinet that contained the names of authors and books by alphabet. She then pulled out several white cards and read them off, saying, "If you go to the bottom level, section nine forty-one, you will find what you want. There are several books on Java Sea and a few on prisoners of war in Asia."

He thanked her and perused the section she indicated. Like she said, it contained many books. Arena managed to find two on the Java Sea engagement and found the Time-Life book recommended by Ballentine. The pictures in Life showed the Brits and Aussies working on the Siam-Burma railroad. They were skin and bones. Only a small number of Americans helped build the railroad, many of those off the *Stuart*. The battle itself was amazing—the Allied battle worn and outdated navies against the new and powerful Japanese navy. The *Stuart* was in several engagements. In each of them she knocked down several Japanese planes. In her final battle she fought until she was out of ammunition. Arena thought, what a hell of a crew. He finished with the books at 11:50 a.m. Time had flown by quickly; he was so absorbed in the reading.

Frankie Jr. was waiting outside the library for him with a big grin on his face. "Congratulate me, Dad. I made the team."

Frank knew how much it meant to his son. Putting his arm around him, he said, "Well done, son. I'm proud of you. Now we have to get home and do our chores. Do you want to drive?"

"Can I, Dad?"

"Why not?" he said as he tossed his son the car keys.

Chapter 12

After signing the daily log book, Arena headed to the back room for a cup of coffee before checking his bin for Ballentine's fax. Danny Wolfe was draining the last drop of liquid from the automatic coffeemaker. Seeing Arena, he said, "Sorry, Frank. You'll have to make a fresh pot."

"No problem," Frank answered, and did so.

While waiting for it to brew, he proceeded to the squad room and took Ballentine's fax from his bin. Dale Alexander of Rockville Center was number one on the list of one hundred thirty-one names.

Wolfe walked over to him, saying, "I poured your coffee. It's on your desk."

"Thanks, Dan. How's the Brentwood murder going?"

"Good," Wolfe replied. "The guy's attorney, Tom Gallegos, is surrendering him to us tomorrow morning. Joe is meeting with Tom this morning in Brentwood."

"It's great having a guy like Sanchez on your team. He sure can speak the language—fluently."

"He should," Wolfe remarked. "He was born in San Juan and didn't come to the States until he was ten." Taking a sip of coffee, he continued, "Gore didn't do you a favor in making you the lead man in the Carlyle murder. Personally, I think it's going to lead us down a dead end street, and then we'll bury it in the thirty day file." A thirty-day file in the Detective Division was like saying that all leads have been exhausted. Every thirty days the detective handling the case would add to it, usually by indicating no progress. Once in a while information would surface that solved a few cases, a very few.

Arena finished his coffee, and then dialed the number for Dale Alexander in Rockville Center. The time was 9:30 a.m. One the second ring a woman's voice answered, "Good morning, Church of All Faiths. Can I help you?"

"Good morning, ma'am, Detective Arena of the Suffolk County Police Department. Is Pastor Alexander available?"

"Is someone hurt?" a concerned voice replied.

"No, ma'am, nothing like that. I'm calling in reference to an investigation of a case I'm working on. The pastor may be able to give us some information."

"Oh, thank goodness! For a moment I thought the worst, like a family member or a member of our flock may have been in an accident. Hold on for a moment. He's out in the yard tending his roses. He just loves them to death, like they were part of his family. I'll go and get him."

Sounds like a nice lady, the detective thought to himself. A minute or so later, a deep baritone voice answered, "Pastor Alexander."

"Sorry to disturb you, Pastor. I'm calling in regards to a homicide I'm investigating. I didn't mention I was a homicide detective to your secretary. The title usually upsets them."

"The lady you mention is my wife, Carol. You did right in not telling her. Is this call in regards to Oki Tashino?"

Arena was taken aback by the pastor's remark. "How did you know Tashino was dead?"

"I read the papers," he answered tonelessly.

"But the newspapers gave the name of Koki Maehara, not Tashino."

"Where are you calling from, Detective?"

"Police headquarters in Yaphank, Suffolk County."

"I have work to do in the afternoon. If you want to talk about Tashino, I'm available this morning."

"I can drive out immediately. Where is Buckingham Road located in Rockville Center?

"Are you familiar with our village, Detective?"

"Yes, somewhat. I know what exit to take on the Southern State Parkway. I have a cousin that lives off Demotte Street."

"Good, so are we. Then you'll have no problem. Go past the synagogue, take the first left on Hopkins, then the next right."

After receiving detailed directions from Alexander, Arena wasted no time in leaving. Once he hit the Southern State Parkway off Sunrise the traffic was light and he made good time. He arrived at the driveway of the church in just over an hour. It was on a corner lot, an old building of wood construction. All the homes in the area were middle to upper middle class, built of brick and stone. On the front lawn of the church was a large marquee, which read, 'Church of All Faiths.' Under the title it read, 'Pastor Dale Alexander.' A third and fourth line gave the day and time of the services. On Sunday there were two services, one at ten o'clock in the morning, the other at seven o'clock in the evening. On Thursday one service was held in the evening at seven o'clock.

The home of the pastor was behind the church. It also was wood construction, but unlike the church, nicely painted in white with a lovely garden. As he approached the front entrance, Arena admired the colorful beds of flowers under the front windows. It was obvious the pastor had a green thumb.

As Arena walked up the front steps, the pastor, having seen the detective arrive, opened the door and greeted him with a smile. He was a tall, slim man of six-two with gray hair, wearing a dark gray suit displaying a white shirt with a white starched collar. Frank's first thoughts were, 'Damn, if he doesn't fit the description of the shooter!'

The pastor extended his hand and said, "You must be Detective Arena."

Frank removed his wallet, took out his identification and gold tin, holding both in the air. With his right hand he greeted the pastor with a warm handshake. Then, answering his question, he said, "Yes, sir, I am. Thanks for inviting me to your home."

"My pleasure. Let's go into my study. It's just down the hall. Mrs. Alexander made some homemade cookies and we have lemonade to go with it."

"That was kind of her," Arena replied cordially, even though feeling a cup of strong black coffee to be preferable.

The pastor's den was small and consisted of an old-fashioned desk old-timers once called a 'secretary,' two chairs, a bookcase on one side of the desk, and two wall pictures. On one wall was a picture of the cruiser *Stuart*, and on the other apparently a picture of the ship's boxing team. High over the desk hung an oil painting of Jesus Christ on the cross. Pointing to the boxing photo, Arena asked, "Shipmates?"

"Yes. The three standing are Bill Shulmelda, Dennis Donovan, and Charlie Cahill. The three sitting are Howie Truman, John Forte, and Tom Jackson."

"One black guy," Arena observed. "If it were a boxing team of today it would be the other way around."

"Jackson was a mess attendant and probably the only true boxer on the squad. I've got to admit he was one heck of a fighter. There was a ship's rumor he once fought as a professional in Jersey City under the name of Kid Hurricane. The guy on the top left was Bill Shulmelda, not much of a boxer but a heck of a brawler. He was our heavyweight. The one standing alongside him was Dennis Donovan, good boxer but not much of a knockout punch."

"How tall are Shulmelda and Donovan?"

"Same size as I am, six-two."

"Did all of the men in the photo survive the battle and the POW camp?"

"Shulmelda died in Thailand. Truman, Forte, Cahill in battle. Jackson lives in California." Then, realizing the import of the question, Alexander said, "You seem to know a lot about the *Stuart*."

"I read The Battle of Java Sea, and Ballentine told me the men that survived the battle became prisoners of war."

"So that's where you got my name," the pastor said.

"Yes, along with the names of the other one hundred thirty of your shipmates that are still alive."

"Then he also informed you we learned from one of our shipmates on the west coast that Tashino was still alive."

"He did, but unlike you he wasn't aware that Tashino was killed. Apparently you forgot to inform him that you read in the newspapers a Mr. Koki Maehara was killed at the Carlyle Hotel on Long Island."

"I didn't think Tashino was important enough. Eventually I would have told him."

"Why didn't you inform the police? According to the newspaper, the murdered man was referred to only as Mr. Maehara, a visiting Japanese businessman. "

"I assumed you had his prints. Once you checked them out you would have known the man was using an alias."

"It doesn't work that way, Pastor, and you know it. If it weren't for the fact that the Tokyo police were as professional as they are, it would have taken us weeks before we found out Maehara was using an alias."

"Did you come here to interrogate me, Mr. Arena, or like you said on the phone, to gather some insight to this mystery Japanese businessman that was murdered?"

Arena realized he was alienating himself, so he changed his method of questioning. Taking a bit of a cookie and a sip of the lemonade, he said, "Tell me about Tashino."

Quick to answer, the pastor described his former enemy. "He was part of yesterday and was trained by the old Japanese regime of the past. For the most part, to our standards, cruel and sadistic. That was fifty years ago. Today, Japan in comparison to the old world, is modern, democratic, and they use their intelligence to constructive ends. Thanks to us, they have become a financial dictator instead of a war dictator."

"Who was Maehara?" the detective asked.

"He was a guard, different from the others. They often made fun of him because he was a little slow and treated us like we were human. He never physically harmed us and saved several of our lives."

"That's interesting," Arena said. "Just how did he do that?"

"How much do you know about the pre-war Japanese culture, Detective?"

"To be honest with you, Pastor, nothing."

"You should read their history. You might find it illuminating. Here in America we're a melting pot, immigrants from all over the world come to our shores. We follow many religions. In Japan, Shintoism and Buddhism are the two main religions. Shintoism emphasizes ancestor worship and the divinity of the emperor. It's also Japan's number one religion. Second is Buddhism, which teaches if you think right your soul will reach a divine state of release from pain and desire. Less than one percent of Japan's pre-war population was Christian, most all of them living in Hiroshima and Nagasaki. Ironically, those were the two cities the atomic bomb was dropped on."

"You're losing me. What's the history lesson you're giving me have to do with Maehara?"

Alexander waited for a moment before he answered, then said, "Maehara was a Christian."

All Arena could say was, "Oh."

Alexander then continued, "Prior to World War Two, in Japan there were two classes—the wealthy and the other. Their nobility despised the white race and rightly so. We treated them as an inferior race. They were an island in the same geographical class as England. To exist, they depended on trade with the outside world. Steel was one of their largest imports. Japan was building an empire with the purpose of becoming the master of all of Asia. After she invaded China, the stories of atrocities became a touchy subject with the United States government. The newsreels showed them killing and torturing the Chinese people. President Roosevelt and Congress voted not to send them any more steel and placed an embargo against the island of Japan. This is probably what their 'powers to be' wanted, and gave them an excuse to declare war on us."

Getting back to the matter at hand, Arena asked, "You said Maehara saved lives. How?"

"When you read about the Battle of Java Sea, did you read anything about how they treated the prisoners of war?"

"No. I only saw photographs of men mistreated and underfed."

"One of the torture chambers we had in Thailand was a box known to the natives as the 'coffin.' To us, the 'hot box.'"

"What was its purpose?" the detective asked.

"It was made of wood and was five feet long and three feet wide. They placed it in an open dirt field and wrapped tin foil around the top. At noon the temperature hit one hundred and twenty degrees. What they called a 'cell' we called a torture chamber."

"You apparently served time in the hot box," Arena said.

"Yes, I did, ten days. We were allowed out one hour a day at dusk so we could walk the wall. This prevented us from being crippled. You see, if we were crippled we couldn't work—and that was our purpose, slave labor."

"What so-called crime did you commit?"

"That's immaterial. The point being, if it were not for Koki Maehara, few of us would have survived. He had night duty and would sneak us additional water and rice, knowing if he was caught he would have been shot."

"Why? It doesn't add up," Arena remarked.

"His Christian faith differed from the way most Japanese were taught. Cruelty was a way of life for the Japanese fifty years ago. Being raised in the Christian faith, he understood we were being mistreated and would die without the extra water. We probably could have gotten by without the rice, but not without the water, because the hot sun would have dehydrated our bodies. At night the mosquitoes sucked our blood and the bed bugs were as big as beetles."

"How the hell did a tall man like yourself survive living in a box five feet long?"

"By folding my legs up against my chest."

"What were the chances of making it?" Arena asked.

"Without help, I'd say fifty-fifty."

"At that rate, I bet a lot of prisoners died."

"Oddly enough, we only lost one man. About seven of us from the *Stuart* spent time in the hot box. We thought Java was bad, but when we got to Thailand we found out they didn't need a hot box—the jungle was our coffin."

"If I hadn't served Uncle Sam in the Army in Viet Nam I would've found your story hard to believe. But I know torture was the Asiatic way of life.

"Let's change the subject. Why do you suppose Hiroshima and Nagasaki were the two cities the Christian missionaries chose?" Arena asked.

"I don't know about Hiroshima. I can tell you why they chose Nagasaki. Back as far as the sixteen hundreds the Dutch discovered the port and it became a trading post. After the sailors came the missionaries. When I was a student of theology in the ministry in Fort Worth, I was curious about Japan and Christianity and checked it out. That's how I am able to answer your questions."

Although the conversation drew his interest, Arena realized he was getting away from his purpose in visiting the clergyman. "Let's get back to why Tashino was murdered. We believe the perp knew him. On the hotel table was a Rolex watch, a gold ring, and a wallet containing six hundred dollars. If he was a crack head he would have wiped the guy out. Not so in the case of our shooter. It was almost as if he were bragging and telling us the killing was revenge and challenging us to identify him."

The pastor laughed at the last remark, then said, "You almost sound as if the man you're looking for is a former crew member of the *Stuart*."

"Is that impossible?" the detective asked, answering his question.

"It's been over fifty years since the *Stuart* went down in battle. Come on, Detective, be realistic."

"The description of our perp is six-two, slim, gray hair. You match that description. How many others of the remaining one hundred thirty have that height?"

"I have no idea," he answered.

"Do you have a group photo?" Arena asked.

"They're available, but I never buy one."

"Since the reunion have any of your shipmates dropped by to see you?"

"Only one," Alexander answered. "Dennis Donovan, from the Boston area. He's a sick man. He has lung cancer and came to see a specialist, a Doctor Jacobson at Stony Brook Hospital in Suffolk County."

A bulb went on in Arena's head. He asked, "When did he visit with you?"

Alexander knew what he must be thinking and said, "Look, Dennis known as the ship's clown. His wife is unaware of just how sick he really is. To tell you the truth, I don't believe even he was aware of the seriousness of his condition until he saw Doctor Jacobson. He's dying."

"I'm sorry to hear that, Pastor. I hope you understand I'm only doing my job. Was Dennis here about the time Tashino died?"

"Yes," he answered, "but Dennis did not kill Tashino. He was as shocked as I was when we read of it in Newsday."

"Did you go with him to Stony Brook Hospital?"

"No, we lent him our car and gave directions." At this point Alexander was showing signs of impatience. "Detective Arena, as I told you on the phone, my morning is free, but I'm afraid I'm going to have to ask you to leave. I've got to prepare for the afternoon's activities."

"Just one more thing, Pastor." Arena reached in his coat pocket for the police artist sketch and showed it to the pastor.

Alexander took it in hand and stared at it for a full minute. "Is this the man you suspect? If so, I can assure you none of the *Stuart* survivors resemble this picture," he said unconvincingly, and handed it back with a forced smile.

Arena pushed it back to him, saying, "Hang on to it. Maybe somewhere down the line the face will spark a remembrance. Please thank Mrs. Alexander for the lemonade and cookies."

As Alexander walked with him to the door, Arena stopped, recalling that another member of the *Stuart* lived on Long Island out east in Mattituck. "John Hughes, I understand, lives out east of here. Do you see much of him?"

"Yes, we're close friends," the pastor replied.

"Ballentine said he was a former cop. Where did he work?"

"He's retired from the New York City Police."

"Oh," Arena said in a surprised tone.

Alexander continued, "As a matter of fact, Johnny was a captain in Manhattan in the same line as yourself—Homicide. I might add, he's also over six-two," he said with a smile.

❋   ❋   ❋

Driving back to headquarters along the Southern State Parkway, Arena had time to ponder his interview with the pastor. When Alexander was shown the police sketch his eyes popped, and his expression gave him away; he knew the suspect. Why did he cover for him? When he read in the newspapers Maehara had been killed, he was aware it was really Oki Tashino. Nevertheless, he didn't notify the police. Why didn't he call Billy Ballentine, the group leader, and let him know Tashino was murdered? He did admit having a shipmate as a houseguest. Is the pastor for real or just a phony clergyman? Then it hit him—Detective Darren Carey of the Rockville Center Police Department. He hadn't seen Darren in over five years since they worked the Babylon rape case. If anyone can fill me in on Alexander, Darren would be the man.

Back in the office, Arena had three phone calls to make before calling it a day. The first was to Rockville Center PD where an Officer Morgan answered. When he Arena identified himself and asked if Detective Carey was on duty, Morgan laughed and asked, "When did you last speak with Carey?"

"Five years ago. Why?"

"He's Lieutenant Carey now, and back in the bag. He's off today and will be starting days tomorrow."

"Oh, he's one of those smart-ass test takers," Arena said playfully.

"He's one of those, Detective. Do you want to leave a message?"

"Yes, could he call me tomorrow morning between nine and ten?"

"You got it, Detective. I wrote it down and it's going in his bin."

"Thanks. What's your first name, Officer? I don't believe you told me."

"It's Joe. Why do you want to know?"

"Just like to know who I'm talking to. Thanks again, Joe."

Hanging up, Arena said to himself, "Son of a bitch. *Lieutenant* Carey." It was five years ago when they first met. Frank handled a rape that occurred at St. Joseph's Catholic Church. It was early in the afternoon and the young lady was alone in a pew close to the rear of the church. She was praying, and paid no attention when someone sat close behind her. Then, without warning, she smelled the ether. When she woke a short time later, she saw a white man pulling up his pants. She pretended she was still out, but got a good look at him. Arena had taken the nervous young lady to Identification at headquarters and she was shown photographs of all previously arrested rapists. Unfortunately, none fit the man who raped her. The following day the story was headlines in Newsday and that afternoon Arena received a call from Detective Darren Carey of Rockville Center. As luck would have it, he also handled a similar case several years previously. The only difference was that the rapist didn't use ether, but raped the victim with an open face, no mask. Two months later the victim was hired as a waitress in Freeport and was working one night when her attacker came in for a cup of coffee. While he was sitting at the counter, she called the police. The rapist was convicted and received a three to five year sentence. When Carey read the story in the newspaper the first thing he did was call Elmira State Prison; just like he figured, the guy had been released early—had been out for several months. After Carey's call, Arena showed the young lady a photo spread he obtained from the Nassau County Identification Bureau; she identified the rapist immediately.

The second call Arena made was at four o'clock to Pat Caputo in New Jersey. He got the answering machine, so he left a message. The third call was to Walter Eilers in Connecticut. "Professor Eilers speaking. What can I do for you?"

"I'm sorry to bother you, Professor. I received your name from a Mr. Bill Ballentine. I'm with the Homicide Bureau and handling the death of a former Japanese guard, a Mr. Oki Tashino, alias Koki Maehara. I'm sure you're familiar with both names."

"I am. As a matter of fact, we learned at the reunion in Boston a week ago that Tashino was still living. How can I help you, Detective?"

"If it's not an inconvenience, I would like to pay you a visit."

"Detective, I know very little about Tashino. I was only under his command for six months, then I was sent to Japan."

"I'd still prefer to talk with you in person."

"It's a long trip from the Island to my home. I'm sure I can answer your questions on the phone."

"I have a few reasons for this request. One is you speak Japanese and have lived in Japan in peacetime. I don't know the language and you might be able to give me some information the other crewmembers of the *Stuart* aren't able to. I'd like to come tomorrow."

"Well, I'm writing my memoirs and trying to keep to a set schedule. Tomorrow I'll be at the university library all day, and Wednesday I'm in a golf tournament. Is Thursday okay?"

"Fine with me," Arena answered.

"Are you close to Stony Brook University?" the professor asked.

"The university is thirty minutes west of headquarters."

"I'm judging how far a distance you have to come. I gave a seminar at Stony Brook and it took me about four hours to get there. Let me give you directions to my home, Detective."

"I looked at the map. Eagleville is a short distance past Storrs. I can follow a map to your town."

"It's very small. Once you enter the village, take the second light, turn left, go exactly a mile, and the house is on the corner of Union and Saxon. It's the only all white house on the block."

Hanging up, Arena was pleased. Now all he had to do was hear from Caputo. Eilers was a strange man. You would think after being a POW under the Japanese for three and a half years would be enough exposure to the Orient. However, he not only learned to speak the language, but also was an exchange student and then taught English at a college in Japan for one year.

Arena's final call was to John Hughes out in Mattituck. He was somewhat curious about Hughes, a former Homicide boss, and was anxious to get his opinion. He spoke to a young girl who identified herself as Donna Hughes, granddaughter. She told him her grandfather was on a fishing trip with friends, so he left a message.

Arena now had three former men to interview that were within driving distance—the pastor, Donovan, and Hughes. He thought for the first time that he was getting somewhere. 'The main suspect has to be Donovan, because he has a good reason and the least to lose; he's a sick man, and even if he's caught, what can he lose but a few months of his life. As for the pastor, I have some doubts. The cop, I won't think about until we meet—then I'll draw my conclusions.'

The phone rang, interrupting Arena's speculations. He picked up the receiver, and before he had a chance to identify himself, the voice on the other end said, "Is this Homicide?"

"Yes, it is. Detective Arena speaking. What can I do for you?"

"Patrolman Depagnier. I'm calling from Bayport. I got an aided case call from Headquarters. It turned out to be a suicide. The dude hung himself in the attic."

"Name of victim?" Arena asked.

"Martin, Bill Martin. He's seventy-six years of age, and according to his wife has been taking drugs for some kind of depression."

"What's the address?"

"One fifteen Bayport Terrace, off Main Avenue."

"Stand by. One of our guys will be over in about thirty minutes."

Both Rubin and Probst were out on grounders. Probst on a crib death, Rubin a pool drowning. Arena's orders were to handle no cases for the present. But since both Wolfe and Sanchez were out, he was the only one in the office. He started to tell Gore he was responding when Rubin walked in. So he handed him the case and said, "You've got a suicide in Bayport."

Rubin gave him a look that could kill. "It's four-thirty. When did you get this case?"

"Came in a few minutes ago," Arena replied.

"Shit," Rubin said, "another twenty minutes and the night team would have picked it up."

"Sorry about that. One of the few bad deals about working steady days. You get all the grounders."

"How long were you in the First Squad, Frank?"

"Five years," Arena answered.

"Add six months to Homicide and that gives you five and a half. I put in six in General Service and five in Homicide before I got the fucking day job last year. You know what I'm about to tell Kelly? To stick it! The heavy investigation comes in and you, Sanchez, and Wolfe work on one case sometimes for weeks. Last week alone I picked up a crib case, a shotgun suicide, a suspicious auto crash supposedly caused by drugs, and an overdose. So I get the weekend off, and today I pick up a suspicious pool drowning and now a fucking hanging." With the last word, he angrily grabbed his set of car keys and stomped out of the room.

The night team supervisor, Detective Sergeant Peter Starr, walked in at that moment. He told Arena, "Rubin's all talk. If Kelly told him he was going back on the clock, he'd squeal like a stuck pig."

Since the relief team leader was early, Arena entered Gore's office with his daily supplementary on the Tashino case. Gore read it over carefully and asked, "This pastor, he didn't tell you a lot—is there something you left out of your report I should know about?"

"Yes. He's covering for someone. Who, I have no idea. When I showed him the sketch his eyes widened and he looked hard at that picture for a full minute before giving me a bullshit answer that he'd never seen the guy before."

"Any other reason?" Gore asked.

"He claims he has no group pictures. He's been going to reunions for fifty years. He has two pictures on his wall of his ship and a boxing team from years ago. Why wouldn't he have any photographs from his reunions? Also, he read about the murder in Newsday knowing the name Maehara was an alias since he was in the prison camp with both of them. He neither called the police or his shipmates."

"Is he a suspect?" the sergeant asked.

"Right height and build. Wrong face. No, he's no suspect."

"So where do you go from here, Frank?"

"I made an appointment for Thursday to see a retired professor in Connecticut. I may have to put some OT in on that one. I'm also trying to interview the ship's cook in Hoboken, New Jersey. I left a message on his machine. Before I check out, I'll call him again. Hopefully, I'll get him. If not, I'll use the County credit card they issued me."

"Let's hope the professor and the ship's cook have a group picture and are not hiding information like the pastor," Gore said.

"It may be wishful thinking, Sarge, but the case is turning out better than I expected."

"Don't get your hopes up too high. We have a long way to go."

Arena had forgotten to mention that the pastor had a visitor during the time of the murder. He did, however, mention Hughes. "We have a retired New York captain out of Homicide residing out east in Mattituck. I called him, but his granddaughter said he was on a fishing trip, so I left our number."

"No shit," Gore said. "A Homicide cop could possibly be some help to us. What's his name?"

"Hughes, John Hughes."

Gore nodded and said, "Incidentally, Dick Purcell called this morning. He was looking over the case jacket and wants to concentrate on the blood type. When you cut down your field of possible suspects, he'll get a subpoena from the State to send to Naval personnel in St. Louis to check out their blood types."

Arena said, "I don't think we need a subpoena. We're dealing with the federal government and we're law enforcement."

"Frank, we have to follow the book. If we make an arrest and we don't go through the proper channels it could hurt the case."

Before Arena left for the day, he tried calling the ship's cook one more time. Once again he got the recording. This time he left a message: "Important you call me anytime after six this evening. The call is long distance, so reverse the charges. Detective Frank Arena, Homicide Bureau, Suffolk County Police Department." Then he gave his phone number and the time he made the call.

Chapter 13

Usually the parking lot at Headquarters had plenty of empty spaces, but not this morning. Arena had to park quite a distance from the main entrance. It was St. Patrick's Day and Suffolk's finest were preparing to board the buses for New York City to march in the parade. Three buses were lined up to take about one hundred marchers, including the Emerald Society Pipe Band. Lieutenant Jim Kelly was tuning up his pipes to the tune of 'Amazing Grace.' Detective Sergeant Kevin Fagan was banging away on the drums. Arena thought Kelly and Fagan looked funny in their kilts, both having hairy, heavy set lets. And he could never understand why the Irish and Scots enjoyed the sound of the bagpipes; to him it was just a lot of noise, something akin to fingernails on a blackboard. The police officers were dressed in their blue uniforms and were all wearing white gloves. Arena waved as he passed them. On the sides of the buses were banners that read, 'Emerald Society of the Suffolk County Police Department.'

"Headquarters will be quiet today," he thought as he entered the building. He would find out how wrong he was. To his surprise there were several people in the Homicide office. Rubin and Probst, the day men who started at 8:00 a.m., were taking statements from two civilians, most likely witnesses. Danny Wolfe was also taking a statement at his desk. Sanchez had two people sitting by his desk—the one directly across from him Arena recognized as Attorney Tom Gallegos. At the attorney's side was a disheveled looking man handcuffed to a large ring attached to the desk. The conversation between the three of them was all in Spanish. The shooter was from Chile.

When Arena was a member of the First Squad he took a two-month course in Spanish. He found the course somewhat helpful, but in reality learned very little. The area's Spanish population had tripled in the past ten years, so learning the language would be useful in his work. On his own time and expense he took a course with the John Jones Agency who guaranteed if you didn't learn to pick up a conversation between two Spanish-speaking people your money would be refunded.

Arena picked up the conversation this time. Apparently the Brentwood attorney had kept his word and turned the shooter over to Sanchez and Wolfe. Anxious to listen to the Spanish conversation, Arena leisurely helped himself to a cup of coffee and listened in.

"Andres cuando entraste en tu casa sabias que Jose elevaba una pistola y sospechabas que se acostara con tu mujer? Esa era la razon por la cual elevabas una pistola?" asked Sanchez. Since he was speaking in Spanish he took a few liberties, trying to put words into the shooter's mouth by asking if he shot him in self-defense. It was obvious he was trying to help the guy.

"Era un puerco y se mercia morir," replied the shooter. He didn't buy in, telling the detective his victim was a pig and deserved to die.

"Te esta tratando de ayudar!" screamed the attorney. "No seas tonto! Dile que tenias miedo." He felt the detective was on their side, but his client was too stupid to realize it.

"Era un puerco las balas no le causaron suficiente dolor. Yo hubiera usado un cuchillo," responded the man in handcuffs. Ignoring his attorney, he called the victim a pig once again and said he should have used his knife.

"Enough!" thought Arena. Going to his bin, he found several messages. One was from Assistant District Attorney Purcell and another from Mr. Seki of the Japanese Embassy in Washington. A third message was from Lieutenant Carey of the Rockville Center Police Department.

Returning to his desk, he made the first call to Purcell. "Dick, Frank Arena returning your call."

"Thanks, Frank. Gore tell you what it's about?"

"You want names so you can get a subpoena to send to the feds in St. Louis to get the blood types of our suspects?"

"You got that right, Frank. How many names do you have?"

"One hundred and thirty-one."

"Good. Send them to me and I'll get started."

"Dick, why send all of the names? Within a day or so I can narrow it down to about a dozen men, maybe less."

"So, when you narrow it down you'll have all the blood types. Send the names over to my office today by courier."

"You'll have them in the afternoon." Arena had little patience with those who generated unnecessary labor on the part of others, but he thought, since he's the guy who's handling the court case, who am I to argue?

At 9:30 a.m. he called Carey. It was good to hear his Irish tenor voice again, saying loud and clear, "Frank Arena, you old spaghetti bender! How the hell are you?"

"As well as can be expected. I see you passed a few tests since the last time we worked together."

"I did, but I sometimes miss working the street. How's the gourmet cook? Still at it?"

"Does a leopard change its spots?"

"So, what's this call all about? To say hello, to invite me to dinner, or are you looking for me to solve another case for you?"

"Remember the Carlyle murder that happened about a week ago?"

"Yeah, I read about it in the newspaper. You the lead detective on the case?"

"I'm the squellman."

"So how can I help?"

"How well do you know the minister or pastor or whatever he calls himself—Dale Alexander?"

"Very well. He's considered a good man. Works with the Hospice program and several of our young officers attend his church."

"I'll be brief, Darren. We have a good description of the shooter, his blood type, and we believe he was a gray haired man. Your Pastor Alexander was a POW in Thailand during World War Two and the victim was a prison guard in the same camp. He fits the description, height and build, but he doesn't match the police sketch—so he's not a suspect, but we believe the night of the murder the shooter either stopped by to see him or could have even stayed overnight."

"What you're asking me to do then, Frank, is talk to my officers who attend his church and feel him out? What's the date and time of the murder?"

"March tenth is the date and time is approximately 10:00 p.m."

"Weapon?"

"Thirty-eight special and a silencer was used."

"How did you tie the pastor in with the victim?" Carey asked.

"The victim was using an alias, calling himself Koki Maehara. His real name was Oki Tashino. The pastor and crew of the Navy ship *Stuart* were prisoners under him in Thailand. He was an unusually cruel son-of-a-bitch. One of the survivors spotted him in California a week or so before the reunion they have every year on the first of March. Seems our government dropped all charges in the early 1950s against all wartime Japanese soldiers accused of atrocities. Someone at that reunion did not take too kindly that Tashino got away with it, so he followed his path from Los Angeles to Chicago to Long Island, then knocked him off."

"You said that mouthful without stopping, Frank. So, Pastor Alexander was a POW in the war. Funny how I never heard about that. I'll do what I can. Give me a day or so and I'll get back with you."

Before going to lunch, Arena had a final call to make to the Japanese Embassy. He identified himself to the operator who answered, and said he was returning a call from Mr. Seki.

"Please hold. Mr. Seki will be with you in a minute."

The detective listened to piano music for about thirty seconds before the voice of Mr. Seki said, "Thank you, Detective Arena, for being so prompt in returning my phone call."

"If you called regarding an arrest, we haven't made any as yet."

"No, just to inform you that like your department we are now aware that the killing of our Japanese citizen could well have been revenge. One question. We have followed the case in the New York newspapers. Why have you not told your news media that Mr. Maehara was using an alias and that his real name was Oki Tashino?"

"Since you use the word 'revenge' I can only assume you have checked with the Tokyo police and have been given the same information as we received," said Arena. "As to your question, I cannot answer that. Sergeant Gore speaks with the press, not myself or any other detective on the team."

Mr. Seki remarked, "Fifty years ago our country was very much different than today. Our children now learn little of World War Two. Most of us learn about the war when we go abroad. We made many mistakes like our allies, the Germans, did, but that was yesteryear. Today Japan is an industrial nation.

"Right now we are going through Japan-bashing in your country. Bringing back the atrocities of World War Two does nothing to bind good relationships between our countries. I can't say I wish you luck in your investigation. Nevertheless, thank you for taking time out to return my call."

Walking to the sandwich shop down the street, Arena was pleased with the way the ball was rolling on this case. He hadn't run into any dead ends yet. He was anxious to return to Headquarters after lunch and meet with Gore to review the case.

Gore opened the conversation after lunch with, "Jim Neill of Newsday called me. Seems some of our men have talked, so he's aware Maehara is an alias name. I'm giving him the go-ahead to print the story. He understands why we held back.

"It's seven days now since the murder. I've looked over your reports and I'm satisfied with your progress. Where to next?"

"I talked with the ship's cook yesterday and made an appointment to interview him at his home in Jersey City tomorrow."

"Basically, what are you looking for, Frank?"

"I'm hoping he has an up-to-date group picture. This way I can break down my suspects by build and height. Purcell is getting blood type info from Naval Personnel in St. Louis on all remaining crew members of the *Stuart*."

"Take home one of the units, Frank. That way you can get an early start in the morning. Do you have many others you want to check out besides the sailor you're visiting tomorrow?"

"Until I see a group picture, I can't answer that question. I would like a man to go upstate and interview a former officer named Jim Meehan. I'm going to Jersey tomorrow and Connecticut the following day. Can you spare a man?"

"Wolfe's going on vacation," Gore answered. "Joey Gentile returns from vacation and will be back next tour. Laurencelle comes off the sick list, so next week we'll have yourself, Gentile, Laurencelle, and Sanchez. Since Joe has just about wrapped up his case, I'll let him make the trip upstate. I'll fill him in on why he's going to see Meehan."

"Thanks, Sarge," Arena replied.

Until he got a group picture, Arena was making an attempt to interview all within driving distance. Meehan's background was impressive—a graduate of Annapolis, he left the Navy after paying back his time. Today he was the owner of three shopping centers; two were run by his sons and one by his son-in-law. He lived in Climax, New York, and according to the report was a wealthy man.

Arena left Gore's office and headed to the back room for the inevitable cup of coffee. The television was on and Wolfe was watching the St. Patrick's Day Parade. Suddenly he shouted, "Hey, guys, our pipers are about to pass the review stand!"

Probst, Rubin, Gore, and Sanchez joined them to watch Lieutenant Kelly and Sergeant Fagan in bare legs. The Suffolk troops looked spectacular in their holiday regalia, hoping to take the crown away from the famous NYPD pipers. They had done this once years back, and every year steadfastly tried to duplicate that victory.

After the Suffolk men had passed and were no longer on the screen, Gore returned to his office, paving the way for Sanchez to indulge in his usual topic of conversation with the other guys. "On St. Patty's Day everyone is Irish. I marched last year and didn't come back to the Island for two days."

"Were you off duty?" Probst asked.

"One of the days I was, the other I called in sick. I picked up this broad. She was wearing a button that said 'Kiss me, I'm Irish.' So I did."

"What happened?"

"We had a ball, then I fucked her for two straight days. She never would tell me her real name, just called herself 'April.' She was probably married."

"Was she any good?" Rubin asked salaciously.

"I wouldn't have banged her for two days if she wasn't. Maybe next year we'll be off duty and I can march again."

Chapter 14

Thursday, March 18, 1993

At 7:00 a.m. sharp he turned onto the Southern State Parkway. Traffic moved at a fast pace. By 8:00 things changed and traffic became heavy. Arena was glad he gave himself more than enough time to get to his destination. At 9:05 a.m. he entered the outskirts of Jersey City. With time to kill, the first order of business was coffee. Pulling into a large shopping center, he found a McDonald's. He enjoyed their coffee and liked the fact that most of them carried the newspapers. Reading the paper would help pass the time.

The weather was made to order. March was usually miserable—cloudy and windy—but not today. A warm front had come in from the ocean, and by noon the temperature should be in the low seventies. At 10:10 a.m. he called his host and was delighted to learn he was only about ten minutes away from Caputo's apartment. He had no trouble finding the place. The directions the ship's cook had given were excellent. When he first pulled up in front of the three-story building, all the parking spaces were filled. But as luck would have it, a car pulled out of one and Arena slipped easily in.

Locking his car door, he noticed the senior citizens sitting out in front of the apartment building were looking him over carefully. The men wore straw hats, the women kerchiefs around their hair. Growing up in an Italian neighborhood, it wasn't uncommon to see the Sicilians wearing straw hats, a custom brought over from the old country where many of them had toiled in the hot sun to make a living. As he passed by, they were talking to each other in Italian, speculating on the stranger amongst them.

Entering the building he checked the mailboxes in the hallway. Caputo's read 3A. He pushed the button and a buzzer went off on the heavy glass door allowing him to enter. The hallway was dark and consisted of a few old chairs and a couch. A sign pointing to the back said 'Elevator.' Once it started up, he thought he should have taken the stairs. The lift, as the Europeans call it, crept and lurched noisily up to the third floor. Finally, the door opened.

The ship's cook was standing in front of an open apartment door. He was a short, fat man, standing about five foot five, bald with the exception of tufts of brownish-gray hair on the sides of his head. Seeing Frank, he shouted, "Over here, Detective!"

Somehow the detective pictured him looking different. As Arena approached his host, the little man said, "You must be Frank Arena."

"In the flesh, Pat, and right on time."

"I was watching you from the window. My neighbors gave you the once-over."

"I guess I made their day. Now they have something to talk about."

"Don't be too hard on them, Frank. They're senior citizens. Part of the way they pass their time is being the neighborhood cops. Nothing gets by them."

Arena was carrying a package under his arm. As he was about to enter the apartment, he handed it to Caputo. "Hope you like this brand of wine."

Opening the package, Caputo raised the bottle in the air and exclaimed, "Valpolicella! Red wine. What's not to like? Like I told you, I'm a good chef, and all good chefs know good wine." Then for the first time, they shook hands. "It's a great pleasure to meet you, Frank." Waving his hand toward the apartment door, he said, "Avanti."

A feeling of nostalgia came over Frank as he entered the apartment. It was like yesteryear. A strong aroma of garlic filled the air. Victorian style furniture, most likely over fifty years old, was covered in vinyl. It was a replica of the boyhood home in which he was raised. The only difference was it was in another state. No doubt this furniture was handed down to Caputo from his parents; he apparently still lived in the past, not choosing to 'move with the times.' With a wave of his hand he motioned to Arena to be seated on the couch.

"Have a glass, Frank?"

"That'd be nice. Thanks."

When Caputo went into the kitchen to decant the wine, the detective walked over to look at a group of framed photographs displayed on the mantelpiece. One was of three sailors hanging all over each other, no doubt all liquored up. They were standing under a sign that read, 'Broadway Joe's.' In the background were dozens of Chinese junks and out further in the bay a large warship, which the detective took to be the *Stuart*. He recognized two of the sailors; one was Alexander and the other, whose name he couldn't recall, was also in the boxing team picture in Alexander's den. A second photo, apparently taken about the same time and place, was of four sailors standing up straight with arms around each other's shoulders. This time he only recognized the ship's cook, with hair. A third photo was young Caputo with a pretty young lady. He was dressed in his Navy whites, and on the bottom it read, 'On my ten day leave after boot camp.' They were standing in front of a marquee, the top part of which read, 'The Glen Island Casino proudly presents the music of Glenn Miller and his Orchestra.' The remaining lettering was blocked out by the young couple.

On the far left of the mantelpiece were three group pictures taken in different cities, all in front of the hotels hosting their reunions. This is why Arena had made the trip. Now he could learn the names of the taller men who served on the ship.

Suddenly he felt the presence of someone standing behind him. Turning, he found his host holding a tray with two glasses of wine and a plate full of hors d'oeuvres. Handing Frank his glass, he put down the tray. And with glass in hand, tapped it against the detective's, saying, "Asoluet!"

The detective nodded and said, "Asoluet."

Caputo said, "I see you're enjoying my photos. They go back a long way, especially the ones on the left taken in Singapore in November of '41."

"I did notice they went back a few years." Then, pointing to the one with the three drunken sailors, he said, "I recognized the pastor, Dale Alexander, in this one, and one of the other guys I also saw in a boxing photograph in the pastor's den."

"A lot of water under the bridge, Frank, since that picture was taken. The other two guys are Tex Shulmelda and Dennis Donovan. They were the macho guys on the *Stuart* and lived for only three things—to fight, fuck, and get drunk."

"Did you go on liberty often with them?" Arena quizzed.

"Are you kidding? I stayed friends, but not close enough to hang out all the time with them. When they got drunk, they were crazy."

"I take it Broadway Joe's was a sailor's hangout."

"For a gob, the best joint in Singapore. Loaded with White Russian whores. And let me tell you, some of them were lookers."

"Walking over to the mantle again, Arena pointed to the picture of the four standing sailors and said, "That's you on the left, isn't it?"

"So you recognized me? I was a young stud in those days. Those are the guys I hung out with most of the time. The guy standing next to me is Fred McLaughlin. Next to him Henry Grant, and on the end, Joe Sandor."

"Are any of them still living?" Arena asked.

"Two of them went down on the *Stuart*. The last one, Sandor, died in Thailand."

"How many of your crew died in the POW camp?"

"I'd say close to a hundred."

"I understand they split your crew up after you were captured."

"We were together for the first six months in Java, and bitched and cried the blues thinking we were in a hell hole. Once we were transferred to Thailand, though, with Tashino to work on that Death Railroad, we realized Java was a country club in comparison."

"What was the purpose of the railroad?"

"It was early in the war. Japan had no idea she was going to lose. Her plans were to invade India. The Burma jungle was India's safety net. So, with a railroad from Thailand to Burma, Japan could move her troops at will."

Arena then said, "I went to the library and looked at the photos in one of the Time-Life books. They showed men working in swamps. They were all skin and bones. Most looked like they were at or near death. Is that why they called it the 'Death Railroad?'" Arena was curious to hear how the little man would describe it.

"Men died by the hundreds every day. The majority were coolie laborers and civilians. They beat and starved the poor bastards. When the men fell down from starvation and exhaustion, they had the coolies dig a big hole. Some were dead and others only near dead when they were buried alive. They were from Thailand, Burma, China, and Java."

"How many slave laborers died?" Arena asked.

"No one really knows. I heard over a hundred thirty thousand."

"What about the Allied prisoners?"

"Since we were POW they were kinder to us and just dumped us into the death house to die by ourselves."

"Didn't the Japanese have any medical facilities?"

"Our doctors had little medicine to work with. When there was no more hope, the Japs didn't want the sick taking up space and eating their rations, so that's where they were put to rest. With one exception—cholera. That spread like wildfire, so they burned them right away. That's how Tex died. He came down with cholera."

"How long did it take to finish the railroad?"

"About a year and a half. It turned out to be for nothing. Our bombers knocked the shit out of it before they ever put it to use. We then spent time repairing the tracks until the war ended."

"I can't possibly imagine how hard it must have been for you guys. First you lose your ship in battle, and from what I've read about seven to eight hundred men went down with her. Then you're captured, beaten, and starved. I think if it was me, I'd have gone out of my mind."

"You'd be surprised how much you can endure to stay alive. Very few Americans have any idea of the torture and death that took place in Thailand. The Brits and Aussies do. They lost about sixteen thousand soldiers. After the war the Aussies named the building of the Death Railroad the Holocaust of Asia."

The detective took a sip of his wine and muttered to himself, "What a fucking way to die."

"What'd you say, Frank?" the cook asked.

"I was just talking to myself. Let's get back to the pictures on the mantle. What years were those group photos taken?"

"The latest one of the far left was taken in Norfolk two years ago. Last year in Chicago I didn't get one. This year it was just eighteen days ago. The reunion was held in Boston. I did order a picture, but it's slow in coming. I think I'm going to call and ask what the delay is." He refilled Arena's wine glass and offered his guest another hors d'oeuvre.

"I see you're in the front row, Pat."

"If I stood in the rear, no one would see me," he laughed. "That's where all the tall guys stand."

"Do you remember the names of all the sailors in the back row?" Arena asked.

"Names? I know their wives, kids, grandkids, and even some of their girlfriends."

"Okay," Arena laughed. "From left to right, who are they?" Arena had his tape recorder playing so as not to miss any of the names.

"Jim Meehan, Art Dromerhauser, Mike Keeley, Everett Busse, Joe Hale, Dick Rafke, Dale Alexander, Dennis Donovan, Ray Cunningham, Johnny Hughes, Mike Manzer, Bob Hill, and Duke Miller. Why do you want to know their names, Frank?"

"Our suspect is a man about six-two, slim, gray hair."

"Frank, you're wasting your time. These guys are like me. They're old. Why are you so stubborn? Believe me, none of them have the strength anymore to kill. If I were a cop I'd be looking at the drug people, not a bunch of senior citizens who survived the Pacific holocaust."

"You're probably right, but it's the only lead we have, so it's my job to follow up on it. Just for kicks, point out the tall slim ones."

Looking over the picture, Caputo said, "Meehan, Donovan, Alexander, Hughes. Those are the ones you would describe as slim. The others weigh too much."

"Tell me about Meehan."

"He was an officer, an Academy grad. Don't know much about him. He didn't come to Thailand with us. He quit the Navy after his hitch and struck gold. Started in the hardware store business. Last I heard he owned three shopping centers in and around Albany. As far as I know he's retired and his kids run the business. I see him at the reunion, but he never talks business."

"What about Donovan?"

"He's a clown and wouldn't hurt a fly. Want another hors d'oeuvre, Frank?"

"No thanks, Pat. I'm saving my appetite for lunch."

Arena then pointed to the photo of Pat and his girlfriend and asked, "Who's the beauty?"

"Rose Acquaro. We were engaged when that picture was taken."

At a loss for words, Arena blurted out, "Did she write you a Dear John letter?" and immediately regretted asking.

"Naw, nothing like that. I got my draft notice, and not wanting to be a foot soldier, I joined the Navy. We thought about getting married, but Rose was her family's sole support. Her dad was sick and her mom never learned to speak English. Her mom helped the best way she could by taking in wash. Since there was no telling where the Navy would send me, we put the marriage off temporarily.

"I was sent to boot camp in Rhode Island. Seeing I was a cook in civilian life, the Navy gave me orders to attend cooking school in San Diego. But before going to the west coast, I was given a ten-day furlough. We had a ball on my leave. I even took here to see her favorite band, Glenn Miller.

"After I finished my eight-week cooking course, they shipped me to a receiving station in San Francisco. My plans were to eventually send for Rose to join me, if only for a few weeks, when out of the blue one night I'm told to pack my seabag. I was being shipped out. Next thing I know, I'm on my way to Manila to replace a ship's cook on the *Stuart* who asked for a transfer to the subs and got it. When I kissed her good-bye the night she saw me off at Grand Central, if I'd known I wouldn't see her for four years, I would have married her for sure."

Arena regretted the Dear John remark. Then, addressing the little guy eye to eye, he said, "That was a bad break, Pat."

"What'cha gonna do? That's life."

"Knowing you were a POW, if she loved you why didn't she wait for you?"

"She thought I was dead. The Japs only let us send home one post card. If she had received it right off, she would have waited. Unfortunately, it took two years to arrive. When she did receive it, she was already a married woman. She married my best friend, Tony Giovanni. He joined the Marines shortly after Pearl Harbor and was hit in the leg on Guadalcanal. They shipped him home. When he visited Rose he was on crutches. At first they talked about me, but as time went on, you know how it is when a boy and girl see a lot of each other, sooner or later something is going to happen. They fell in love. You gotta understand, Frank, Rose thought I was dead."

Arena was a sensitive man. The story upset him; he had only met the little guy a few hours ago but immediately took a liking to him.

Caputo pointed to another picture on an end table. In this one he was holding a baby. He handed it to Arena. "That's me with my godchild, Patsy Giovanni. They named their third little guy after me. Rose had the first two before I was freed."

Looking over the picture, the detective said, "How old is your godchild?"

The host laughed, and then said, "Time waits for no one, Frank. The kid is now a mother with three kids of her own."

Arena decided it was time to get back to the matter at hand. "Tell me about Tashino."

"It's been a long time, Frank, but some things in life you never forget. Sergeant Tashino is one of them. He was a tall man for a Jap. Most of the guards were five-three to five-five. He was about five-ten. He carried a silver and brass swagger stick and often used it to hit a subordinate who failed to respond quickly to his orders. His one feature I will never forget were his beady eyes. A vulture might have eyes like that. Anyway, I was lucky—being short. He hated the tall men, especially the macho ones."

Arena interrupted, "It's hard to believe, under the conditions you describe, that anyone would have the balls to be macho."

"Only in the beginning. By the time Tashino got through with them, the only macho ones were the dead ones."

"Apparently some of the sailors stood up to him. Who were they?"

"Tex Shulmelda, Johnny Hughes, Dennis Donovan, Dale Alexander, and Ben Ramondi."

"In what way did they get to Tashino?"

"We were given rules to follow by the Base Commander, Lieutenant Saito. One rule was to bow to all Japanese guards, as well as the Korean guards, at all times. If we failed to do so, we would be punished. These five men I mentioned were the ship's tough guys. Four were boatswain mates. Ramondi was a gunner's mate. Johnny Hughes was the kid of the crowd. He lied about his age and joined the Navy at sixteen. On January thirtieth of forty-two we celebrated the kid's seventeenth birthday. He was then officially old enough to be a sailor. He's the one that started all the trouble."

"How did he do that?"

"Dale, Dennis, and Tex took a shine to the kid and got him to work with them as a boatswain mate striker. In reality he was a seaman first class doing boatswain mate's work. In case you're not aware of what a striker is, in civilian life you might call it an apprentice. I gotta say this for the three big guys, they wouldn't allow the kid to go into the bars with them and kept him in line by letting him know if he broke their rules he'd never make boatswain mate."

"They were sort of like his big brothers then?"

"That's about the way it was, Frank. We were only in the POW camp about a week when the trouble began. They woke us up at six in the morning and we had our usual cup of rice and tin can of water. Then we had roll call before they marched us out to the fields to work for the next twelve hours in the boiling sun."

Caputo then took a sip of wine before continuing his conversation. "The kid was half asleep and forgot to bow to the Korean soldier on duty. The guard hit him on the side of the head with the butt of his rifle, knocking the kid down. Tex stepped out of the line and conked the Korean. Tashino blew his whistle, bringing down a dozen guards to attack the big Texan. Believe me, sometimes it took a dozen guys in a bar fight to knock the big guy down. The guards were all over him, hitting him from all angles with their rifles. Donovan, Ramondi, and Alexander then joined the fight and were getting the best of the guards. Tashino drew his revolver and fired one shot, hitting Ramondi in the head. Lieutenant Saito heard the commotion from his headquarters, which sat right behind where we had roll call, and came running out. When he saw Tashino had fired his gun, he ordered him to stop. That saved the lives of the other sailors involved in the fight."

"I don't get it," the detective remarked. "Why weren't they all shot? From what I've read and been told by you and other sailors, the Japanese soldiers thought nothing of killing."

"True, but Saito was different. He wasn't your typical Japanese soldier. He was educated in the States. We were told he went to college in California. Like Tashino, he was a wounded veteran of the Chinese campaign. When we were imprisoned under his command, he always talked about how he honored the Geneva Convention. We realized after the war that, although he violated the laws of the treaty in every way possible, he no doubt was the best of the enemy commanding officers. He stopped the beating and ordered a trial."

"What a break for our guys," Arena said.

"Not really. The trial was a kangaroo court. When you think back, he had no choice. If our guys had got off for beating on his guards, he would have lost face. All of them were found guilty."

"What was the sentence?"

"He gave Shulmelda and Hughes two weeks in the hot box. Alexander and Donovan got ten days."

"I heard about the hot box from Alexander. From what he told me it may have been better to have been killed like Ramondi was."

"You should have seen the poor bastards when they were released. It took them a day or so before they got their legs back."

"Did Alexander ever tell you that the guard Koki Maehara was the one that probably saved their lives by sneaking them extra rice and water during his night shift?"

"You know, Frank, I only found that out at the reunion in Boston two weeks ago. I don't think too many people knew that one of the enemy saved their lives."

"Why didn't they at least tell you guys after the war?"

"I guess during the incarceration they kept it to themselves to protect Maehara, and once we were freed it didn't seem an important matter anymore."

"I bet Tashino was pissed when the four of them walked away from the hot box alive."

"He was, but the Japanese never bucked their superior. Lieutenant Saito was a fair man. As far as he was concerned, they served their penalty."

"Now, tell me about Alexander. How did he find religion?"

"Life is strange, Frank. He was a barroom brawler when he was on liberty. He lived from day to day like there was no tomorrow. It happened in Thailand when Dale came down with malaria. He overcame that temporarily, but then he came down with diarrhea, followed by diphtheria. He was useless to Tashino on the railroad gang and took up a bed in the hospital. The British doctors did all they could with the little medical supplies they had. So Tashino ordered him to be put in the death house. This is where the bodies were laid to die. I went in there once. The stench made me throw up. Flies swarmed all over the skeletal bodies. Don't forget, all of them had diarrhea, and what little food they ate came out, if you know what I mean."

"God, how did Alexander ever survive?"

"Good friends. Shulmelda, Hughes, and Donovan. After they finished up their twelve hours on the railroad, they would save part of their food and water. Barney Epstein snuck some medical pads out of the infirmary and I supplied bowls of hot water. They washed him, cleaned up his body scabs, and Hughes managed to get some native ointment to help stop the diarrhea and it worked. In a few weeks time he was strong enough to move, so they carried him outside the death house and set up a small tent under a tree. It was a miracle. In some way, God was watching over him."

"What about the guards? Didn't they try to put a stop to it?"

"Hell, no. As far as they were concerned, the trio was wasting their time. However, if they did help him get well it would be another body to put back to work on the railroad."

"So, how did he find religion?"

"I really don't know other than giving my own opinion. When you're near death like he was, and manage to survive, the one you become close to is your maker. Dale, as far as I know, was not a man who prayed or went to church until he met the Reverend Worthington."

"The Reverend Worthington was a chaplain, I presume?"

"He was a Brit, a Scot I believe, and like you said, a chaplain with the Brits. He was an older man, gray hair, gray beard, and a red nose. Kinda reminded me of Santa Claus. He would stop by the Death Hospital every day, but most of the patients were out of it, so he talked a lot with Alexander. Dale suddenly looked forward to his visits."

"He preached a good sermon most likely," Arena said.

"He gave Dale a Bible and the two of them read aloud to each other. Little by little you could see the man was suddenly talking like the Reverend Worthington," Caputo said.

Arena observed, "You see it in the movies and read it in books that 'there are no atheists in foxholes.'"

"More wine, Frank?"

"No thanks, I had enough. You've been more than helpful to me, Pat. You gave me more insight into Tashino that I had hoped to get. I have a personal question to ask you. It has nothing to do with this particular case. Do you mind my being inquisitive?"

"Ask your question."

"How do you feel about the American Japanese that were wrongly incarcerated during World War Two getting a payment of twenty thousand dollars each from our government?"

"It sucks," replied Caputo. "When we returned home, Congress voted to give us a dollar a day extra for the time we spent as prisoners. I got over twelve hundred dollars and thought that was a big deal. Sure, they were humiliated, but so were we. So why doesn't Japan give us twenty thousand dollars? Hell, they beat us, starved us, and treated us like animals."

Arena wasn't surprised at his answer or the emotion the question engendered. He did not agree with him, but knew enough to drop a touchy subject. On a lighter note, he asked, "Did you ever see the comedian, Pat Cooper?"

"Are you kidding? He was named after me. His real name is Patsy Caputo."

"Was he really named after you?" Arena asked, surprised.

"Naw, I'm pulling your leg. We both have the same name, so I tell people that. Some believe it, others know better."

"I guess I'm gullible. You had me believing you."

Standing up, the host stretched and said, "You hungry?"

"Starved."

"Then let's cut all the bullshit about police and war talk, and eat. I made a special lunch for you, paison."

The kitchen and dining room combination in the apartment was a surprise to Arena. It was outfitted like a fine restaurant. The meal was already prepared beforehand and was now simmering on the stove, waiting to be served.

"Sit, Frank, and let me do the honors. I've skipped the antipasto, having served that with the drinks. So, we begin with Minestrone Genovese soup."

The amateur cook only had to take one spoonful to know it was the beginning of a real gourmet meal. The soup was followed with a dish of pasta seasoned with basil and garlic. The main course, or 'pesce e carne,' was scampi oreganato, consisting of shrimp in a sauce of basil, garlic, and oregano butter, accompanied by risotto and ratatouille. Formagi, an assortment of fresh fruit and various gourmet cheeses followed this. Dessert was a delicious Italian rum cake. After the meal, the chef opened a box of cigars and offered one to his guest.

"No thanks. I don't smoke."

"Ah, you don't know what you're missing. After a large meal I always enjoy my cigar with my demitasse coffee."

"Well, this demitasse is superb. I assure you it's enjoyable with or without a fine cigar," Arena commented.

After thirty minutes talking about food, the host stood up and said, "Let's return to the living room and finish our conversation in there." Pat sat in his favorite chair and enjoyed his cigar. Arena sat on the couch, feeling stuffed, knowing he ate too much. Nevertheless, he enjoyed every mouthful.

"Pat, I'd like you to come to my home in North Babylon for dinner. This time I'll be the chef."

"Did you enjoy your meal?" Pat asked.

"You know I did. I cleaned my plate on every course. It was truly a fine gourmet meal."

"That was only lunch. Next time I'll make something in the evening," Caputo said.

"Not until I get the chance to be the host. When can you come to Long Island?"

"Hey, just because I cooked you up a meal doesn't mean you have to invite me!"

The detective was not only impressed with the little man's cooking, but he had an idea he was also lonely. The man never married, and most likely all the relatives close to his age were no longer around. Besides, he wanted to show off, so he answered, "If I didn't want to invite you, I wouldn't have. You'll love Eleanor, and I'd like to have an opinion of my cooking from someone whom I consider an expert."

"Since you put it that way and want to show off, you name the date. I'm retired and have all the time in the world."

"I'm off Friday and Saturday this week. I need a day to prepare, so how about coming to my house Saturday afternoon? We can talk, have a few drinks, and then dinner."

"You said your wife's name is Eleanor? Do you have any kids, Frank?"

"Two, but as luck would have it, neither one will be home Saturday. Frankie Jr. is spending the weekend at a friend's and Jamie is attending a weekend seminar given by her college. So, there'll just be the three of us."

Smiling and nodding his head, the gourmet chef agreed. "You got a date, Frank. What time?"

"Anytime after five."

"I'll need directions."

"Take the Southern State Parkway all the way out until you see the sign for Deer Park Avenue. I believe it's Exit 39. Go north; you'll be crossing over the bridge. Hang a left on August Road. It's about two miles down before you'll see Cherry Drive. It's a short block with only one house. I'm on the corner of Cheryl and Gaulton Drive. My house number is 23 Cheryl."

As he was about to leave, Arena said, "Oh, I almost forgot." Then, opening his briefcase, he pulled out the police artist sketch and showed it to Caputo. "This is a sketch drawn by our police artist from a description of the shooter. It's supposed to be a good look-alike. Is the face familiar to you?"

Taking the sketch from the detective, Caputo studied it carefully for several minutes, and then said, "I can't put my finger on who this guy resembles. I know I've seen him before, but where I just can't remember."

"Keep the sketch. I've got more copies. Study it once in a while, and if it comes back to you, where you may have seen this face before, call me. Here's my number." Arena then handed Caputo a business card.

It was late in the day when he arrived back at headquarters. His team was gone for the day. Detective Sergeant Kevin Fagan was on duty. Checking his bin, he found several messages; one from Purcell, another from Gore telling him to hang onto the unmarked car for a few days. The third message was from John Hughes. The time was now 7:20 p.m. He was curious, and dialed the retired homicide detective's number. This time he was lucky when a male voice answered.

"Mr. Hughes? This is Frank Arena of the Suffolk County Police."

"Ah, Detective Arena. I've been expecting your call."

"No need to go into why I called. I'm sure by now you know."

"That I do. Someone killed the animal."

"Yes. When we try to establish facts about the case, seems like the crew of the *Stuart* always comes up."

"So how can I help you?" Hughes asked.

"I have a few questions to ask. And since you're retired out of Homicide, who knows, maybe some advice."

"Don't pull my leg, Detective. When do you want to question me?"

"Not question, sir. Interview would be more like it. How about next Saturday? You name the time."

"I usually go fishing. However, this is more important. Say, noon?"

"That's fine. I know how to get to Mattituck. You're just past Riverhead. Just tell me where to turn off Main Street."

"You know where the high school is?" Hughes asked.

"Yes," Arena replied.

"Take the first right past the high school. It's a residential block. Our house is the fourth on the right hand side, color gray. You'll see my white Saturn in the driveway."

"Thank you. I'll see you around noon on Saturday," Arena said.

"I'll have sandwiches and coffee, so don't eat lunch," Hughes said, and then hung up the phone.

Chapter 15

Friday, March 19, 1993

Getting the okay from Gore to take the unmarked police cruiser home was a break. It saved Arena over an hour not having to go to headquarters first. It was 6:50 a.m. when he entered the Southern State Parkway off the Deer Park Avenue exit. Traffic was moderate and the moving vehicles were all going at a fast pace. It only took him a little over an hour before crossing the Bronx city line into Connecticut.

The warm spell that covered the entire east coast was still with them and the sky was blue. It was going to be a beautiful day. At Storr he turned off the Wilbur Cross Highway and followed the directions that Professor Eilers had given him. He arrived at his destination slightly past 11:00 a.m.

The professor's home was on a corner lot and the grounds were enormous. The house itself sat back about fifty yards and the scene reminded Arena of the movie setting in Gone with the Wind. The house was painted white. The driveway was lined with trees, most of them as tall as the house. Arriving in front of the home, the driveway now became circular. Under the bay windows on both sides of the house were red Ixora out in full bloom.

As he approached the front door it opened. Standing in the doorway was the professor who was about five-five with snow-white hair. His skin was pale and he had navy blue eyes. With a friendly smile he extended his hand to greet the detective and then said, "I presume you are Detective Arena."

The detective greeted him with a handshake, and then removed his wallet, displaying his gold tin on one side and his identification card with his picture on the other. Eilers looked over the identification, then welcomed his visitor into his home, saying, "Let's go into the living room. Nico was kind enough to fix us a plate of sandwiches, a pot of coffee, and hot water in the event that you're a tea drinker. She's getting dressed to go riding. Thursday is her riding day. She will join us in a minute."

"Nico, I presume, is your wife, Professor?" the detective asked.

"Yes," he replied. "I'm sorry I didn't mention her to you in our conversation. Blame it on old age."

While waiting for Nico to join them, Arena tried to find some small talk to pass the time. "I drove by Connecticut University to get here and was surprised to see open fields with cows grazing."

"Many years ago Connecticut was an agricultural state. They still teach it at the university."

"I noticed most of the buildings were old, with greenery and vines climbing the walls. Over in the distance, one building taller than the others seemed out of place."

"That was probably the gym. We have a fine basketball team and play in the Big East."

"So, your wife likes to ride horses?"

"Very much so. Years ago when she was younger she was a member of the Riding Academy Equestrian Team. Now she just rides her beloved prize horse, Kanazawa, for pleasure."

"Sounds Japanese. Where did she get that name?"

His question was answered by a petite, dark haired lady who said, "It's a seaport in Japan where I was born. I named the horse after the city."

The detective was somewhat taken aback. He didn't expect to find the wife of the professor to be of Japanese ancestry. The lady extended her hand to Arena and said, "I'm Nico Eilers, Walt's better half."

"Detective Arena," he replied. "Feel free to call me Frank."

Taking him by the hand, she led him over to the large bay window on the north side of the house. Then pointing to a large barn in the rear, she said, "At one time we had several horses. That's why we built that large barn in back. Now Kanazawa has the barn all to herself."

"She treats that horse like a baby," the professor said, laughing.

"So do you, dear," she answered back.

"Where did you two meet?" Arena asked.

"In Japan. I was a college professor teaching at a small college in New England. Many countries offer American teachers an invitation to come over on an exchange program. I spoke Japanese, having picked up much of the language as a prisoner of war, and a two-year course in Japanese in the States. I was accepted into the program and later found out why. Not too many Yanks spoke Japanese. As it turned out, Nico's father was the headmaster of Sophia, the school where I was assigned to teach. He was an officer in the Japanese army during the war. He sought me out and quizzed me about my experiences as a prisoner, having been told very little in Japan. One Saturday he invited me over for tea. A beautiful butterfly waited on me hand and foot. I was hooked by the butterfly from that day on."

"From what I've read about Japanese customs, it probably took you a long time before you dated her."

"Too long. That semester we dated a few times, always with a chaperon. Then the summer ended and I returned to the States lovesick. The next summer I put in once again to be part of the teaching exchange at Sophia in Tokyo. This time I was accepted immediately since I not only spoke the language, but Nico's father, Mr. Morita, requested me. You're right about strict traditions. The Japanese people wrote the book on them."

Nico listened politely to the conversation, most likely having heard it many times before. She stood up and walked over to her husband and kissed him on the top of the head. Then, addressing the detective, she said, "Frank, it's been a pleasure meeting you. Come again sometime with your wife. I love hearing police stories." Then she said to her husband, "I'll leave you two alone to talk over business."

When Nico departed, Eilers led his guest over to the dining room table where the lunch sandwiches and coffee were waiting for them. "Help yourself," said the professor. "Nico made ham and cheese, pastrami, and chicken salad, a nice variety."

The detective had been anxious to get down to business, but seeing the food deterred him. It had been a long ride and he had not eaten all day. He had only drunk one cup of coffee. Why not eat?

After lunch Arena made the first move, saying, "Tell your wife the sandwiches were wonderful. I've got to admit I forgot how hungry I was until I took the first bite. Now I'm ready to get down to business."

"Fire away, Frank. I'll answer your questions to the best of my knowledge."

"I have visited two of your shipmates, Dale Alexander and Pat Caputo. Dale doesn't purchase group pictures and Pat had one that was two years old. Do you have one taken on March first?"

"Yes, I do. It came in the mail yesterday. Have another cup of coffee. I'll go to my den and get it."

The detective took his host's advice and poured himself his third cup of coffee. Then said to himself, 'Thank the Lord someone has an up to date group photo.'

Eilers returned with the picture and a large book that resembled a high school or college yearbook whose cover read '40th Anniversary.' The professor put the book down on the table and handed Arena the group picture. The detective took out his notebook, sat down, and pointing to the men in the back row, said, "These guys would be the ones six foot and over, right?"

"Give or take and inch. All I know is that the taller men are in the back row."

"Can you name them?" Arena asked.

Sitting alongside him Eilers pointed his finger from left to right, then said, "Everett Busse, Joe Hale, Duke Miller, Art Dromerhauser, Ray Cunningham, Jim Meehan, Dennis Donovan, I don't know the next man, Dale Alexander, Dick Rafke, John Hughes, Mike Keeley." Pausing for a moment, the professor turned to the detective and asked, "You don't really believe that a sailor off the *Stuart* murdered Tashino, do you?"

"We have no suspects, only a motive—revenge. Witnesses state that they saw a man coming and going that stood six-one or maybe six-two and he was slim. Our Identification Division found gray hair during the investigation, so we have to presume our shooter is not a young man.

"Our victim's name was Koki Maehara, or so we thought. Our investigation, along with the help of the Tokyo police, revealed that his real name was Oki Tashino, a man wanted for questioning by the War Crimes Committee at the end of World War Two. Since they thought he was dead already, he no longer was a wanted man. For half a century he has used an alias. Until a few weeks ago nobody was aware that he was in the States except for the sailors who served on the *Stuart*. Whoever killed Tashino knew who he was."

"You say you have a description of a possible suspect. I read the papers, and according to the FBI sixty percent of crimes are committed for drugs. Who's to say the man who killed Tashino wasn't an addict?"

"Nothing of value was taken. The shooter left cash and very expensive jewelry, then proceeded to clean up after himself to cover his tracks," Arena answered.

"I doubt very much if most of our guys could plan a murder. They're too old and just not capable of it."

"The mind, Professor, is very complex. When it snaps it can change a human being into whatever he wants to become. He may be a well-educated man, a religious man, or a Caspar Milquetoast type who lets people walk all over him. A strong hatred, especially one laid dormant for many years and then brought to the surface by circumstance, can transform even the best of us. Eighteen days ago we believe someone at that reunion, upon learning of Tashino's existence, went bananas. It had to be someone so abused that if Tashino had been caught by Army Provost Marshals to appear before the War Crimes Committee way back then he would have been at the trial and, who knows, maybe even would have attempted to kill him then."

"You make a convincing argument, Frank. You should have been a lawyer."

"Let's get back to the group picture. You saw all of them at the reunion. Who are the really slim ones, say, the ones that go about one hundred and fifty pounds?"

Eilers studied the picture and said, "I can only help to a point. I can't tell if a man is one hundred fifty or one hundred seventy-five, but I'll do my best. You're looking for a man six-one or six-two, so that leaves Busse and Dromerhauser out. Both are six-five. Hale is only about six foot, so is Cunningham. Keeley and Duke Miller are overweight. All go well over two hundred pounds. The only four that qualify are Meehan, Donovan, Alexander, and Hughes."

Arena checked this information against the names in his notebook, the ones given him by Caputo. He discovered one missing, and asked, "What about Broderick?"

"He died about six months ago."

"The man standing between Donovan and Alexander, you say you never saw him before. How did he get into the picture?"

"A few of the guys brought guests. He's probably one," Eilers replied.

Arena counted the men in the photograph; there were one hundred forty. The photo included some guests, and a few had family members with them. Eilers then handed him the large book, and said, "Maybe this can help."

Arena skimmed the pages at first, then realized what the professor had handed him was worth its weight in gold. "Wow, you guys had a forty year book printed up?"

"It was Ballentine's idea. We had two hundred sixty members then. When we put the book together we had no idea it would take us close to a year to get it started, and it was costly."

"This book is amazing. How did you do it?"

"Every ten years we have a memorial service and invite the families of all our shipmates, so we had all the addresses. As you can see, we have a picture of what the sailor looked like before the war and a little background about him. Here on page one is Alexander yesteryear and today. Below him is Eddie Allen killed in battle; we only have the one picture of him. In the back of the book we have snapshots taken over the years and managed to get a few pre-war pictures, too."

"Can I borrow the group picture and the book?"

"Be my guest, but guard the book with your life. A reunion picture can be replaced, but not that book."

Finished with his questioning, Arena could now sit back and talk with the professor about his personal life and the war. "When did you join the Navy, Walt?"

"When I graduated from high school in June of forty-one."

"What was your rank when your ship went down?"

"Signalman Third Class."

"During the battle, where were you stationed?"

"On the bridge. At first I thought we were going to fight our way out. They kept coming and coming, one destroyer after another. Then the motor torpedo boats and finally the big ships. We help our own until we ran out of ammunition. Then we never had a chance."

"Since you saw all that was going on, no doubt you were pretty scared."

"One by one I watched them blow up one gun turret after another. I heard the men screaming, saw bodies mutilated, and prayed to God that if I took a hit I would die immediately."

"How did you get to Java?" Arena asked.

"When the bugle was blown to abandon ship I had my life jacket on. The skipper hollered for everyone to jump over the side. He jumped, we followed."

"How long were you in the water?"

"God only knows. I lost the others and found myself alone. I knew land was close by, but the tide was against me. I remembered my training from my high school years when during the summer I was lifeguard in Reis Park in the Rockaways. It reminded me to take off the heavy water-soaked life jacket, and then I swam. It was almost daylight when I came ashore."

"Being alone, how come the Javanese didn't hack you to death? I understand the Japanese paid them for every sailor they hacked up."

"God was with me. I came ashore where the Japanese landing barges were, so they pulled me out of the water and took me right over to start unloading supplies. There I was joined with both American and Aussie sailors."

"Then what?"

"They marched us to Borger where I was jammed into an old movie theater. That's when I first saw Sergeant Tashino. He was the executive officer under Lieutenant Saito."

"What did you personally think of Tashino?"

"He was a mean bastard, not one to cross swords with or he would make life miserable for you."

"Tell me a little about Tashino and the camp in Java."

"We worked twelve hours a day, six days a week. Two things you learn fast. One, never slow down or look exhausted if you don't want a gun butt over your back. Two, don't talk to the man alongside you. If you did, they thought you were planning an escape."

"So Java is where you said you met Tashino?"

"That's right. It was the morning after we arrived. Lieutenant Saito spoke first, introduced himself as the commanding officer and advised us of the rules in an unemotional, business-like way. He introduced Tashino when he was finished. And Tashino really enjoyed himself laying down his law to us."

"How did you size him up when you first saw him and heard him speak?"

"He was taller than most all of the Japanese soldiers in the camp. I was standing in the front line and was pretty close to him. I think what frightened me the most was his eyes. They looked right through you."

"Did he ever strike you?"

"No. I played his game and bowed whenever he passed me, and I made sure to stay out of his way as much as possible."

"I understand several of the men broke ranks and caused a fight. Tell me about it."

"One of the POWs was struck down by a guard for failing to bow, so I heard later. I was assigned to a different detail, so I didn't witness it. Big Tex Shulmelda went to his aid and hit the guard. Then all hell broke loose and Donovan, Alexander, and another guy, I don't remember his name, oh yes, it was Ben, Ben Ramondi, they all jumped in. Tashino blew his whistle and a dozen guards joined in, hitting our guys with their gun butts. Tashino fired one shot, killing Ramondi, and was stopped from shooting the others by Lieutenant Saito. Saito wasn't a mean bastard. That's the only reason all of them weren't killed right on the spot."

"According to Alexander, they were sentenced to time in the hot box. That was cruel and unusual punishment."

"You can say that again. None of us thought that any of them would come out alive. Much to our surprise all of them lived. At the time we thought it was because they were tough. Just a few weeks ago, though, at the reunion in Boston, we learned for the first time that a Japanese guard snuck them water during the night."

"Koki Maehara," Arena blurted. "Do you think he was ultimately murdered by Tashino?"

"We'll never know. During the last days of the war our planes bombed the Japanese compound, killing several of our men and a lot of Japanese guards."

"I don't get it. Why would our aircraft bomb a POW camp?"

"They didn't. Some of our men were being used by the Japanese as laborers on the railroad. Our side had no idea that POWs were in the compound."

"Given the cruelty of the Japanese during this time, why in the world did you ever get involved with them as a civilian?"

"I know it seems unlikely. But as I mentioned before, I was a professor at a small Catholic college in New England, and Sophia in Japan is also a small Catholic college. They sent several of their teachers and students to our school and we did likewise. The fact that I spoke Japanese was probably the main reason they chose me."

"The gods were with you," Arena remarked. "If things were different, you never would have met Nico."

"True, and not being close to a Japanese family I may not have ever really understood the Japanese people. Sometimes I wonder if they really understand themselves."

"Their thinking does seen quite opposite to ours."

"I really didn't get to understand many of their customs until my second visit. When I returned to the States I wrote a book called *Understanding Japanese Culture*. It never sold much on the open market; however, it's in many of our university libraries throughout the country."

"So tell me about your book."

"I explained the different customs, etiquette, etcetera, and basically tried to explain that the Japanese of today are unlike those who lived in Japan prior to World War Two. Although many of the old ways still exist, Japan is no longer a dictatorship led by a wealthy hierarchy but is more of a democracy. I gave us credit for many of the changes; many occurred during the time General MacArthur was in command."

"I see what you mean. Our culture has changed over the years, but theirs has changed quite dramatically."

Eilers continued his history lesson. "In Japan today the history of World War Two is not taught in the schools. They have erased Pearl Harbor from the textbooks. They do, however, cover the atom bomb forays on Hiroshima and Nagasaki. On the anniversary of those cities' destruction, films are shown of the aftermath—the suffering and damage. Many of the old-timers that survived tell their stories to the children. Like the Holocaust in Europe, it's a time they feel should always be acknowledged by future generations."

"How do you feel about our government compensating the Japanese-American citizens who were incarcerated during the war twenty thousand dollars each?"

"I'm all for it. They weren't the enemy. They were American citizens. Our government should have apologized years ago."

"Somehow I thought you would feel that way," Arena said. "I agree with you."

"We, the Americans, along with the Brits, Aussies, New Zealanders, Canadians, and Dutch are trying to get the same amount of money out of Japan. We have a four million dollar claim against them for violating the Geneva Conference, to compensate the war widows and vets for the suffering, beating, and brutal treatment we went through as prisoners. The Canadians have filed this claim for each of the two hundred thousand of us still available."

"What're your chances of getting it?" Arena asked.

"We have as much chance as a snowball in hell. To admit brutality would open a real can of worms. Every Asiatic country would file a suit."

Looking at his watch, the detective saw it was time to leave. He stood and shook the professor's hand. "I can't thank you enough for your cooperation. I'll get the picture and the book back to you in good condition."

Professor Eilers walked the detective out to his car. Arena was sitting at the wheel when he realized he hadn't shown the professor the artist's sketch. Removing one from the briefcase on the passenger's seat, he handed it to him and said, "Look this over."

Eilers accepted the drawing and studied it carefully. "Is this a look-alike for the suspect?"

"Yes, and it's supposed to be a good one. Do you know that face?"

"I've seen him before, but I can't put a name to him."

"Really?!" This remark was the best the detective heard since the start of the investigation. "Keep it, Walt. Please study it, and when it comes back to you, call me." He then handed the professor his card. "If by any chance we do make an arrest, I'll put you on my 'promise' list?"

"What's a 'promise list,' Frank?"

"So far I've promised three people that if we solve the case, either myself or my sergeant would notify them. So, now you're also on my promise list."

On the way home Arena thought that if the sketch was someone Eilers had met it surely wasn't one of his suspects. He had felt some hope a few minutes ago, but now figured it was probably just a resemblance to someone in Eiler's past.

The traffic on the Connecticut Turnpike moved freely. It wasn't until he hit the Bronx that traffic slowed down to a snail's pace. He drove off an exit in the Bronx to have supper, and hoped that when he resumed his trip that the traffic would be lighter. It was 7:05 p.m. when he arrived back at headquarters. He was now on overtime and still had about another hour's work before heading home. Team One was on duty, but two of them were out in the field, so there was an open desk to use in order to type up the supplementary he needed to leave for Gore. Arena would be off the next two days and had a lot to tell him.

Before checking his bin for phone messages, he walked down the hall to Identification. To get in, a buzzer had to be pushed to let the men working inside know they had a customer. Once inside you enter a small room with a large glass window. If it were a civilian requesting help, the detective would get what was needed and then hand it through the opening. Seeing it was Arena, Bill Senior, the detective on duty, buzzed him in.

"Hello, Bill. Is Maureen Snyder on duty?"

"She left for the day, but will be here in the morning. Anything I can help you with?"

"I want her to call me in the morning." Indicating the book from Eilers he held in his hand, Arena said, "Could you put this in her bin? I'll give you a note to attach to it." He scratched out a note and handed it to Senior. "Thanks, Bill."

He returned to the office area he found a message to call Lieutenant Darren Carey in Rockville Center. He dialed the number right away and only had to go through one other person before connecting with Carey.

"Frank! Glad you called."

"What'cha got, Darren?"

"One of the officers that goes to Alexander's church was at the service the evening the man from Japan was killed. The service lasted until nine. Then when the congregation was having coffee and cake afterward, he overheard the pastor's wife say, 'I'm worried about Dennis. He's not back. I wonder if he got lost?' And the pastor put his arm around her and said, 'Dear, don't worry about Dennis. He'll find his way home.'"

"My vibes told me right along that the pastor was covering for someone. Thanks for the info. It could be just what I need to close this case."

"If it is, old buddy, I did it again and solved your case for you!"

With that they both laughed. Before hanging up Carey said, "Let me know if the info was any good."

Arena walked back over to Identification and began looking through the book Professor Eilers had loaned him. He spent the better part of an hour searching it for a clue, one page at a time. The book would have the answer if it included nicknames of the men, but he was having no luck.

Returning to the office area, he made out his supplementary report and called his wife to assure her he was all right and would be home in forty minutes. Then he signed out in the logbook. The time was 8:35 p.m.

Chapter 16

Sanchez arrived in the sleepy little village of Climax around mid-morning. He bought a USA Today at a newsstand before going into the local eatery for breakfast. After bacon and eggs and three cups of coffee he still had time to kill before his noon meeting with Meehan, so he finished reading the newspaper. As he paid his tab he asked the frowsy blond waitress for directions to Fiddlewood Lane. She referred him to the real estate office next door.

As he entered the office a chubby faced dark haired man was sitting behind a desk talking on the phone. Sanchez seated himself in a chair in front of him and waited patiently for him to finish.

"Can I help you," the man asked politely after hanging up the phone.

"Yeah, I hope so. Can you direct me to Fiddlewood Lane?"

"Going to see Mr. Meehan?"

"Yeah, how did you know?"

The man laughed. "All twenty acres of land on Fiddlewood belongs to Meehan."

"Sounds like the whole town," Sanchez remarked.

"Not quite, but if you owned three shopping centers you could afford to own the best property in the area."

"So how do I get there?" the detective asked once again.

"Take a right at the corner. Follow it four miles until you hit Meehan's property. You can't miss it. There's a six-foot wired fence on the outside. Drive a block or so till you hit the entryway."

The directions were good and the ride scenic. Fifteen minutes later Sanchez drove through the front entrance to Meehan's property. He passed open green fields for a quarter of a mile. Several horses were serenely eating grass. Pulling into the large driveway, Sanchez saw the house reminiscent of a Swiss chalet. The exterior was mostly stone with just enough wood to make it interesting. He had once seen a movie called The Sound of Music, which took place in Switzerland or Austria, he wasn't sure. Wherever it was, that's what the house looked like.

A voice from an upper verandah shouted to him as alighted from the car, "Take the stairs behind the garage!"

As he entered the room at the top of the stairs, Meehan greeted him with a friendly handshake and they introduced themselves. Meehan offered coffee and said, "Let's knock off the formalities. Call me Jim."

"Joe," Sanchez answered. He observed Meehan carefully as he poured the coffee. In no way did he resemble the police artist's sketch. True, he was about six-two and slim, but the likeness ended there. Although he was probably in his early seventies, his hair was sandy with very little gray. Also, his nose was short, unlike the sketch, and he poured with his right hand. Arena's note had said to make sure to look him over carefully to see if he was a lefty.

"So, Joe, from what you told me on the phone you're investigating the murder of Tashino. Is that right?"

"Yes, sir. That's why I'm here."

"I've heard from the grapevine that your department has already been in touch with a few of our crew members."

"That's right. And we intend to contact several more," Sanchez remarked.

"Why, exactly, are you here to interview me? In what way can I help?"

"We're looking for a tall, slim man about six-two with gray hair. A man of that description was seen entering and leaving the hotel the night of the murder."

"I see. And you're here to look me over since I fit the description. How do I size up?"

"Are you a southpaw?" Sanchez asked.

"No," Meehan replied.

"Then you have two strikes against you as a candidate. We're looking for a lefty, and you look nothing like the artist's drawing." Removing the sketch from his briefcase, Sanchez handed it to the businessman, saying, "Is this face familiar?"

Meehan seemed to study the sketch for a few moments, then handing it back to the detective, replied, "Don't know the man."

"Hang on to it," Sanchez said as he pushed it back to him.

Meehan accepted the sketch, and then gave his opinion, "Sounds to me like your department is on a fishing expedition with no fish in the lake. A few weeks ago we all thought Tashino was a dead man. Turned out he outfoxed both our government and his own and has been living right under their noses in Tokyo. Think about it, Joe. He disappeared nearly a half century ago, way back in nineteen forty-five. I've long since buried that part of my life and I think I speak for the rest of the guys as well. The good Lord will see he gets justice when he faces him."

"Tell me about your life as a POW," Sanchez requested.

"You want my life story?"

"No, just start from when you graduated from the Naval Academy."

"Fifty-two years ago," replied Meehan. "A long time ago. I was twenty-one, a green ensign who hoped one day to become an admiral. The *Stuart* was my one and only ship. When we were captured I thanked the Lord that I was an officer. Lieutenant Saito, their base commander, came from an elite Japanese family and believed officers were special. So we became the overseers, the pencil pushers, the arbitrators, et cetera. The enlisted men worked in the hot sun six days a week, twelve hours a day."

"Did you ever see Tashino mistreat any of our men?"

"No, he left the dirty work to the Japanese and Korean guards. Tashino often struck his own soldiers with a steel swagger stick he always carried. It was common in the Japanese Imperial Army for a sergeant or officer to strike a subordinate if he was displeased with him. If a guard didn't punish a prisoner for even the smallest so-called infraction and Tashino witnessed it, the guard would get the full brunt of the swagger stick across his back. So they often hit the prisoners with their gun butts just to keep themselves safe."

"Can you name any of the *Stuart* crew that received, let's say, cruel and unusual punishment?"

"I wouldn't call being hit by one of the guards unusually cruel—that was a way of life with them. But the hot box, or 'coffin,' now that was sadistic by any standards."

"How did that work?" Sanchez asked.

"If one of the sailors broke their rules they had a 'trial.' If found guilty, they were put in a box no more than five feet long and three feet high. The box was placed out in the hot sun and boiled all day. From what I was told they were only let out a short time each day and given little food and water to survive on."

"Do you recall any of your men who were put in this box?"

"I remember them all. As officers we sat in on the 'trials' and tried to stop them from going so far as to put our men in that death trap."

"Let's have the names."

"Alexander, Lazo, Brown, Donovan, Hughes, Shulmelda, and let me think a moment…yes, George Fecke."

"Are any still living?"

"Only four—Fecke, Donovan, Alexander, and Hughes."

"How tall are they?"

"Donovan, Alexander, and Hughes are my height. Fecke is five-six. You're fishing again. Joe, I know these men and none of them resemble the sketch you showed me."

Meehan also had a forty-year book. He showed it to Sanchez, but refused to part with it. Instead, he took him into the study that doubled as a business office and made a clear copy of the Boston reunion group on his copy machine.

It was a few minutes past three when Sanchez entered the New York Throughway. The weekend traffic already was beginning to show. By the time he turned onto the Long Island Expressway, the traffic was moving at a snail's pace. Not only was the work force heading home to Nassau and Suffolk Counties, but many of the city dwellers were heading to the Hamptons for a weekend of fun.

It was 6:15 p.m. when he signed out in the logbook. He rushed home and immediately headed for the shower when he walked through the door. After his shower he set his alarm for 8:00 p.m. and lay down to get a little shuteye before hitting the town. He was hoping to score and be up a good part of the night. Friday night was pick-up night. After some rest he would get dressed and stop at the local diner for a steak dinner and then onto Huntington for a night of fun at his favorite disco where the broads came in pairs, alone, and in groups—blondes, brunettes, and redheads. The Golden Boy Disco was the hottest ongoing meat market in Suffolk County.

It was 10:30 p.m. when he approached the entrance of the disco. The line was half a block long with customers waiting to pay their five-dollar cover charge. He ignored the line and walked through the door. The big bouncer, knowing he was a cop, winked in his direction as he passed by.

He entered the foyer where a circular water fountain with a gold-plated statue that represented the name of the disco adorned the center of the room. The wallpaper was gold, giving off a glittering effect. Sanchez thought this is what "fool's gold" must be like. On both ends of the room were large murals of several nude women. Entering the adjoining room he passed the first circular bar already full to capacity and crossed the dance floor where he spotted several empty seats; he thought he'd better get settled before the outside crowd streamed inside.

Pete Gallagher, the bartender, placed a Scotch and water in front of him and said, "The brunette in the black dress two seats away is a sure thing." He winked at Joe and then moved down the bar to serve another customer. The bartenders knew Sanchez and his tastes well, and since he was also generous with the tips, they were willing to respond with 'tips' of their own.

Sanchez observed the girl in black over the edge of his drink, and he liked what he saw. Her silk dress was so skin-tight her 38-Ds were popping out. Putting on his most smoldering Latin persona, he walked over and tapped her on the shoulder. She turned to him chewing a wad of gum a mile a minute, which was a turn-off, but...

"You alone?" he asked.

"Sort of. I'm with some girlfriends."

"Want to dance?"

"Why not?" she answered.

The first few numbers were fast dances. He liked her moves, but wanted a chance to talk. Then a slow dance finally came on, and from that moment she didn't shut up. He couldn't stand women who talked too much and wasn't too happy with a broad who, when she wasn't yakking, chewed gum constantly. Oh, well, sometimes you have to put up with these things for a good piece of ass.

When the band finally took a break and Joe was walking with her back to the bar, he suddenly noticed a beautiful blond staring at him. She was sipping a tall drink through a straw. "God, she's gorgeous!" he almost said aloud. He looked away for a moment and then turned back again; she was still staring at him. She was wearing a gold lame minidress that glittered like the wallpaper in the outside entryway. "I think she has the hots for me, but how do I ditch this dingbat I'm with?" he thought.

"How about buying a girl a drink? I'll have a seven and seven," said the brunette.

Still dazed by the beauty of the blond, he came slowly back to reality. He would be stuck with this bimbo unless he could get by with one of his old tricks. He asked her, "Can you lend me a fin?"

She laughed. "Stop the bullshit, and order me a drink."

"With what? I ain't got no money."

"Don't bullshit me. I watched Pete put a drink in front of you when you came in."

"Did you see me pay for it? Pete's a friend of mine and knows I just picked up my last unemployment check."

"Then how did you get in here? They charge five bucks."

"Look, that was my last fin. Today I got kicked out of my apartment for being three months behind in the rent. Now I've got to live out of my '87 station wagon until I find another job."

She rolled her eyes and said as she turned away, "Why do I always pick the losers?! If you think you're going to squeeze any dough out of me with your phony charm, you picked the wrong girl. Go find another sucker." She left her seat and only walked a few stools away before another wolf on the prowl snatched her up.

Pete had been watching the whole performance. The blond called him over when she saw the brunette walk away, and whispered something in his ear. Pete nodded to her, poured another Scotch and water, and carried it over to Sanchez. "What's with you, Joe? Why did you pass on the brunette? That broad's a snake in the sack."

"Talks too much, and I'd be afraid of waking up in the morning and finding wads of gum stuck all over my pad."

As he placed the drink in front of Sanchez, he said, "The good-looking blond bought you a drink. The one in the gold dress. I can't help you here, old buddy. Ain't ever seen her before."

Looking at her across the room, Sanchez tipped his drink and said in a whisper, "Thank you." She nodded and smiled. "Wow," he thought, "I've screwed a lot of broads, but none as beautiful as her. He walked over.

"My friends call me Joe."

"Hi, Joe. My friends call me Patti."

"Are you alone?" he asked.

"Sure. What about you?"

"Same. I'm a free man."

"What about the slinky brunette?"

"An old friend. She joined her boyfriend a few stools away." When the music started up again, the couple sitting next to her at the bar got up.

So Sanchez took advantage of the opportunity and took the seat next to her, moving as close as he could. Her long golden hair was almost a match for her dress and her green eyes shone like emeralds. His heart began to pump and he thought, "I'm in love."

"What attracted you to me, Patti?"

"I just love Italian men, especially with hard bodies," she breathed.

"So she thinks I'm Italian," he thought. "Typical dumb blond and a nympho to boot."

She was breathing heavily and her eyes started to glaze as she moved her hand slowly up his thigh and felt the hard hammer of his penis as it began to grow in response. He had made love to a lot of women and knew she was more than ready; he certainly was. "Your place or mine?" he asked.

"I share an apartment with two other girls in Huntington," she answered.

"You're in luck tonight, babe. I've got my own pad. Let's go."

As they left, the Latin lover said to himself, "Tonight you are Italian."

Chapter 17

Although it was Frank's day off, he had a lot to do. With his gourmet guest coming for dinner, he had prepared ahead of time to make sure tonight's meal would be special. Many years ago when he moved into North Babylon, in order to buy the special ingredients he needed, he had to go to Aldo's Gourmet Deli in Corona. Over the years, with the exploding Suffolk population, good Italian delis moved in and were now all over the Island. He only had to go a few miles away in Sunset City to buy his products. A few days ago he had called Gino's Deli and placed his order. At noon today he would pick up the few items he did not have at home. Then he would stop at Jean Calibries' Liquor Store and pick up his William Wycliff wine. The sauce was always the big item. Early that morning he had prepared it and left it on the stove to simmer throughout the day.

The house was in good shape. Eleanor always made sure of that, and Frankie Jr. would cut the lawn when he came home from baseball practice. Eleanor came in from her garden with some fresh-cut flowers and was placing them in a vase. Frank was tasting his sauce. As she was arranging the flowers, she said, "You would think that the Pope was coming instead of a cook."

"Don't ever call him a 'cook,' Eleanor. He's a gourmet chef."

"Oh, I'm sorry if I said a nasty word about His Lordship. I suppose it's off with my head."

"Honey, try to understand. You love your garden, and it's like another child with you. I see you out there for hours on end cultivating your plants. Being a gourmet chef means the same to me. It's only for one night, so grin and bear it. Besides, once you meet him you'll love the little guy."

"Don't worry. I'll be at my best for your guest."

Just then the phone rang. Her son had just finished baseball practice and was asking to be picked up. "I'll be there in about fifteen minutes," she replied.

As she was leaving, Frank walked out to the car with her and said, "Since you're going to the high school, and Sunset City is only a few blocks away, do you mind stopping at Gino's Deli and picking up my order? It's ready."

"No, I don't mind," she answered.

"Oh, one more favor—Jean Calibries' Liquor Store has set aside an order of wine for me. She's only a few doors from Gino's." If looks could kill, Frank would have been dead. Nevertheless, she agreed to pick up both items.

At noon Sanchez called to report what he learned in Climax, New York, at the home of Jim Meehan. "Morning, Frank. Sorry I'm late in calling you, but I had a heavy night."

"No problem, amigo. I appreciate your calling, since it's our day off. Fill me in."

"First off, he looks nothing like the police sketch. Second, the guy doesn't seem to have a big hard on for the Jap. Seems he was an officer, and they didn't have it as rough in Java as the enlisted men. Third, he's not a lefty. I asked him if any of the men would have a reason to kill Tashino. His opinion was, no. Then I asked him if Tashino abused any POWs. He said, only the ones that went through the torture of the hot box. Do you know about the hot box, Frank?"

"Yes, I have all the facts."

"Meehan gave me about seven or eight names. Only five are still living: Alexander, Donovan, Hughes, Dromerhauser, and Fecke. The first three—Alexander, Donovan, and Hughes—fit the description. Fecke is only five-six."

"Anything else?" Arena asked.

"Yeah, he showed me a forty year reunion book. But I couldn't get him to part with it."

"No problem there. I have it. Anything else?"

"He's a businessman and has a top notch copy machine in his home office. He made a copy of the Boston Reunion picture for you."

"I have that, too."

Arena then heard a female voice in the background, "Honey, come back to bed."

"Sounds like you have company, amigo."

"Yeah, I'll tell you about it Sunday over coffee. Gotta go, Frank."

Frank hung up the phone and smiled at the thought of the Latin lover. Then he wondered why Maureen Snyder hadn't called. With his family still in town and his sauce simmering just the way he wanted, he dialed police headquarters using the direct number to Identification.

"Detective Bilton, Identification," a male voice answered.

"Bob, this is Frank Arena. Snyder working today?"

"Robbery has her tied up doing a sketch on a supermarket stickup man. Anything I can help you with?"

"No. It's nothing to do with drawing. She's the only one that can help. When she's free, can you have her call me at home?" Arena gave Bilton his number, and while hanging up the phone he noticed that his family had returned. Eleanor came in carrying her packages, and Frankie Jr. headed into the garage to get the lawn mower.

Working in the kitchen was a labor of love, and Frank was more than pleased with the progress of his gourmet menu. At 2:30 the phone rang. Eleanor answered, and then called to her husband, "It's for you, Frank. It's a female police officer."

Picking up, Frank said, "Maureen?"

"What other police female would be calling you at home?"

"You have the book and my message?"

"I have them, Frank. What do you want me to do with them?"

"I guess you noticed that some of the men are shown in two photographs, how they look today and how they looked over forty years ago. Could you match up the composite drawing you took from the witness and compare them to two names I'm going to give you?"

"What's your point, Frank?"

"I think one of the two names I'm giving you is the shooter. Now, I know you already did a composite. Witnesses sometime don't see it one hundred percent. So compare them, and maybe, just maybe, you'll see something that could match."

"Let me get this straight. You will give me two names, right? Then I take the picture out of the book that's forty years old and put some makeup, lines, etcetera, and see if there is a likeness to the sketch I made?"

"Good girl. You understand what I'm looking for."

"Give me the names."

"Dale Alexander and Dennis Donovan."

"When do you need the drawings?"

"I come back Sunday. Are you working that day?"

"Yes, I am. See me when you come to work. I'll have them for you."

"Thanks, Maureen. You're a doll."

Arena was pleased with his idea. Take the picture taken pre-war, age it, and then match it up with the drawing Maureen took from the witness, Miyako.

Entering the kitchen, his wife asked, "What time is our guest arriving?"

"Four o'clock."

"Well, you'd better take a shower and get dressed. It's almost three."

"Thanks for reminding me." With that, he headed upstairs and into the shower.

Chapter 18

Saturday, March 20th (continued)

Four o'clock came and went and still no Caputo. He's probably lost, Frank thought. He poured himself a glass of wine, and sat down with the latest copy of the evening paper. Flipping idly through the pages, his eye caught the headline of Troy Pool's column that read: Suffolk Police Dragging Their Feet on Tashino Case. "That scumbag," he growled. "One day after I retire I'm gonna meet up with that piece of slime and punch him in the kisser."

Pool was a controversial columnist who wrote about everyone in a backstabbing manner. He regularly tore apart the police, politicians, government, and well-known public figures; anything and everyone to stir up the pot. He received more mail than any writer on the paper's staff, and smiled all the way to the bank. Ninety-five percent of the respondents were telling him off. Nevertheless, his editor could care less, because he knew that people were reading the column and that meant they purchased the newspaper. Before Arena had a chance to read this particular column, the doorbell rang.

It was 4:15 when he opened the door to find a smiling Pat Caputo with arms outstretched, a bottle of wine in one hand and a bouquet of roses in the other. "I have arrived. Sorry about being late. You gave me the right directions, but when I got off the parkway, I went south and ended up near the water."

"Who cares as long as you made it safe and sound," said Frank. "Welcome to the Arena abode."

Caputo followed his host into the living room, placed both the wine and roses on the coffee table, and sat down on the couch. Frank walked over to the staircase and hollered up to his wife, "Honey, our guest has arrived."

"Be down in a minute, dear," she answered in a sweet voice.

Returning to his guest he asked, "Glass of wine, Pat?"

"I'll pass until your wife joins us."

The words were barely out of his mouth when Eleanor descended the stairs wearing a black silk dress with matching black shoes and a white necklace. Both the dress and shoes went with her jet-black hair. Frank did not expect her to make such an effort tonight, but was pleased and once again very much aware of her striking beauty.

"Sophia Loren is joining us, Pat," joked Frank, then added, "Meet my better half, Eleanor."

Rising from the couch, Pat picked up the roses and handed them to her. "It's a pleasure meeting you, Mrs. Arena. May I be so bold and call you Eleanor?"

"How thoughtful of you, Pat" she said of the flowers. "By all means, call me Eleanor. Excuse me while I find a vase for these lovely roses."

Frank and Pat made small talk until Eleanor returned and placed her vase of roses on a small side table. "Now, Pat, how about that glass of wine?"

"Sounds good to me."

"How about you, Eleanor?"

"No, dear, I'll just have a Diet Coke." Then, addressing Pat, she said, "I rarely drink alcohol except with dinner. Then I do enjoy a glass."

Pat took a sip of the wine Frank handed him, moved it around his mouth, and swallowed. "Valpolicella, one of my favorites." He then took a large cigar from his inside pocket and was about to prepare it when he had second thoughts. Looking across at Frank, he asked, "Do you mind if I smoke, Frank?"

"No, not at all, Pat," he replied equably.

"How about you, Eleanor? I know smoke sometimes offends people."

She lied when she answered, "You're a guest in our home. Please make yourself comfortable." To herself she thought, I'm going to kill that man of mine. He knows how I hate smoking. He should have informed his guest that neither of us smokes.

Pat removed the wrapper from his cigar with a small pocketknife. He cut both sides of the Havana, wet it, and put the knife back in his pocket, took out a lighter and lit the cigar. Moments later he was blowing smoke rings into the air with a look on his face of a kid eating a chocolate bar. The smoke was killing Eleanor, but she managed to survive.

For the next half hour the trio discussed politics. Frank refilled the drinks and excused himself to put the finishing touches on the meal he was preparing in the kitchen. Pat and Eleanor continued in conversation. Since they were both of Italian origin, Pat asked, "Are your parents also from Sicily?"

"No," she answered, "Salerno."

"So you're Calibrese?"

"My grandparents were. My mother and father were both born in the Bronx."

"I see. Second generation Italian." Changing the subject, he asked about her children. "Both your children are grown, I understand. I would like to have me them tonight."

"Yes, Frankie Jr. is staying overnight with his best friend. Jamie, she's the older of the two, is attending a weekend seminar at C.W. Post College."

"Frankie Jr. is a high school student?"

"Yes," she replied.

Frank then returned to the living room, and seeing that Pat's glass was empty, he refilled it. "We'll be ready to muncha shortly."

"So what's on the menu?" asked Pat.

The amateur gourmet cook kissed his hand to the air and enthused, "We begin with antipasto, Calamari and Mussels Caruso, followed by a cup of soup. Tonight we are having Consommé Vermicelli. The soup is followed with Alavarese Caesar Salad. Then we relax with a glass of wine before I serve my special pasta dish, Spaghetti Bolognese, then Scampi Oreganato, shrimp in a sauce of basil, garlic, and oregano butter, accompanied by risotto and ratatouille. After the main meal, we serve Gorgonzola cheese, and don't pass up my Apricot Ricotta Pie. Like most Sicilians, we enjoy fresh fruit to cleanse our palette. Then we top off the meal with demitasse coffee. Need I say more?"

"If you have prepared the meal you have described the way a gourmet cook would have put it together, then I'm in for a hell of a treat."

"You won't be disappointed. Let's move to the dining room and get started." Frank seated his wife at the table and waited for his guest to get settled before sitting down himself.

As Pat Caputo ate the first course, Frank watched him from the corner of his eye, looking for any reaction. Pat gave none. On the table was a carafe of wine. It was Frank's favorite, William Wycliff. He doubted his guest could guess this one, since it was not popular like Valpolicella. When the main meal was served, once again Frank watched for a reaction. This time Pat said, "Excellent, Frank. Excellent."

Pleased as punch with this remark, Frank reached across the table and poured out a glass of wine for Pat, who took a mouthful and rolled it about in his mouth like a professional wine taster, and swallowed. "William Wycliff burgundy. Very good."

Frank was amazed. "You really know your wines."

"Yes, I do," Pat said simply. "What is your favorite, Frank?"

"Just what we are now drinking, William Wycliff. I discovered it a few years ago and really enjoy it."

After the meal, two hours later, the men returned to the living room where Frank suggested they enjoy their demitasse coffee. A contented Pat Caputo sat down with a comfortable sigh. "Your dad taught you well. You're a better gourmet cook than many of the so-called professionals I have worked with over the years."

Removing another large Havana cigar, Pat once again went through the same routine before lighting up, only this time he didn't ask permission. Taking a puff, he said, "A friend of mine, he's Canadian, recently went to Havana on vacation and brought me back a box of Havana cigars. Best in the world."

Frank was still in semi-daze at the good rating from Pat on his cooking. "Thanks for the compliment, Pat. Coming from you it means a lot to me. I only wish my dad could have met you. He came to America and never really got a chance to show off his ability in the kitchen to the big hotels. He did all right, though. Raised five kids and we always had plenty to eat."

Pat noticed Eleanor was missing and hollered into the kitchen, "Eleanor, come on out and enjoy the demitasse with us. You can do the dishes after I've gone."

Popping her head out the door, and knowing her husband would like to spend time alone talking to his guest, she replied, "I'm too full to drink or eat anymore. I'll join you after I finish the dishes."

Shaking his head, Caputo looked across the room at Frank, "Why is it women have this fetish that the dinner dishes have to be washed right away?"

"Maybe it's because they think like a housewife and you don't. In your kitchen, you had dishwashers. As a housewife, Eleanor just can't stand to see a mess in her kitchen."

"I guess you've made a good point," Pat chuckled, "I just never thought of it that way." Then, changing the subject, Caputo asked, "Tell me how your homicide case involving Tashino is coming along."

"No shop talk, Pat," he said genially, "You're my guest."

"I'm just curious."

"I didn't invite you to my home to interrogate you," the detective replied.

"Hey, come on, Frank. I know why you invited me—to show off your cooking *and* to learn my opinion. Since you last talked with me at my home, I've been told through the grapevine that you made a trip to see Walt Eilers and Jim Meehan."

"You guys have some grapevine."

"We have, Frank. Understand, we're a close-knit group. Ballentine is our leader, and whoever you talk to calls him and tells him when you were there. None of us believe it was a sailor off the *Stuart* that knocked off that animal, Tashino. But we'd still like to know what's going on."

Frank saw no harm in discussing the case, so he answered, "Eilers was a lot of help to me. He gave me the latest reunion photo and the forty-year book. How come you never mentioned the book, Pat?"

"To tell you the truth, I completely forgot about it. As for the photo, mine only came in yesterday's mail. How can the forty-year book help you, Frank?"

"Let's say I come up with a suspect off the *Stuart*. I would take his photo from the book and have our artist make him look another ten years older. Then we could show the photo to our two witnesses who saw him the night of the murder."

"Do you have a suspect?"

"That's police business."

"What about Meehan?"

"My partner interviewed him. He claims that being an officer he was treated differently from the enlisted men. Seems he never left Java. He was thankful that Lieutenant Saito wasn't hard on officers, gave them clerical work and not the brutal details in the hot sun. He knows little about Tashino, as he served under him only six months."

"He's telling you facts. In Java the officers had it made."

"Eilers is married to a lovely Japanese lady named Nico."

"He's a Jap lover," Caputo replied curtly.

"I take it you and him don't get along?"

"You said a mouthful. I avoid him at the reunions like the plague."

"Why is he a Jap lover? Because he married one? Or did he collaborate with them in the camp?"

"He was treated like everyone else when we were in Asia. Like Meehan, he stayed in Java when the rest of us were shipped to Thailand.

But I really don't know if he stayed in Java or shipped to Japan. We never talk to one another."

"For Christ sake, Pat, the war has been over some fifty years. So he married a Japanese lady. So did hundreds of other GIs."

"Maybe so, Frank. I guess I'm one of those hard-nosed ginnys that can't forget those bastards who killed, starved, beat, and treated us like animals for three and a half years."

"It was war, Pat. Did we not also kill?"

"I'm not referring to war. I'm referring to the sadistic manner in which they treated us while we were prisoners of war. They starved us, beat us, humiliated us. We lived in filth, no medicine, fed us food I wouldn't feed to a starving dog. That's what I can't forgive."

"Not having lived through what you have, I rest my case," Arena said.

"So, getting back to the book," Caputo said, leaning forward, "You're going to take one hundred thirty-one pictures and blow them up and show them to your witnesses?"

"No, we're only blowing up a few—the tall ones who fit the perp's description." Arena walked out of the room for a moment to retrieve the photo taken at the Boston reunion. Then he showed it to Caputo, pointing to the man standing between Alexander and Donovan. "Who's the man between the pastor and Donovan? Have you seen him before?"

"Yeah, that's Pat Donovan, Dennis' brother. He came as a guest to the reunion. Dennis was the co-chair and invited him. He only came to the dinner on Saturday and was there for the snapshot. He was close to Dennis' age and looked almost like him, too, before Dennis lost all that weight."

"What weight?" Arena asked.

"Dennis was close to two hundred, but at the reunion he looked like he's down to about one hundred fifty. I asked him was he on a diet and he said the reason was stomach problems. I told him he better see a doctor."

Wanting to know more about the boatswain mates, Arena said, "You told me you rarely palled around with the boatswains, but according to pictures, you were close to them."

"They buttered me up, Frank. On a large ship in the Navy the three rates the sailors get close to are the ship's cooks, the yeoman, and the storekeeper. The storekeeper is in charge of the pogey bait, known to you as candy, and the smokes. If he closed and a guy needs a smoke and has an in with him, he gets what he wants. Now the yeoman, that's another story. He's the man that has a lot to do with making ship's liberty, and you want to make damn sure you get on his good side. And when on a night watch and hungry for a loaf of hot bread and cold cuts to go with your coffee, you butter up to the cook. I always took good care of the boatswains."

"Sounds like you were afraid of them."

"Hell, no. The word is 'security.' When we went ashore in Manila, Singapore, Hong Kong, or any other Asiatic port, most of the time we ended up in the same joint with a bunch of leathernecks. I'm a small guy and an easy target, so I made sure I sat next to the boatswains. Get it? You scratch my back, I'll scratch yours."

"Outside of reunions, have you ever been in contact with them?"

"No. Dale and Hughes live on Long Island, and Dennis lives in Massachusetts. We got nothing in common. I think seeing them at reunions is enough."

"Donovan. He was on the boxing team. Was he any good?"

"No knockout punch, but a damn good boxer. He was a southpaw and usually took the early round by screwing them up, then his skill did the rest. I could never get close to Dennis. No matter what I said, he made light of it. To him everything was a joke."

Without realizing it, Caputo said the magic words, 'he was southpaw.' So was the shooter. Frank began to think that Donovan was looking more and more like the perp. He fit the description, and who had a better reason? He watched Tashino gun down the Aussies in cold blood. Then, so did Alexander, for that matter.

Picking up the carafe, Frank was about to pour Pat a glass of wine. "No more, Frank. I have a long ride ahead of me. If I get stopped for some reason, I want to have my wits about me."

Eleanor entered the room and joined them, sitting next to her husband. "The kitchen's all cleaned up. I hope I gave you two plenty of time to talk about cooking."

Pat answered her, "You did, Eleanor." Then, looking at his watch, he stood up and said, "It's almost nine o'clock. I'd better get going. It's been a wonderful evening. The cuisine was the finest and the company first class."

Eleanor replied, "Such kind words. We do hope you will join us again for dinner. And I promise my children will join us next time."

"I have your phone number and Frank has mine. I would enjoy meeting your children."

Frank and Pat walked to the car together. When Pat got behind the wheel, he lowered the car window and took Frank by the arm. "I wasn't born yesterday. All those questions about Donovan and Alexander. If you're thinking what I think you are, remember this, Dale is a man of the cloth, Dennis is a clown who wouldn't deliberately hurt a fly nor does he have enough brains or cunning to pull off a murder. As for Hughes, he's a retired NYPD captain. Save yourself some shoe leather and look in another direction." Then Pat waved back to Frank as he drove from the house. Arena hadn't heard a word he said. All he could think about was, Dennis Donovan is a southpaw.

Chapter 19

Saturday, March 20, 1993

Mr. Miyako was given permission to go through Mr. Maehara's luggage to obtain special agreement papers between Fairfield Electronics and the Japanese company, Yoshio, in Tokyo. With him to see nothing else was taken was Detective Falk of the Fourth Squad. Removing the papers, Miyako noticed an item missing from the luggage. "Mr. Maehara's silver swagger stick is not here," he said.

"What's that?" Falk asked.

"Mr. Maehara's swagger stick—he had it during the war and it was always in his possession. I know that it was packed for the New York trip in this particular suitcase."

"Is it valuable?"

"No, no monetary value—sentiment only."

"I'll mention it to Sergeant Gore," Falk said.

❊   ❊   ❊

Sunday, March 21, 1993

Arriving at work at 8:30 a.m. Arena parked in the front parking lot. During the week this would have been impossible; however, on the weekends most all of the civilian workers and the brass are off duty. His appointment with John Hughes wasn't until noon, so he had a chance to sit down with a cup of coffee and review his case jacket to date. As soon as he got comfortable, Gore, who was also at work clearing up loose ends from various cases, summoned him to his office.

"Have a seat, Frank. I have some information for you on your case."

"Somebody confessed," Arena joked.

"Not quite, but we did come up with an important piece of information. Miyako says a silver swagger stick that his boss always traveled with is missing. Miyako said it was like a part of him. Apparently it was part of his past identity, his 'signature piece' from the war."

"So we assume the shooter took it? Subconsciously left his own signature, showing he was in the POW camp with Tashino?"

"Either that or maybe he was *deliberately* letting us know that someone from the *Stuart* crew got revenge."

"Well," said Arena, "this throws some new light on the case."

"I understand you're going to see John Hughes, the retired NYPD captain, today. When is that?"

"My appointment is at noon."

"I've filled Kelly in on all the particulars of the case to date," Gore said. "As you know, his dad is a retired deputy inspector out of the NYPD. Kelly called him, and it turns out he knew Hughes quite well, said he was one hell of a cop and a top Homicide man."

"Good. Maybe he can be of some help."

"Are you leaning toward a possible suspect, Frank?"

"Nothing concrete, but yes. I have feeling, that's all."

"Mind sharing it with your whip?"

"Really, it's just a feeling right now. But all roads lead to a crewmember who lives in the Boston area. His name is Dennis Donovan. He fits the bill—right height and weight, and gray hair. Plus, he's a lefty and was on the Island the night Tashino was murdered."

"So what are we waiting for? Why don't we pick him up?" Gore asked.

"It's all circumstantial. Give me a little more time."

Traffic was heavy going east, but moving at a fast pace. Mattituck was on the South Shore and was known as the town where the legendary pirate, Captain Kidd, was supposed to have buried some of his treasure. Traffic slowed somewhat when he hit the village of Riverhead, and smooth sailing into Mattituck. Arena had no trouble with the directions

Hughes gave him. The house was large and entirely made of red brick. The lawn was neatly trimmed and the flowerbeds were abundant with daffodils and tulips.

Hughes' greeting was as inviting as the exterior of his home. He stood tall in the doorway, lots of white hair, clear blue eyes, and a big smile. "Top of the morning to you!" he said heartily. He had a strong handshake and looked very fit.

"Let's go into the den. I have coffee and sandwiches ready." When they were seated comfortably, Hughes said, "Please help yourself. Don't be bashful. There's plenty to eat."

"Thanks," Frank replied. "The sandwiches look delicious. Did your wife make them?"

"That she did, just before she left to visit one of our daughters. She's a cop's wife and knows we'd like to be left alone."

"Who takes care of the flowers? Your front lawn is quite a showplace."

"She does. It's sort of her hobby, like mine is fishing."

"Fishing? That's mine, also."

"You have a boat, Frank?"

"Yes, a nineteen foot Key West. I keep it at the Bayshore Marina. Usually I try to go out in the Great South Bay at least one of my two days off."

"I've always found it relaxing," Hughes said. "I love deep sea fishing, especially. So when I retired I bought a thirty-four foot Hatteras. I keep it down at the dock in Mattituck. How about joining me for some real fishing out in the ocean?"

"I'd like nothing better, Mr. Hughes, but it will have to wait until this case is over."

"Frank, cut the crap. We're both cops. Call me Johnny. Everyone else does."

"Johnny it is," the Suffolk detective replied, and helped himself to the refreshments.

"So, Frank, let's cut to the chase. I've heard from the *Stuart* grapevine that your department seems to think one of our crew killed that son of a bitch."

"We have no other suspects, Johnny."

"Why the *Stuart*?"

"From what I've learned from other crew members, Tashino was a sadist. He mistreated all of you and was responsible for many of your shipmates that died."

"That's all true, Frank, but did you take it under consideration the crew of the *Stuart* are all old? We go in age from late-sixties to the eighties."

"I'm aware of that, Johnny, but being a former cop I'm sure you have dealt with killers that were seniors. Age, as far as I'm concerned, has no bearing on this case."

"I'm not up on all the aspects of the case—just stuff from the newspapers and from the *Stuart* alumna grapevine. Fill me in as to why you think it was one of our crewmen."

"Our suspect was over six foot, a senior citizen according to one of our witnesses, and we believe he was aware that Tashino was coming to stay in Hauppauge at the Carlyle Hotel."

Hughes raised his hands in astonishment. "Now, how would you know this?"

"A man calling himself Monahan phoned electronics companies both in California and here on the east coast claiming to represent another company, was professional, and asked particulars concerning Tashino's schedule. He eventually knew that night that Tashino would be having dinner out and would return fairly early. He waited for him in the hotel lobby, and when Tashino and his secretary go in the elevator, entered with them."

"Sounds plausible. So you think your suspect followed Tashino to his room."

"Not quite. Since the secretary was in attendance, our man let them out first and followed them down the hallway. He simply observed the room number Tashino entered, and knew at this point he was alone as his secretary went into another room. He used a silencer, so no one heard the shots."

"Any fingerprints or witnesses that came forth later?" Hughes asked.

"None other than his secretary, the doorman, and a young bellhop."

Arena then opened his case jacket and drew out the police sketch. "This is a composite of the suspect given to our artist."

Hughes looked at it for several seconds without any discernible expression, and then said, "He was wearing a hat and dark glasses. Is that all you got?"

"That's about it."

"So, am I a suspect, Frank?" he laughed.

"We have five or six that fit the description, including yourself. But in my opinion, I doubt a man with your background would have committed murder. You know it's almost impossible to get away with it. However, I would like your feeling about the case." Arena was careful not to mention the swagger stick, the blood, or that the killer was a lefty.

Hughes answered his question. "If it was my case the first thing we want to know is the time of death, check for blood samples, hair samples, question everyone that stayed on the same floor, the help, the clerks, people who own shops at the hotel, hotel security. With crack cokeheads on the loose, who's to say they didn't knock him off?"

"Nothing was taken, Johnny. Cash and items of value within plain sight were left behind."

"They could have been scared off."

"No way, Johnny. He used a silencer. His secretary was in a room on one side and a honeymoon couple on the other. No one heard a shot or even a scuffle."

"What about the secretary? He probably hated Tashino like the rest of us."

"Tashino's behavior in the Maehara identity was nothing like that of years back. He was a successful and respected businessman."

"Sounds like you did your homework, Frank."

"So what about the sketch?"

"As a former cop, I say 'no good.' Too much of his face is covered. Frank, I believe you have a suspect, but you're keeping the name to yourself. I don't blame you there. That's good police work; let the public know a little, but hold back some of the info from the press."

"It's a tough one, Johnny. Who knows? We may never solve it."

"The guy that murdered Tashino deserves a medal. We all feel that way. I hope they never catch him."

"I understand. One last question. Where were you that night?"

Hughes laughed. "How about reading me my rights?"

"You don't have to answer," Arena said.

"I've nothing to hide. I took the Hatteras out for some night fishing. I was alone, but I'm sure the security guard at the marina saw me leave as I usually go out when it's daylight. I left around 5:00 p.m."

"Just routine, Johnny, you know that. You didn't have to answer if you didn't want to."

When the required questioning was over, Johnny Hughes and Frank Arena parted in good humor, with tentative plans to go fishing in the near future.

Arena was thorough in his investigation, however. Before leaving Mattituck he drove down to the docks where Hughes' boat was kept. He wandered about for about ten minutes before finding a guard named Charlie Neil, about sixty, tall and lean with stooped shoulders, wearing thick glasses. When Arena identified himself and asked to see a logbook, Neil became testy.

"Well, I don't know, this is a bit unusual. Folks around here like their privacy."

"Look, Mr. Neil, if I have to I'll call the Southold Police. They'll tell you the same—let the man see the books. Or, if that doesn't work, we'll go to the courts. I don't think your 'folks' would like that."

"Let me see that badge again." Neil was stubborn, but finally agreed to let him see the logbook. "Come on over to the guard shack."

As Hughes had said, he was duly noted in the logbook as departing at five-fifteen and returning the next morning at eight. "Much obliged," he told the guard politely, and took his leave.

Deep in thought while making his way back to headquarters, he was more than ever convinced that the man he wanted was Dennis Donovan. Not one member of the crew would identify him, however, from the sketch—especially Captain Hughes, since Dennis was like a brother to him. Their grapevine was very effective and they formed a formidable roadblock. He was aware their seeming disinterest in whether Tashino had lived or died was a blind. They all hated him so much they wanted to pin a medal on his murderer. No way were they going to help the cops with this one.

Johnny Hughes phoned Dale Alexander as soon as Arena left his house. "Dale, it's Johnny. The Homicide cop, Arena, was just here. He's still trying to pin the killing on one of us."

"He's doing his job, Johnny, just like you did when you were a detective. You sound worried. Are you?"

"Why should I worry?" he said. "I'm clean. By the way, how is Dennis doing?"

"Not good. Mary's worried. We better visit him soon."

"Both of us have seen a lot of deaths, Dale. But losing Dennis will be hard to take. I'm free when you can get away."

"Good. I'll call Mary and have her pick us up at Logan Airport in Boston. How about tomorrow?"

"Fine. You pick the time."

"I'll call MacArthur in Islip, get the flight schedule, and call you back. And Johnny, I know you're not a man who prays a lot. But I know you love Dennis as much as I do, so pray to the Almighty."

Chapter 20

Monday, March 22, 1993

At 8:50 a.m. Frank Arena pulled in front of headquarters. Getting out of his car, he heard the screeching of tires; it was Sanchez racing into the lot—he was always in a hurry.

"Hey, Frank, hold on and we'll walk in together."

"No hurry, Joe. We've got ten minutes."

As they walked to the front entrance, Sanchez put his arm around Frank's shoulders, "I'm glad Gentile and Laurencelle are back. We've been working our asses off. I like overtime, but I also like to play, and the job has been cutting in on my love life."

They found Gore, Gentile, and Laurencelle already in the office. Laurencelle was sitting at his desk with his feet across an open drawer, reading the Sunday Newsday. Gentile was sipping coffee and looking out the window in a daze. Frank asked him, "How was your vacation, Joey?"

Coming back to life, he responded, "Great, Frank. We took the kids out West and showed them what our forefathers went through to build up this country. The scenery was breathtaking. In only wish we had another week."

Sanchez broke into the conversation, "I'm glad you're back, Gumba. With you and Adrian out we've had to work a lot of overtime."

"My heart bleeds for you. Put another nickel in the jukebox and play the song the guy plays on the fiddle," Laurencelle shouted across the room. He enjoyed teasing Sanchez, because he knew it upset him. And the more upset he became, the more Adrian rubbed it in.

"Up yours, Adrian, go back to sick bay. We were better off without you, Mr. Doomsday."

Arena said to Laurencelle, "You look a hell of a lot better than the last time I saw you in the hospital, Adrian."

Laurencelle, a tall six-two Frenchman, responded, "Thanks, Frank. I feel a lot better. The last place I ever want to see again is the inside of a hospital."

Sanchez, still steaming, finally thought of a retort to Laurencelle's dig and said, "Adrian—what a name. Sounds like they named you after a broad, not a man."

"Shows your ignorance and how little you know of history. My great-grandfather's name was Adrian. He was a general in the French army."

Arena, in an attempt to cool down this oral exchange, took Sanchez by the arm and led him to the back room where he poured out two cups of coffee. "I don't know about you, Joe," he said, "but unless I have one of these when I get here I can't get going. Nothing like a fresh cup of brewed coffee to start the day."

As they returned to their desks, Joey Gentile pointed towards Gore's office, "Gore wants to see both of you in his office."

They entered Gore's office and he gestured for them to sit down. "Frank, you've done a hell of a job cutting down the field of suspects. Since Sanchez and Wolfe have wrapped up the Brentwood case, I'm assigning Sanchez to work with you until your case is finished. I know you wanted someone to work with you on this one. Joe's your man. Take him out and bring him up to date."

Arena filled Sanchez in on all the facts he was not already familiar with. He told of his suspicions of Dennis Donovan since learning that Donovan was a southpaw; he was the leading suspect. Donovan was a houseguest of Pastor Alexander in Rockville Center the date of the murder. He was dying and came to see a Doctor Jacobson who is at Stony Brook Hospital.

When Arena finished, Sanchez said, "I gotta admit, when Gore made you the lead detective in this case I felt he handed you a bag of worms and stiffed you with it because you were the junior man, but you've surprised me in getting this far. Where do we go from here, partner?"

Going over to his bin, Arena removed two large photos and showed them to Sanchez, "The one on the left is Dennis Donovan. The one on the right is Dale Alexander. Dale has an alibi. He held church services the night of the murder. That doesn't mean that he didn't help in the planning. I'm going to show these two photos to my two witnesses. Purcell has obtained the fingerprints of the remaining one hundred thirty-one crewmembers from the *Stuart*.

"I thought he'd just seen too many TV shows and wanted to play cop. However, since he's the Assistant District Attorney we have to work with, we played along with him."

"Callahan picked up a partial thumb print in the bathroom as well as numerous other prints. It was Callahan's opinion that most of them belonged to the cleaning people. He was right on two occasions. The others were put into our NCIC computer, with negative results, which simply means none of them had a record.

"We know the shooter changed in the bathroom where we found gray hair, and we know he was hit with the victim's cane which most likely caused the bleeding. No doubt the shooter removed his gloves to wash off the blood on his head, and that's where he slipped with his thumb."

"How good of a partial is it?"

"It's not smudged, so we have a shot at it being good."

"I'm reading your mind, Frank. Let's head down the hall to Identification."

Detective Tuiet buzzed them in at the ID Bureau. "You guys are just in time for coffee and doughnuts. Maureen brought them in this morning from Hanson's Bakery."

"Hey, sounds good to me," Sanchez said.

As they entered the back room, Maureen Snyder had just taken a bite of a white powdered jelly doughnut, with predictable results; the powder fell all over her uniform. "Shit, I did it again. When am I going to learn to stay away from powdered doughnuts?"

Callahan laughed, "Never, Maureen. You say that every time."

Arena helped himself to coffee, Sanchez to coffee and a doughnut. Frank waited for everyone to devour his or her doughnuts before addressing Snyder.

"You did a real good job on enlarging the photos."

Taking Frank by the arm, she walked him over to the computer. "We're in the nineties now, Frank. This baby does it all. I took your photos out of the book, enlarged them, and then played a little. All I had to do was add ten years, and that was easy. Both were pepper and salt, now full gray. Both slim with fair complexions and blue eyes. So I added a few wrinkles, dusted the hair a little, and we have what they look like today. Any questions?"

"Yes. Your sketch taken from the witness, Mr. Miyako. It doesn't match Donovan or Alexander. I thought for sure he gave you a good description."

Maureen nodded, "It may have been. Who's to say either of these two guys is the shooter? One thing I know, having taken many sketches from witnesses, sometimes no matter how close the witness is to the subject, when he gives his description he misses something. For example, all three have something in common. Complexion, eyes, and except for one feature, look very similar. Look for yourself."

Frank and Joe studied the two photos and the sketch together. "It's the nose that's different," said Sanchez. "Donovan's is pugnacious like a boxer's. Alexander's is average—not small, not large. But the guy in the sketch has a large Roman nose."

Arena studied the three, also, then replied, "You're right, amigo. It's the nose. I guess we all know it's possible even if a witness eyeballs a person, he is not usually one hundred percent right.

"What about nationalities? It's obvious they're not Latin, Italian, Greek, or from the Mediterranean. It's also obvious that Donovan and Alexander are from the British Isles somewhere. What about the man in the sketch?"

Snyder answered his question. "More like a Brit, a Scot, Welshman, English, or Irish from across the sea Irish. All of them are fair-skinned and blue-eyed. The high cheekbones on Alexander give me the opinion, along with his name, that he's a Scot. There's no question Donovan is Irish. He has a square chin. As for the man in the sketch, he's one or all of the above."

Arena said, "We can find out who the perp in the sketch is, probably right now. I have my opinion of who the shooter is."

"You think it's one in the pictures we have just seen?" Callahan asked.

"It's Dennis Donovan. I believe Alexander allowed him to stay at his house. However, although he may be in conspiracy with Donovan, he never left his home. And we have a good thumbprint, although only a partial.

"Callahan, you do have the fingerprints of the *Stuart* crew, don't you?" Arena asked.

Callahan, a pipe smoker, took a leisurely puff and blew smoke. With a sly cat-who-ate-the-canary smile, he said, "I received a package from St. Louis containing a fistful of fingerprints. When they came, I couldn't believe we requested so many prints when we didn't even have a suspect."

"Great," Arena said. "You don't have to check all of them. Donovan's the man; just check him out. Joe and I will be in the office. Please call us as soon as you get the results."

Returning to Homicide, the partners conferred with Sergeant Gore and filled him in on what had occurred at ID

When they finished, Gore, with a sullen look on his face, said, "Before going to the staff meeting, Kelly told me the Police Commissioner is burning up over the article written by Troy Pool. He's also upset at what he described as excessive overtime, and wants Chief Francis to get on the back of his commanding officers."

"I hope Kelly told him we're understaffed."

"I'm sure they know that, but balls have to be broken by the chain of command, from the P.C. to the Chief of Detectives, right on down to the squad bosses. So for a little while we better cool the overtime."

They left Gore's office and returned to the squad room. Sanchez took the case jacket to study; maybe he could find some overlooked clues. The phone rang and Frank answered. It was Callahan.

"Frank, I've gone through about half the crew's fingerprints. Came up with one good one so far."

"Who?" Arena asked, holding his breath.

"Dennis Donovan," Callahan replied.

"He's my leading suspect. Is the partial good enough to convince a grand jury to indict him?"

"In itself, maybe not enough, but you have other proof like the photos. I still have half the crew to go. Let me get back to work."

Sanchez had overheard the conversation. "Did I hear right? Donovan print looks good?"

"You heard right, Joe. I know damn well the shooter is off the *Stuart*, and when Callahan is finished checking all the prints, Donovan is our man."

Standing behind his partner who was looking at the latest reunion photo, Sanchez said, "Point out Donovan to me."

"He's the one standing between Hughes and Alexander. The three of them are real close buddies. Alexander was a first class petty officer and a boatswain, Donovan second class and a boatswain, and Hughes was an apprentice under them on the *Stuart*."

Sanchez laughed, "I can tell you were a dog face in the Navy. A sailor going for a rank from seaman to a petty officer is called a striker."

"So he was a striker."

"They do look somewhat alike."

"My vibes tell me Donovan is the shooter. Alexander has an excuse or alibi; nevertheless, I have a hunch he knows Donovan killed Tashino."

"What about the third guy, Hughes?"

"He's clean. I interviewed him at his home. He's a retired homicide dick out of NYPD."

"Why is he clean? Because he's a cop?"

"No, he told me he went night fishing when Tashino was killed."

"Sounds like a fish story to me," Sanchez said.

"Why? Because he went night fishing?" Arena asked with a smile.

"Yeah. Who goes fishing at night?"

"I do, for one, Joe. And so do hundreds of other fishermen."

"Then I presume you checked out his alibi?"

"I did. He keeps his Hatteras docked at the Mattituck Marina. To take out the boat, you have to go through Security, which keeps a log time in and out. He checked his boat out at 5:00 p.m. and returned at 8:00 a.m. the following day."

"Okay, but I think because he's a cop maybe you're not looking hard enough at this dude."

"Lieutenant Kelly knows of him, and said he was a top-notch homicide investigator."

"The question remains, Frank, who's the lead investigator on this murder case—you or Kelly?"

Arena nodded, "Amigo, I think you have a point."

"Do you have a close friend in the FBI you can call?" Sanchez asked.

"I know some agents, like you do, but none I would feel comfortable enough to talk with regarding a fellow police officer."

"I have a good friend in the FBI in Boston," said Sanchez. "Indirectly he got his promotion from the Long Island office with my help. He owes me one."

Sanchez dialed and a husky female voice answered, "Federal Bureau of Investigation. Can I help you?"

Turning on the charm, Sanchez said, "I love your voice. You made that monotonous speech come to life."

"Do you need help, sir?" she responded with a bored sigh.

"Yes, is Gary Owen Murphy available?"

"Yes sir, but he's on the other line. Who shall I say is calling?"

"Detective Joe Sanchez, Homicide, Suffolk County Police."

"Would you like to leave your number or would you prefer to hold?"

"I'll hold, but tell him it's an emergency."

Arena had picked up his phone and was listening in. "Why does this guy owe you a favor?"

"When I was in the robbery squad some years ago we had a rash of bank jobs all over the Island. It was a Mutt and Jeff team and they hit once a month like clockwork. The feds got a hot tip they were going to hit a bank in Patchogue. So with the complete Fifth Squad dicks, all the plainclothes men, and a dozen FBI agents, they staked out every bank in Patchogue. I had a grand jury case and was late heading for the stakeout. As I left court, I put the car radio on, and they were talking about a bank stickup in Bellport. They got stiffed.

"I was heading over to Bellport when a young cop came up with a description of a car and a suspect. A man in a deli nearby said a young man parked his car in front of his store and walked toward the bank wearing a black leather jacket and denims. So I said to myself, this mother is heading for the Long Island expressway. I sat at the entrance and waited. He came, all right, going on the expressway heading west. I asked for assistance, and who backed me up, none other than Gary Owen Murphy. We both made the collar, but being it was a federal case, he took over. The stickup man, a junkie, had held up nine banks. Needless to say, I got a commendation. Gary Owen Murphy was promoted and sent to the Boston office. It's payback time, Frank."

"Do you think he'll help us? Most of the time I've dealt with the FBI they ask you questions, but when you ask them, they tell you it's confidential."

"Murph's not like that. He's a cop first, an agent second."

"We're lucky he's in. It's Sunday," Arena mentioned.

"They work seven days a week just like we do. He's in, so no doubt he's working," Sanchez replied.

Gary Owen Murphy got a note placed in front of him that he had an emergency phone call waiting on another line from Detective Sanchez of the Suffolk County Police. Although he was on the phone with another agent, he ended the conversation, saying he'd call him back.

"Joe, it's Murph, what's the emergency all about?"

"No emergency, Gary Owen. Just my way of getting you on the phone."

"I haven't heard from you in over a year. Then when you do call, you break my balls. Joe, you'll never change."

"Hey, you Irish hump, it's a two-way street. When's the last time you called me?"

"Okay, we're even. What can I do for you that's so important?"

Sanchez gave him the details. It took about ten minutes. Murphy never interrupted. He used his tape recorder so as not to miss any of the facts. When Sanchez finished, he said, "So that's the story, Murph."

"Tell me, Joe, what do you need from me?"

"If we call the local department and ask them about one of their own, I'm sure they would want to know why, and rightly so. Since he's only a suspect, we need to know something about him, like, was he considered a good cop? Where does he live? What department did he work out of? What rank did he hold? Just anything that might help."

"I see you point, Joe. Why give the guy a bad name with his department if it turns out you fellows have the wrong suspect. I can get this info to you in about an hour. I have your number, but don't panic if it takes me a bit longer."

"I can't ask for more than that, Murph. You're a real friend."

"Keep in touch, Joe. Next time I make a trip to New York, I'll call you. We can meet and have a cold one together."

When they hung up, Arena said to Sanchez, "I guess there's nothing as bad as checking on one of your own. Like you said, amigo, we have no choice. We have a job to do. I'm curious, though, why do you call him Gary Owen instead of just Gary."

"That's his name. Let me tell you how this came about. The name of General Custer's marching song for the famous Seventh Cavalry was called Gary Owen. The legend goes that one day the general heard this Irishman from the old country playing the catchy song on his mandolin. When he asked the name of the tune, the Irishman replied, 'Gary Owen.' 'Who wrote the tune?' Custer asked. The Irishman replied, 'I did, sir.' 'Why do you call it Gary Owen?' 'It's me name,' he replied. Custer then asked the Irishman if he would mind if the Seventh Cavalry used it as a marching song. Of course, the man was delighted. The legend also says the Irishman rode with them in the Battle of Big Horn. Murphy's parents name him Gary, and at his confirmation he was given the name Owen. When he learned of the legend, he became 'Gary Owen.'"

"That's a fish story if I ever heard one," Arena replied.

Sanchez laughed, "Maybe so, but don't ever say that to Murphy. You'd be calling him a liar, and he holds a black belt."

The time was 11:50 a.m. Sanchez, addressing his partner, said, "Toss you for who goes to the deli for sandwiches. We're eating in today."

Arena lost the toss.

❉   ❉   ❉

It was 2:05 p.m. when the agent returned the call. An anxious Sanchez picked up the receiver and said, "Took you long enough, Murph. So what's the scoop?"

"I did what you should have done instead of hiding behind the blue coat of honor—I checked with two sources, one Internal Affairs, two a close friend in the Emerald Society. Your man comes up smelling like a rose."

"All right, cut the crap, and spill it. Let's hear what you learned."

"Seems way back when he was in the Detective Division one of the police officers in his station was accused of stealing, and Hughes was the dick handling the case. The charges had been brought up by then Captain Patrick O'Brien. Hughes went out of his way to show that the young cop was innocent, and bucked O'Brien all the way. Bottom line was, the rookie was cleared and kept his job. Years went by and Hughes made a name for himself as a top boss in Homicide. That's as far as he ever went. Civil service tests only go as high as captain. To make deputy and move up the line, as you know, is all political."

"I take it you're telling me Captain O'Brien had something to do with that?"

"That's what I'm telling you. He was now Chief O'Brien."

"What's the second fact you learned?"

"Hughes is a member of the Honor Legion, he has broken a dozen top profile murder cases, and his record is flawless. That's all I could find out."

✳   ✳   ✳

Callahan called back shortly after Sanchez's telephone conversation with Murphy. "Good news, Frank. The only crew member whose print matches on the partial is Donovan."

"We'll be over in five minutes."

Turning to his new partner, Frank said, "Donovan's partial comes up affirmative. Let's go to Identification."

Callahan was sitting smoking his pipe and looking at some old photos taken of his plane and crew when he was an Air Force tail gunner. He looked up when the two homicide dicks came in and said, "Hopefully we have a suspect."

"How good a partial is it?" Arena asked.

"It's not a smudge, so we have a good shot of it being accepted."

Seeing Arena and Sanchez, Maureen Snyder called to them, "Over here, guys. I've finished matching today's photos with the ones you gave me of Donovan, Alexander, and Hughes. Let's have a look there in the other room."

As they walked in, she said, "Thank God we're in the nineties and have all the machines to make it easy for us." She then pointed to a large machine. "This baby did it all. I took your photos out of the book, enlarged them, and then played around a little. The rest was easy. All of them have gray hair now and blue eyes. As far as ethnic background, no doubt all of them are Celtic. Now we do have some differences. Alexander has the smaller nose of the three and a round face. Donovan has an Irish square chin—I should know, all the micks in my family have square chins. Hughes has the larger nose of the three. But, in general, if I was a witness it would be hard to really pick out the shooter unless I saw him up close, without the shades and fedora he was wearing."

Frank and Joe studied the three photos. "You're right," Frank said, "the only real difference is the nose. Like you said, Maureen, it's possible the best eye witness is not always one hundred percent right." Arena then asked Maureen to make up half a dozen copies.

When they were leaving Identification, it was shortly after 3:00 p.m. Frank suggested they take the photos over to the Carlyle and show them once again.

"You know what Gore said about overtime," Sanchez cautioned.

"Screw the overtime. We're getting close. Let's go."

The shift at the Carlyle changes at 4:00 p.m., so they made it just in time to catch both the day and evening crews. They headed for the manager's office and espied Bauman and Sacca. Frank asked Bauman to get the day crew together before they were scheduled to go home. "We have three photos to show them."

"As you wish, Detectives." He then gave instructions for his day crew to be paged.

"Thank you, Mr. Bauman. We appreciate that."

One by one they entered the office—DeMarco and all the day staff. After they were settled, Arena said, "We have three sketches here. Please look at them and see if you recognize the photo. What we're looking for is identification that one of the three was here that night."

It took about ten minutes. All but one clerk said they had never seen any of them that evening, and DeMarco picked out Donovan. Arena then said, "Mr. DeMarco, we need a statement from you." Turning to Sanchez, Arena said, "Joe, work with the clerk who said he did see a party that resembled the photo."

"What office can I use, Mr. Bauman?" Arena asked.

"Take him into Bob Hart's office. He has a typewriter on a desk and a couple of comfortable chairs."

At 4:15 p.m. Arena and DeMarco entered the office along with Bauman, who addressed Hart, "Bob, the detective wants to take a statement from Pat. It won't take long."

The big guy with the red nose and chewing on his usual cigar, said pleasantly, "There's the desk, Detective. It's all yours."

A reluctant doorman sat opposite Arena who sat behind the typewriter. Arena took out his tape recorder and said to DeMarco, "We're doing it both ways. Mr. DeMarco, state your name and address."

"What for? I was told you were going to show me a photo."

"We are, sir," Arena replied. "The recorder is for office use only. And the statement is for use in court."

When they got the preliminaries under way, Arena asked, "On the evening of March 10th, what was your duty?"

"I'm the doorman at the Carlyle Hotel."

"You stated you had seen a stranger about to approach the hotel, but he hesitated, and before you had a chance to speak with him a taxi pulled up with customers."

"That's right."

"What time was it?"

"About 8:30 p.m."

"How far away was he?"

"About twenty feet or so."

"Was it light enough to see him?"

"Yes, the outside is well lit."

"Then you did get a good look at him?"

"Yeah, when he saw me he stopped and made like he was looking for something. I got a good look and I never forget a face."

Arena opened his briefcase and removed the three photos. "Which one was him?"

Without hesitation, he doorman stuck with the original one he picked out. "That's him."

"You pointed very fast. Are you positively sure?"

"That's the guy I saw. He was wearing a hat and glasses, but that's him. I never forget a face. Is that the killer?" he asked.

When Arena finished the statement of the conversation, he handed it to DeMarco and said, "Read it. Then sign it."

"What about the reward?" DeMarco asked with a surly expression.

"We have nothing to do with the reward. You will have to talk to Fairfield Electronics about that."

Arena excused the doorman and called out to Bauman to send Conway in. This time he did not take a statement, just asked a few questions and then showed Conway the three photos. He took a lot longer than DeMarco to study the photos. Then, pointing to Donovan, said, "He's the man I saw."

"Are you sure, Len? Why did you hesitate?"

"I had to take off the hat and glasses and study his face. I remembered he had a long chin. He's the man I saw."

Arena had a smile on his face when he rejoined Sanchez in Bauman's office. Sanchez said, "One of the clerks said a guy that looks like one of these perps checked into the hotel about three in the afternoon."

A shocked Arena said, "Come again? Am I hearing right?"

"I took a statement. He couldn't be positive which photo, so I didn't push. He checked the records, and found the man called himself John Smith from Buffalo, New York."

"Our guys checked with all the clerks. How did we miss that one?" Arena asked, speaking to Bauman.

"What's the clerk's name?"

"Paul Moody," Sanchez answered.

A flustered Bauman said, "Let me check his record." It took a few minutes before he came to the date of March 10th and the time 3:00 in the afternoon. "The clerk, Paul Moody, went on vacation on the 11th, and the hotel was not able to locate him, since he went out of state. Sorry about that. I guess it was our blunder."

Arena then asked Sanchez what else Moody had to say. "Smith had no baggage, and Moody asked him to pay up front, figuring maybe he was a cheater, then assigned him to a room he specifically requested."

"Which was?" Arena asked, almost knowing what it was.

"He asked for a room on the tenth floor, saying it was his lucky number—room number 1006," Sanchez laughed. "That's the room Hart gave us for our command headquarters because it was unoccupied. Along with the killer's prints, the room contains our prints."

"Is 1006 occupied at the present?" Arena asked Bauman.

"It's not," Sanchez interjected. "I already checked it out and took the liberty of calling Identification. They're sending over a team to dust it. But my guess is the only prints they'll find are the cops."

Taking the photos and looking them over, Bauman said, "So this is what our killer looks like. You guys know your business. Somehow I thought this case would go unsolved."

"Why did you feel that way, Mr. Bauman?"

"Nothing was taken. It wasn't a kid or a middle-aged person. From what you told us he was a man up in years. Somehow I felt it was a sour business deal or a hit job."

On the way back to headquarters, Arena remarked, "You know, Joe, I never gave it a thought, but the guy did have a good reason to kill Tashino. How come we never thought of it the first day of the investigation?"

"Because a good homicide team never comes up with any type of conclusion until every angle is checked out. In Tashino's case and with the help of the Tokyo Police, we established the reason within a few days."

Chapter 21

Sunday, March 21, 1993

Lately he had been sleeping a lot. It was those damn pills Rochford prescribed. It seemed to hit him in the evening, usually right after supper. He tried to fight it off, but with each passing day his body became more listless. He knew he was dying and could probably live another six months to a year, but who the hell would he be kidding, it would only prolong the agony and drain what little money they had in the bank. Why give it to the drug stores and doctors when those bloodsuckers had enough already.

Out in the kitchen Mary was finishing up the evening supper dishes. With the kids gone and only the two of them living in the house, she preferred to wash the small amount of dishes by hand rather than use the dishwasher. She felt lonely lately. Dennis shut her out and the home she loved in the past had become just a place to eat and sleep. An avid reader, she found comfort in going to the library twice a week. This morning she went and picked up three novels, two of them romance books.

When she was finished in the kitchen, she checked on her husband in their bedroom. He was stretched across the bed sound asleep. Retreating to the living room, she picked up one of the romance novels, curled up in the corner of the living room couch and began reading.

At 8:05 the phone sitting on the end table alongside the couch rang. It was Dale Alexander. "Dale, I was hoping you would call."

"I called Johnny. We're taking the 2:30 out of Islip MacArthur tomorrow afternoon. Can you pick us up at Logan Airport at 4:50 or so?"

"Of course. I know Dennis will be glad to see you, even though he told me 'no visitors,'" Mary replied.

"Hogwash," Dale said. "See you tomorrow, then. We're on Flight 612."

* * *

Monday, March 22, 1993

Dale brought up the Tashino murder on the flight to Boston, saying, "What're your thoughts about Detective Arena, Johnny?"

"He has no case, so he's fishing by putting the finger on a bunch of old men."

"Seems to me the police have done their homework, learning about us in Thailand."

"So they found out Tashino was a sergeant on the Death Railroad by checking the war records."

"Fishing or not, I think the Suffolk Police Department did a hell of a job finding that information in such a short time," Alexander said.

"Well, whoever killed the bastard should get a medal. And I'm sure every Brit, Aussie, Canadian, New Zealander, and the crew off the *Stuart* agree with me," Hughes said with a lot of heat.

"What did you think of the sketch Arena is showing around?"

"It's half a sketch—a man wearing a fedora and shades, you can't see the hair or the eyes."

"You will agree the description of the killer fits all three of us—Dennis, you, and myself—height six-one or so, senior, possibly gray hair, slim in build," Dale interjected.

"Let's talk about something else," Johnny grumbled. "What did that Doctor Jacob say when Dennis consulted him?"

"The doctor's name is Jacobson," Dale said.

"So, what was his opinion when Dennis consulted him?" Johnny repeated.

"Dennis never went to see him."

"Why? I don't understand."

"He left my home on the morning of the 10th. It was past midnight when Carol and I retired and he still hadn't returned. On the morning of the 11th when he came down to breakfast, he said he visited a relative in Central Islip after his appointment with Jacobson, and time just flew. He also said the doctor was going to call him with the results after he went home."

"So how do you know he never saw Jacobson?" Johnny inquired.

"I called Jacobson's office. No Dennis Donovan ever had an appointment with the good doctor."

"What made you check up on Dennis?" Hughes asked.

"I didn't right off, but when I saw the headlines in Newsday, 'Japanese Businessman Murder at the Carlyle Hotel,' and showed it to Dennis, he didn't seem all that interested. My instinct told me something was wrong, so that's when I called the doctor's office."

Hughes sat with a blank expression for a minute or so before asking, "You don't think for a minute Dennis killed Tashino, do you?"

"I don't really know what to think, Johnny."

As they got off the plane, they were carrying overnight suitcases, so no luggage to check out. Mary was waiting as the passengers of Flight 612 arrived. Seeing them, she ran over and hugged both of them one at a time. They picked up Mary's car at short-term parking, and then headed for Needham, on the outskirts of Boston.

When they arrived at the Donovan home, Dennis was still sleeping. Dale said to Mary, "Don't wake him. It will give the three of us a chance to talk, and maybe figure out where we are going."

Mary led them into the living room and asked if they wanted coffee. "No thanks, Mary. Let's talk. From what you have told us, Dennis is not in good shape. We need to get him into a hospital."

"He won't go to a hospital, Dale," said Mary

"The man has no say in the matter. He's dying and needs help. He's going to a hospital," Dale said with grim determination.

Mary looked exhausted as she said, "Dennis is a proud man. He and I had a long talk. He begged me to let him die at home. I gave him my word, and I can't go back on it."

"Mary, if he were in a hospital they would see he eats, if only through tubes. He could live a year, maybe more. Why are you doing this?"

"He would be just another basket case hanging on. He doesn't want it that way. He wants to die at home."

Hughes sat alongside of Mary and put his arms around her. She was crying. She knew she was wrong, but it was something she promised she would not do. Consoling her, Johnny said, "Do what you think in your heart is best for Dennis."

Alexander, seeing it was a waste of time, then asked, "What about Hospice? Do you have someone coming in?"

"I've tried to get him connected with Hospice, but he's stubborn and refuses to see any of them."

"I work with those people. They do one heck of a job. Their people are well trained and will help you cope as well as console Dennis and his family. Mary, why didn't you call Johnny or me when you found out Dennis had cancer?"

"He hid it from me for several months. Then, when he lost his appetite and began losing weight I became suspicious and called Doctor Rochford, our family doctor. He was surprised that I was not aware of Dennis' condition. I was shocked and hurt at first that Dennis didn't tell me, but when I knew the situation I worked with him daily. One of the promises I made was not to call friends. He said he wanted no pity."

"What are friends for, Mary? Johnny and I are blood brothers to your husband. He's closer to both of us than our own brothers."

Mary began to cry again. Johnny consoled her once again, and then said, "Forget about what she should have done. Let's talk about what we can do now."

Dale nodded in agreement. "When he came to my house, he arrived the evening of the 9th. The next day he had an appointment to see a Doctor Jacobson. Were you aware of that, Mary?"

"Yes. Before the reunion Doctor Rochford mentioned his name as a specialist on Long Island."

"Did he tell you he saw Jacobson?" Dale asked.

"He said he did," she answered.

"He fibbed, Mary. He never did see Jacobson. Seems like our Dennis, the life of the party, has no will to live anymore."

"What can we do, Dale?" Mary asked.

"We're here to cheer him up tonight. Tomorrow, if you and Johnny have no objection I would like to spend some time alone with him."

"I understand, Dale. Like, if you were a priest and he was sort of giving you a confession," Mary ventured.

"Something like that, Mary. We'll talk some about God."

"Why are we all talking so glum? What about seeing another specialist?" Hughes asked.

"Nobody can help Dennis. He's dying, and the sad part of it all is, he wants to die," Mary replied with tears in her eyes.

"Why? I don't understand. This isn't the fun-loving Dennis we all know," Hughes said.

"You are aware Dennis played the stock markets. It was like a Bible with him. A few years back in '88, he lost his shirt. We never did recover. Denny had an ace in the hole. He carries a large insurance policy. He often said if he had to go, I would be well taken care of. He has ignored Doctor Rochford's advice, takes only pain killers, no medicines, refuses chemo, and won't go to the hospital where he belongs."

"Hogwash," Dale said in exasperation. "The man has Medicare, his business had a good backup policy. So, what you're telling us is no excuse."

"I'm aware of that. So are our children. But we're dealing with a stubborn man who feels he's lived a long life and is ready to meet his maker."

"Then he's not very smart, is he, Mary?" Dale said in dismay. Then he thought, I do believe his mind has slowed up this past year. He's had cancer for some time now, and if Mary had not eventually found out, he would have passed away without Johnny and I ever being aware of his sickness. Poor Mary, my heart goes out to her.

Suddenly there was a banging on the floor above. Mary said, "That's Dennis. He's awake. He gets my attention by banging his cane on the wooden floor. Why don't you guys go up and surprise him? He doesn't know you're coming."

The two shipmates went up the stairs with Johnny Hughes leading the way. He walked up to Dennis and hugged him. "You look great," he lied.

Speaking in a whisper, Dennis smiled, "You always did know how to throw the blarney, Johnny." The remark broke the tension and all three of them laughed at Hughes' boner.

Addressing Johnny, Dennis asked, "You heard any good Pat and Mike jokes lately?"

Answering with an Irish accent, he said, "That I have, lad. That I have. Did I tell you about the time Pat and Mike went to Confession?"

"You probably did, but tell me again. I forget the punch line."

"Well, the two of them went to Confession. Pat went first and came out and told Mike, 'Now it's your turn to get new information. I did the last time, and Father Pickering will know my voice.' So Mike went in, and when his turn came he entered the Confession box. Mike told his usual sins, and then suddenly blurted out, 'Oh, one more thing, Father. I forgot to tell you, I've been sleeping with one of the town widows who is also in sin.' 'Is it Mrs. Pearce?' the good Father asked. 'No, Father,' Mike replied. 'Then it has to be Mrs. O'Grady.' 'No, Father,' Mike again replied. 'Then it's someone new in town I'm not aware of. Say ten Our Fathers and ten Hail Marys.' Outside, Pat was anxiously waiting. Seeing Mike, he asked, 'Well?' Mike smiled and said, 'We got two more leads. Mrs. Pearce and Mrs. O'Grady.'"

The silly joke broke up the sick patient who laughed so much he had a coughing jag. After talking together for almost an hour, Dennis began to show signs of being tired.

"It's time to let you get some rest. You have a good night's sleep, and we'll see you in the morning," said Dale.

In a low whisper, Dennis said, "It's great seeing both of you."

Dale and Johnny descended the stairs and rejoined Mary who had made coffee and sandwiches for them.

✳   ✳   ✳

Tuesday, March 23, 1993

Mary made a hearty breakfast, and both visitors were surprised to see Dennis at the dining room table. After breakfast they went into the living room where they talked about old times and Mary showed photographs from the Hughes' many family albums. About eleven o'clock Dennis asked to be excused and returned upstairs. He woke up shortly after one, and found the pastor sitting alongside his bed reading the Bible.

In a low whisper, Dennis said, "Hey, I'm not dead yet."

His remark took Dale by surprise. "You're awake. Good. We have to talk." Closing his Bible, he went straight to the point, "You know you're terminal."

"Where's Johnny?" Dennis asked, ignoring the pastor's statement.

"He took Mary to the store." Handing Dennis a newspaper article, he said, "Can you read well enough to look this article over?"

Dennis pushed it back, saying, "Read it to me."

"It's a short article giving the description of the man seen at the Carlyle Hotel the night Sergeant Tashino was killed. He's about six-one, slim, possibly gray hair, and carrying an overnight suitcase. Do you have something you want to tell me, Dennis?"

"Like what?" he asked.

"Where did you go when you left my home? And why were you so late?" Dale asked.

"Why're you quizzing me? You know I had an appointment with Doctor Jacobson. After the appointment I stopped to visit my cousin, Jim Doyle, nearby in Central Islip, and we talked for hours before I realized the time; it was getting near midnight."

"Let's talk straight, Dennis. You're terminal, so it's no use lying. You never meant to see Jacobson. Did you go to the Carlyle Hotel?"

"I thought Johnny was the cop. Who gave you a badge, Dale?"

"I've known you for over fifty years. You've visited my home dozens of times. Never once did you mention a cousin Jim Doyle. Did you go after Tashino?"

"What're all the questions for? You would think Tashino was a saint. The man should have been hanged in 1945. It's 'cause luck was with him that he lasted another fifty years or so."

"Dennis, what you tell me now is between pastor and church member. Level with me. Did you see Tashino?"

Dennis leaned forward and grabbed Dale by the arm and whispered, "I'm not stupid. Just why are you accusing me?"

"When I picked you up at the airport you were carrying a small black suitcase. You came to my house alone on the ninth and said you had an appointment to see a liver specialist at Stony Brook Hospital. Mary was supposed to be with you, but couldn't make the trip. Carol offered to drive you to the doctor. Then you gave Carol a cock and bull story that you had relatives living in Central Islip and would be visiting with them. You asked to borrow the car and begged off having Carol go with you. You didn't get back to my house until well past midnight."

Dennis interjected, "You can check with Mary. She was going with me until she received a call from our daughter. She had a miscarriage."

"I'm aware of that. I wonder if you didn't just take that as an opportunity to implement this other plan of action." Alexander continued, "When Carol and I saw you the next morning you had a cut on your forehead, saying you ran into a door in the dark. We wanted you to see a doctor and you refused. When the story came out in the newspaper describing a tall slim man wearing a hat and carrying a small black suitcase, I froze. After I thought about it awhile, I called Doctor Jacobson at the hospital and learned he never treated you, or for that matter, ever heard of you. Also, you and Mary have visited us many times over the years and neither of you ever mentioned any relatives on Long Island. The reason is because you have no relatives on Long Island."

"So, what you're saying, Dale, is because Tashino was killed the night of March 10th and I was not in your sights until sometime past midnight, then I killed him."

"I have more to say. The night of the reunion when we learned Tashino was alive, you questioned Fecke closely, regarding was he sure of his identification and of the names of the companies listed in the newspaper. Somehow you found out Tashino was going to be staying at the Carlyle—then you made your plans."

Dennis was smiling now. "Like I said before—you, not Johnny, should have been a cop. One thing for sure, you know how to interrogate."

"I thought everything over before accusing you. The only reason I'm telling you all this, is because I don't want you to die with this on your conscience."

"If you believe I murdered Tashino, why don't you make a citizen's arrest?"

"You're not listening to me, Dennis. Let me be your priest and hear your confession. Ask for forgiveness. As a Catholic, you were taught 'I shall not kill.'" Dale pleaded.

"You make me laugh, Dale. I haven't been to church since my wedding. Before that when I was growing up, the only reason I ever went was my parents made me. Besides, you can't hear my confession. You're not a priest. Let's drop the subject, Dale."

Ignoring him, but changing the subject, the pastor continued talking, "What about Hospice?"

"What about it?" a sarcastic patient asked.

"Have you considered it?"

"I don't need Hospice. I got Mary."

"You're a selfish man, Dennis. You say you love Mary, yet in your dying days, instead of getting help, you expect her to wash you, feed you, and wait on you hand and foot."

"She's my wife and doesn't mind doing it," he said stubbornly.

"You have to be at least six months terminal to get Hospice, but they'll have a nurse come in to feed and bathe you, read to you, and give Mary some time to herself. Once or twice a week a doctor will give you an examination. It won't cost you a nickel. You're under Medicare and your supplemental insurance will cover the full cost."

"I'll think about," Dennis replied.

From below they heard the sound of voices. Johnny and Mary had returned. Johnny took the stairs two at a time and came into the room with a smile on his face. Taking a chair and sitting alongside the bed, he said to Dale, "Now it's my turn to entertain. Dennis, did I tell you the one about the time Pat and Mike went to Sean Finnerty's wake?"

"No," Dennis replied, laughing.

Dale left the room and joined Mary in the kitchen. She was putting groceries away. You could hear Dennis laughing from the upstairs bedroom. Mary looked at Dale and said with a smile, "Johnny is the best medicine he's had in weeks."

✲   ✲   ✲

Tuesday, March 23, 1993

At 9:00 a.m. the team met in Kelly's office with Purcell on hand. Kelly, sitting behind his desk, started the conversation. "Dick has been informed that both witnesses picked out Dennis Donovan as the man they saw the night of the murder. Armed with the facts that our suspect's blood type matches the blood we found on the walking cane and the rug, the identification of the partial thumb print, and the statements given by both witnesses that he was seen on the premises the night of the murder, Dick will meet today with Judge Thomas to have a felony warrant signed."

Addressing the Assistant District Attorney, Kelly said, "Dick, take it from here."

The jovial attorney smiled and stood up. He began what he thought was going to be the biggest case of his career. "I'll have the warrant signed by Judge Thomas as soon as possible and it'll be on my desk this afternoon. Good hunting!"

✳   ✳   ✳

Wednesday, March 24, 1993

Unknown to the detectives, Dennis Donovan passed away in his sleep in the early morning hours before dawn. Hughes and Alexander stayed over to help with preparations for the funeral. Mary called all her children and made arrangements to have Dennis viewed at home the first day, an old Irish custom, then to Casey Funeral Home on Friday. Both Hughes and Alexander called home to notify their wives to catch the next plane to Boston.

Chapter 22

Thursday, March 25, 1993

At 8:05 a.m. Arena and Sanchez boarded Flight 333 out of MacArthur, heading for Logan Airport in Boston. Arena felt twenty pounds lighter, and was relieved, knowing the time and effort he put into the case was finally paying off. An hour later they picked up their rental car at Avis, with Joe Sanchez the wheelman and Frank the map reader. Needham, a city of about 28,000 people, was off Route 128 according to the map. As they drove along, Sanchez said, "Frank, my stomach is crying out for bacon and eggs. How about some breakfast?"

"Sounds good. Let's stop at the Needham PD first to let them know we're in town."

"C'mon, Frank, breakfast time will be over. I say we eat first."

"Okay, you win. Stop at the first restaurant we see when we enter Needham."

Sanchez spotted a Denny's. Without further consultation with his partner he pulled into the parking lot. As they walked in, he spotted a newspaper stand and bought the morning paper. "The Mets played the Braves last night. Got my fingers crossed they won."

They sat in a booth and were immediately approached by a bleached blond waitress carrying a container of coffee. "Would you gentlemen like coffee?" she asked.

Sanchez answered, "Do we want coffee? Does a camel want water? Pour darlin', pour."

She smiled and asked if they were ready to order.

"Bacon, eggs, home fries, and an extra order of toast for me."

Arena said, "Same for me, but just one order of toast."

Frank got out his reports and was rereading them while Joe was leisurely reading the sports section of the newspaper. Then he shouted, "Dammit, Tom Glavine beat us in a close game!" He read some more, and then said, "Frank, did you know Glavine came from Massachusetts? It says here he's from a place called Billerica."

Sanchez eventually turned to the front page of the local Needham paper. Suddenly he hollered out loud, "Holy mackerel! He's dead!"

"Who's dead?" asked a startled Arena.

"Dennis Donovan, the perp!"

Knowing Sanchez as a sometime practical joker, Arena said unbelievingly, "Right, Joe. Nice try. What you need is a cup of coffee."

"No shit, Frank. He croaked last night. Here, read it yourself."

Frank snatched the paper from Joe's hands and read aloud, "World War Two Hero Dies. Yesterday morning Dennis Donovan passed away in his sleep. Mr. Donovan was a wounded veteran who received the Bronze Star and served three and a half years in a Japanese prisoner of war camp. His ship was sunk in the Battle of Java Sea off the coast of Java. He will be buried Saturday at 10:00 a.m. at St. Joseph's Catholic Church in Boston."

Next to the short article was a photo of Donovan. Arena then turned to page six and continued to read:

"Dennis Michael Donovan passed away March 24th at his home on Cabot Street in Needham. He is survived by his wife, Mary; sons, Patrick of New York, Timothy of San Diego, Michael Jr. of Rochester, NY; daughters, Nancy of Milton, MA, and Virginia of Brockton, MA; and six grandchildren. Wake service will be held at 120 Cabot Street, Needham, this afternoon between 2-4 p.m. and at Casey's Funeral Home in Boston tomorrow afternoon between 1-4 p.m. and in the evening between 7-10 p.m. A memorial mass will be held on Saturday morning at St. Patrick's Catholic Church in Boston. In lieu of flowers the family requests donations be made to the American Cancer Society."

Frank looked over at his partner and whistled, "Wow, he was a heavy hitter."

"You can say that again. Can you imagine if this guy wasn't sick? We would have had to sneak him out of the state. So where do we go from here, Frank?"

"First, we finish our breakfast. Them I'm going to call Gore and dump this case right in his lap."

At 11:10 Frank dialed the office and got Gore on the line.

"Problem, Frank?"

"Big one, Jerry. The perp is dead."

"Oh, great. Give me the details," he groaned.

"Apparently he was carrying a heavy case of liver cancer for some time and it caught up with him yesterday afternoon."

"That's a bummer for you, Frank. You worked so hard on this one. You had no idea he was a sick man?"

"I should have picked up on it when Caputo told me that Donovan looked like death warmed over at the reunion."

"Without the man and no weapon, we're going to have to shit can the case. Get a plane out of there and let us know when to pick you up."

"I have a request, Sarge. I'm going to the wake this afternoon. Before I make any plans I want to see what the shooter looked like."

"I can understand your feeling. You work a case, live with it, and when it's over you feel like you lost something. The problem is, we're off tomorrow, so if you don't get back today I can't put you in for OT. The chief would have me by the throat."

"No problem. We understand. If we're a little late, we won't expect overtime."

After he hung up, Sanchez asked, "What's all this bullshit about overtime?"

"The boss wants us to head back home. I told him I wanted to go to the wake this afternoon and then head back home. If we can't get a flight today, we may have to go tomorrow. And since that's our day off, it would mean heavy OT"

"So why are we going to the wake? It's all over, Frank. Let's go home." Arena tried to explain, "It's like writing a book, Joe. When an author finishes, he's sad. He's lived with the characters and feels like they're a part of him. I've lived with the characters in the Tashino case, and I'm curious. I want to see what Dennis Donovan looks like."

"It's early. The wake doesn't start for a couple of hours. Let's call the airport and book a night flight before all the seats are full," Sanchez suggested.

They booked an eight o'clock flight and called Homicide headquarters and made arrangements to be picked up by one of the night team. With time to kill, and although all coffeed-out, they stayed on at the restaurant and ordered two more cups at the counter. Sanchez took a sip and said, "Life's funny, Frank. You work your balls off to get enough evidence to get a warrant, and then boom—it's all over. The perp leaves you hanging. He up and dies."

"I'm satisfied, Joe. The case wasn't a complete washout and we had to put it in the thirty-day file. At least we can close this one out and with no flak. The Japanese government will be happy. I don't know or give a damn how the boss will handle Newsday, as long as the Chief of Detectives and the P.C. know we did our job."

At 1:30 p.m. they asked for directions and headed for Cabot Street. As it turned out it only took twenty minutes to get there, so they parked a few houses away from 120 Cabot Street. The block was a clean residential one and looked like a middle class development on Long Island. Most of the homes were Cape Cod style and the residents kept up their properties. All the lawns were green and most all displayed spring flowers under the living room window or along the driveway. Several cars were in the driveway of the Donovan home and a few more were parked in the street. Sanchez remarked, "Funny having a wake at home instead of a funeral parlor."

"Years ago the Irish always held wakes at home. Donovan probably wanted it that way. Besides, tomorrow's the big one."

At 2:00 p.m. they locked their car and headed for the home of the deceased. Several other people entered the home at the same time.

A tall young man standing about six foot four, his face the map of Ireland, his eyes blue and his cheeks red, greeted them. He stood up straight and had a good speaking voice. Extending his hand to the two detectives and giving them a warm handshake, he said, "I don't believe we've met. I'm Patrick Donovan."

At a loss for suitable words for the occasion, Frank simply said, "We're police officers. We came to pay our respects."

"Very kind of you, sir. Won't you sign the book? Then, pointing to an open door, Patrick added, "The family's in the living room. If you would like to see them, just go on through."

The room was full, mainly family who had been there for hours. The coffin was by the far wall surrounded by wreaths of flowers. Sitting close to it was a lady in black, no doubt the widow. Arena recognized two men sitting close beside her, Pastor Dale Alexander and John Hughes. Quietly seated behind them were some young people and a few children.

The two detectives knelt by the coffin, each blessing themselves. Arena was thinking that the funeral home did one hell of a good job on Donovan. For a guy who was supposed to look like death warmed over, they had brought him back to looking human again. It was obvious he had been a big man by the size of his hands. On his chest were his bronze star and Purple Heart medals. What a waste, he thought; the widow should pass them onto one of her sons. Then, on second thought, maybe it's only for show and she will later. Donovan had a strong face, a Roman nose, and a full head of gray hair. Damn if he didn't fit the sketch Maureen Snyder put together from Miyako's description.

Others were behind them, waiting to pay their respects, so both Sanchez and Arena stood and saluted as police officers do for a fallen brother. They backed up and turned to leave. As they did, Alexander rose, excused himself to Mary, and followed them. Once out of the main room, he approached Arena, saying, "Can we talk alone, outside?"

"Why not?" the detective answered, and then followed the tall Alexander out through the kitchen door into the backyard. Dale, as a pastor, was wearing a gray suit and shirt with a white starched collar. In just a few seconds, Hughes also joined them.

"Thanks for meeting with us, Detective Arena."

"No problem. I'm glad you invited me. There's a few things I'd like to get straightened out."

"So have I, Detective. Why are you here?"

"We came to arrest Dennis Donovan for the murder of Oki Tashino."

"Since Dennis is no longer with us, can you tell me what gave you the idea he was the murderer?" Dale asked.

"Let's not play games, Pastor. Both of us know he was your houseguest the night of the murder."

"I never lied to you when you interviewed me at my house. I told you Dennis visited with me."

"That you did. But you never said he was gone until the wee hours of the morning."

"I really didn't think that was important, Detective."

"In my mind you were playing a game with me. What about when I showed you the police sketch? You said you never saw the man before. After viewing him his afternoon, I'd say the sketch was close to perfect."

"It was a good look-alike, I admit. Look at it from my point of view. I knew Dennis was a sick man, and the last thing he needed was to be interviewed by the police."

Johnny Hughes broke in and spoke for the first time, "Frank—you don't mind if I call you Frank?"

"No formalities," he replied.

"In all fairness, you showed Dale a sketch of a man wearing a hat and shades. Yes, put the hat on Dennis and the shades, and it was a good sketch—but not good enough for him to finger a man he considered a brother."

Returning to the pastor, Arena said, "Did you suspect Dennis?"

"Yes. I told him to think of me as a priest and ask God for forgiveness."
"I take it he never admitted it?"

"Not to me, he didn't. I had no real proof and probably was out of line accusing him. He's past all that now and with his maker," Alexander answered.

"What's next?" Hughes asked.

"We go home and put the case to bed."

"Since he's no longer with us, do you have to give this story to the media?" Alexander asked.

Hughes added, "It wouldn't be fair to his family. Losing Dennis was a hard enough blow."

"I can assure you the media will never get this story from Joe or myself. And judging from my telephone conversation earlier with my boss, the Bureau also wants to put it to rest."

Hughes decided it was time to change the subject. "Still want to go deep sea fishing with me, Frank?"

"Call me in a few weeks when things die down," Arena answered.

The foursome shook hands. Alexander and Hughes returned to the funeral parlor. Arena and Sanchez headed to the Logan Airport to turn in their rental car and head home.

❋   ❋   ❋

Monday, March 29, 1993—Five to One Tour

Returning to work after being off two days, Arena walked toward Kelly's office. He had been called at home and asked to come into work fifteen minutes early. When he arrived at the boss' office, Sanchez and Gore were waiting. Both of them also were advised to report early. The reason, to put the Tashino case on the back burner or, in police language, the dead file.

The tall, heavy-set, bespectacled commanding officer was in a good mood, and why not? The Police Commissioner at staff had given him an "attaboy" in the presence of all his peers. He, in his turn, now commended Arena and Sanchez on one hell of a job. "Although we still are carrying an open case, as far as we are concerned, it's a dead one. I gave the facts to Jim Neil and explained we had enough to arrest Donovan on a warrant, but a weak case unless we had an admission or a weapon. Since we had neither, Jim won't print the story, knowing his paper would have a helluva lawsuit from the family. As for Troy Pool, he was told to back off. The Japanese government was also notified we were closing the case, and they were quite pleased."

Arena responded, "I'm glad for the family's sake you're not giving his name to the media. I'm not condoning what he did. He's a murderer. But since he's dead, why bring slander to the innocent, his family."

For the first few hours after Kelly left, all was quiet. Sanchez was enjoying a hot cup of coffee when the phone rang. Joey Gentile answered. It was Sergeant Scull of the Third Squad. "We got a do-er for you in East Islip."

"What are the details?" Gentile asked.

"You familiar with an attorney named Beauchamp?"

"He's a well-known criminal lawyer."

"Seems he was away on business. When he arrived home this afternoon he found the front door wide open. He called out for his wife and got no answer, so he went into the bedroom. The window was open and his wife was lying on her back spread eagle. She'd been shot."

Sergeant Gore had been given the high sign by Gentile and was listening on another phone. He cut in and asked, "Norm, it's Sergeant Gore. Who's been notified?"

"Two Third Squad dicks are on the scene. Identification's on the way. The duty officers and the medical examiner have been notified. Now all that's missing is the Homicide dicks."

"What's the address?"

"Fourteen Kit Carson Drive. The house is right on the Bay, and from what the sector car operator told me, worth a couple of mil."

"I know the area. Notify the duty officer that Team Two of Homicide is on the way."

Placing the phone back on the cradle, Detective Sergeant Jerry Gore called to Joey Gentile, "Grab a set of keys. You're riding with me. Joe, you and Frank follow us in the Plymouth. We've got another heavy to roll on."

Chapter 23

Mid-April 1993

Three weeks had passed since the Tashino case had been put to bed. Arena was finishing up the last day of the day tour when Rubin, sitting two desks away, called to him, "Frank, pick up extension forty-seven. Some guy wants to talk to you."

It was Johnny Hughes. Pleasantly surprised, Arena asked, "John, how've you been?"

"Fair to middlin', as the old Yankee catcher, Bill Dickey, used to say. Remember I said I would take you fishing, old buddy, so how about it?"

"Wow, my weakness. No way can I pass up that offer. When?"

"Anytime. I go out almost daily, so you pick the time."

"Let me call home and check. I'm off tomorrow, and if my wife hasn't booked us, I'd like to go tomorrow."

"Go ahead and call her now. I'll stand by for your answer."

Eleanor answered on the second ring. "Ellie, it's me. You remember me telling you about a retired New York captain that offered to take me deep sea fishing?"

"Vaguely," she answered.

"I met him on the Tashino case. He was one of the prisoners of war men off the *Stuart* that served under Tashino in the POW camp."

"Yes, now I remember."

"The captain wants to take me out deep sea fishing tomorrow. What's our schedule?"

"You were supposed to do the lawn. Other than that, nothing. The following day we're going over to Marilyn and Norm's."

"So, I'm free!" Frank said joyfully.

"Frank, fishing is to you what gardening is to me. It's like a shot of adrenaline. Go fishing—and make sure you bring home some fish."

Frank went back to Johnny on the other line. "The ol' lady give you the okay, Frank?" he chuckled.

"It's a go, John. What time and where do I meet you and what do I bring?"

"I have the rods, the bait, a basket full of sandwiches, and a cooler of beer. I like an early start, so we leave at 6:00 a.m. I don't have to tell you how to get to the Mattituck dock. You've been here before."

Frank thought as he hung up, no doubt Security at the dock informed him that I was checking up on him.

Frank got up at 4:00 a.m., took a quick shower, then before going on the parkway he stopped on Deer Park Avenue in Sunset City in North Babylon for a hard roll with butter and a container of coffee. He took Exit 39 off Deer Park Avenue on the Southern State, getting off at East Islip, and then taking the Sunrise Highway. Traffic was very light going east, unlike west where most of the commuters were heading into the city of Western Suffolk or Nassau County. It was a free ride, no traffic lights until arriving in Riverhead. Once past Riverhead he went through Laurel, then Mattituck, arriving a few minutes before 6:00 a.m.

Hughes had the boat gassed up and running. "See you made it on time, Frank!" he called out.

As they took off from the dock with Hughes at the helm, it began to rain slightly and Hughes remarked, "It's April, Frank, and like the weatherman says, 'April showers.' Thank God it's only a mist."

Hughes guided the Hatteras through Peconic Bay. They passed Shelter Island, then Gardiners Island, past Montauk Point, and finally out into the Atlantic Ocean. The rain had stopped, the weather was in the high fifties, and there was a cool breeze. Hughes remarked, "It's a perfect day for fishing, Frank." Suddenly the boat captain stopped his engines and said, "This is a good spot, Frank."

Two captain's chairs were set alongside each other and there were several fishing poles. Arena picked one he liked, put on his bait, and was optimistically all set to haul in a load of fish. Hughes settled in alongside him. Hughes made the first kill—a bluefish. Frank followed with cod. Hughes certainly knew a good location; within the first hour both had two strikes.

"Hungry, Frank?"

"Starved. Something about salt sea air that pumps up my appetite."

"Take your choice, Frank—ham and cheese, or roast beef. And help yourself to a beer. We've got Heineken and Coors."

Frank helped himself to a ham and cheese sandwich and a Coors. He pulled the tab on the beer and took a big swallow. "Ah, that hit the spot." For the moment they forgot about fishing and enjoyed munching on their sandwiches and swigging beer.

Hughes brought up the Tashino case out of the blue, saying, "I know your department felt Dennis was the one who killed Tashino, but if you had arrested him it would have been hard on his family, especially since he was innocent."

Arena responded, "He committed a crime, John. If he hadn't died, no doubt he would be in prison now."

"Since the case is over, can you answer a few questions for me?"

"Sure. What're your questions, John?"

"It was obvious the killer left his signature, since he took nothing— leaving behind some valuable jewelry and cash. What evidence did you have on Dennis?"

"Putting the whole picture together, we had two witnesses that identified the police artist sketches, a partial thumb print and Type O Negative blood that matched Donovan, and, although we kept it quiet, Miyako, the secretary, told us someone took Tashino's silver swagger stick with his initials on it."

"Did you ever find the swagger stick?" Hughes asked.

"We figured Dennis took it, but no, we never did find it."

"So, the weapon was never found. The only thing missing was never found. And all you really had was a partial thumb print that came back to Dennis Donovan."

Arena interjected, "Plus the two witnesses that picked him out from the police sketch."

"It's just my opinion, Frank. But as a former cop, I doubt a grand jury would have indicted him on that skimpy evidence."

"Well, that's a matter of opinion, John." Just at that moment, Arena's line began to jerk and he shouted, "I got another one!" Hauling it in, he added another bluefish to his score.

Hughes was anxious to talk more about the case, and waited until Frank settled down once again in his captain's chair.

"I have a theory, Frank. Want to hear it?"

Arena was not really interested, but being polite, he answered, "What's your theory, John?"

Hughes postulated, "I believe more than one person was in the hotel when Tashino was killed. Dennis left Dale's home early. He headed for the Carlyle, arrived say ten or eleven o'clock, then booked a room for one day only, paying cash and using a phony name, say a name like Bill Linn. He did his homework, knew Tashino would be staying at the hotel, and knew he would be out for the evening. So Dennis waited in his own room that was also on the same floor, and felt maybe ten or ten-thirty would be a good time to knock on Tashino's door. Before leaving his room, he made sure the hallway was clear. When he knocked and no one answered, he tried turning the door handle and was surprised to find it open.

"He enters and finds the room lights on. And he spots Tashino lying in the middle of the room on his back with his eyes wide open. Dennis isn't wearing gloves, since he only planned to shoot the guy and then leave. So, although he's careful, in his shock he touches the cane. Then most likely he wipes it, but doesn't do a thorough job and leaves a partial thumbprint. Dennis, baffled, returns to his room, but doesn't leave right away. He waits until the wee hours of the morning. Since he has his car parked in the hotel lot, the doorman doesn't notice him when he leaves. He gets back to Dale's home before dawn, so as far as Dale and Carol know, he came home about midnight as he said he did. That's my theory."

"But, whoever killed Tashino had to know his expected time of arrival at the hotel and that he would be going to a business dinner and most likely return to his hotel room around 9:30. So, I can't buy your theory," Arena responded.

"Just my theory," Hughes said with a smile. "Let's forget the case and catch fish."

Both had another strike, then more sandwiches and a few more beers. Relaxing in his captain's chair, suddenly Hughes' line began to jerk hard. He shouted to Frank, "I got a really big one this time. Give me a hand."

The two professional fishermen maneuvered the line together. Hughes then hollered, "Frank, help! It's circling the boat just like a shark does! I think maybe we got one."

"I never felt a line this hard," Frank answered.

"Don't let it get too close or the line will snap. Get the gaff, Frank, and we'll pull it in the boat."

The big fish eluded him on the first try, but Frank eventually managed to get the gaff hook into it, and started to haul it in.

"Don't get too close to it, Frank. It can still take a bite out of you."

The big fish fought for a few minutes, and then finally the fight was out of him. Smiling, Hughes said, "Frank, you're my lucky charm. We just caught ourselves a Mako shark."

Catching the shark was a thrill for Frank. All in all, a very satisfactory and relaxing time. He also noticed during the course of the day, as even on off time a police officer is still observant, that Hughes was a lefty.

❉   ❉   ❉

At breakfast the following morning, Eleanor said, "How was your day yesterday? It was late when you got home, but why didn't you wake me?"

"We caught us a big Mako shark, took pictures at the dock, then John had it and the other fish we caught to a fish store he sometimes deals with to have them cleaned and filleted. I brought home some pretty nice pieces and put them in the freezer."

"Wow, you caught a shark," she said in awe.

"By the way, Frank, a package came special delivery for you while your were fishing yesterday. It's in the den on your desk."

Frank didn't hurry through breakfast. He continued to tell his wife about the fishing trip and especially the shark catch. When he went to the den, he saw the package, which was about two feet long and slim. When he opened it he found a long silver baton of some sort. It was quite heavy and had some Japanese lettering on it. He knew this was the missing swagger stick belonging to Oki Tashino. He sat there for a moment dumbfounded. Then he noticed it was mailed from Grand Central Station, one of the busiest places in the US, on the day before the fishing trip.

He recalled yesterday's conversation with John Hughes. At the time he had dismissed Hughes' theory as over-imaginative rambling—that two men went to the Carlyle separately but with the same murderous intention, and the one that succeeded in doing the deed was not Dennis Donovan. Could it be true? Was Hughes trying to tell him something in the way of a confession? Was he the one who had the package mailed? Or was he covering for Dennis and just trying to confuse the issue? Arena was confused. He knew he had to follow up with this as soon as possible.

He had promised Eleanor to mow the lawn, so he made short shrift of that chore and grabbed his car keys. "Honey, what time are we supposed to meet with the Sculls for dinner this evening?"

"At four this afternoon."

"I have to go out for a few hours, but I promise I'll be home by three at the latest."

"Oh, Frank, you have a habit of being late. Please don't embarrass me."

"You got my word, honey. I won't let you down. But there's something I've got to do that just won't wait." He was then on his way at ten o'clock to the Carlyle Hotel to get some answers.

DeMarco who was wearing his usual red uniform and hat with the gold braids greeted him. "Hey, Detective Arena. Back again?"

"You've got a good memory for names," Arena replied.

"Nah, only Italian names. Some others I may remember, but I never forget an Italian name."

A slim blond youth with a pockmarked face was manning the front desk. His name was Jim Gardiner, according to the nameplate on his chest. Arena asked to see Mr. Bauman, the hotel manager, and introduced himself to the young man.

"Oh, you must have been on the murder case here. I was off, but all they talked about when I got back was the murder. I'll just let Mr. Bauman know you're here."

Bauman was not happy to see Arena when he entered his office. "I thought the case was over."

"It is. I just have a few things to tie up, and need your help. On the day of the murder, March tenth, I need to see the log book."

"Sure, Detective. We keep them all for a year before sending them to the main office." He went to a closet and pulled the March log. "Be my guest."

Frank turned to the March 10th entries. He was only interested in the morning check-ins. He was not surprised to read the name of Bill Linn who checked in at 10:15 a.m. He noted that the clerk on duty for that time was Bill Gardiner. Handing the book back to Bauman, he said, "Did any of our detectives question Gardiner?"

"I don't believe he was here when your team came to the hotel."

"Can you explain that?" Arena asked sharply.

"Jim's grandmother passed away in Boston. He asked if he could work a half-day. I believe he left on the tenth at noon. He's the one on duty now if you'd like to question him in here. I have two others to cover for him at the desk." Arena nodded, and Bauman got on his intercom to the front desk.

Very shortly the blond youth entered, and Frank greeted him cordially. "How's your memory, Jim?"

"Pretty good, sir," he answered.

"The day you left at noon—do you remember how many single males you booked into the hotel?"

Jim thought for a moment, and then said, "Was that the same day of the murder?"

"Yes," Frank replied.

"I do remember two—an Izzy Horowitz and a William Linn."

"You do have a good memory," Frank said with a smile. "But how come it's so clear?"

"A private investigator came in about a week after the murder and showed me his identification and a gold shield. He wanted to know if any single men booked with me the morning of the tenth. I checked for him since the March book was still out, and like I just told you, I found two names—Horowitz and Linn."

Bauman, hearing this, gave the young clerk a look of disapproval and said, "Jim, you're not supposed to give out that kind of information."

Gardiner lowered his head and said, "I know, sir, but the man seemed bona fide to me. And I'm sorry, but I did give him the information."

"How old is Horowitz?" Arena asked.

"In his early thirties."

"Describe Mr. Linn to me," Arena requested.

"The first thing I noticed about him was his Boston accent. I asked him was he from Boston, and he just nodded. I guess he didn't want to talk. He booked for one day, paid cash. He must have been in his seventies, and he was tall and kinda thin and sickly looking."

"Now," Arena said, "describe this investigator as best you can."

"Well, he had a very likable personality. He was about the same size as Linn, over six feet. And his hair was white. He must have been around the same age as Linn, but was well built and looked healthy enough. He said his name was Ted McKrell."

"You say he showed you a badge?"

"Yes. It was gold, and looked like a police badge."

"Did he find who he was looking for?" Arena asked.

"No, sir. He claimed neither Mr. Horowitz nor Mr. Linn was the man he was after. He thanked me and left."

"Thank you for your help, Jim. That's all the questions I have."

After dismissing the young man, Bauman turned to Arena and said, "I'm going to have a serious talk with that kid. What he did was against all our rules and regulations in giving out that kind of information without checking with management."

Arena said placatingly, "He's young, Mr. Bauman. But a good talking-to won't hurt him; maybe he'll be more careful in the future."

"I thought the case was finished, Detective. Why more questioning?"

"It is all over, like I said—just wrapping up a few loose ends."

Standing, he shook hand with the Carlyle manager and thanked him for his cooperation.

✤   ✤   ✤

Returning to work on the night tour, Arena approached Sergeant Gore, sat him down, and filled him in on the conversation with Hughes on the fishing trip, receiving the swagger stick in the mail, Hughes dropping the name Bill Linn, the interview at the Carlyle with the clerk who booked Linn on the tenth, and the reason they missed being able to interview Gardiner earlier. The fact that there really was a Bill Linn who fit the description of Dennis Donovan, Gore listened carefully.

Absorbing all Arena had to say, Gore said, "I'd say this John Hughes is a piece of work. No doubt he pulled a fast one on us. Our artist drew what the witnesses saw. Both Hughes and Donovan look enough alike for it to be confusing to the casual observer. We have no proof whatsoever that Hughes was the murderer other than he practically admitted it to you. He has an alibi, which is a good one—but when you stop to think, he could really have docked anywhere and left the boat for several hours. As far as the department is concerned, the case is closed. Look at another way, Frank. Tashino beat the hangman's noose when he took the identification of a dead man, Koki Maehara. So he lived another fifty years. In my opinion he beat the odds anyway."

On the ride home, Arena mulled over his conversation with Gore. He agreed with him; Tashino was a butcher, and many suffered and died because of his cruelty. Why not "an eye for an eye?" After all, sixteen thousand Brits, three hundred Americans, and one hundred thirty thousand Coolies died building what the POWs called the "Death Railroad."

Epilogue

After Dennis Donovan passed away Dale Alexander became interested in the article he read to the big guy before he died. He had brought up the idea of a group trip to Thailand during the March reunion but was turned down. Most of them wanted to forget those POW days ever existed.

Every April 25th a commemorative service was held at the two graves of the POWs who did not survive the Death Railroad. The two gravesites were in the town of Kanchangburi. That was where they had lived in the bamboo barracks. Dale convinced Johnny Hughes to go by telling him they had never visited the grave of Tex Shulmelda. So, along with their wives Carol and Pam, the foursome flew from New York to California, then onto Tokyo, and finally arriving in Bangkok where they had rooms booked at the beautiful Oriental Hotel.

The wives were not too happy about going into the jungle, having heard so many stories of the past. To appease them, the couples stayed three days in the city of four and a half million, visiting the National Museum on the first day in the morning and the National Art Gallery in the afternoon. On the second day, they took a tour by boat, a must-do for tourists. And on the third day, they saw the area known as China Town by rickshaw. The wives wanted to stay longer, so the sailors promised them they would return a few days earlier from their visit to Kanchangburi.

Checking in with the tourist center, they were advised that the town in the jungle was no longer what they had departed from fifty years ago. After the movie, "Bridge Over the River Kwai," curious visitors to Bangkok took the eighty-seven mile trip to see the famous bridge that was used by the Japanese twenty months before they were annihilated by Allied warplanes in 1945. The Thai government quickly acted to have the bridge rebuilt. The merchants, hotels, and restaurants were built shortly thereafter, and today the town thrives on the tourist trade. During the incarceration the POWs were, as part of the brainwashing effort, told that the nearest city was five hundred miles away from their camp; in reality, it was very close.

The four departed by an air-conditioned bus at 9:30 a.m. on the fourth day and arrived at The River Kwai Hotel located in the center of town on Saengchuto Road. By noon both men were shocked to see how the area had changed—no bamboo barracks, native huts, or muddy roads. In their place were modern hotels, restaurants, and municipal buildings. After cleaning up, they had lunch and walked to the tourist office located on the same street as the hotel. The map showed many guesthouses in the town besides hotels; also, a police station, post office, banks, and museums to visit. One of the museums was out of town a short distance, and they were told it displayed articles and photos and was a must-see. Founded by a monk, it was called the JEATH War Museum. The letters stood for Japan, England, America, Thailand, and Holland. They were told that it might take them all day to visit the graves, since there were two graveyards containing about fifteen thousand headstones. The foursome took a cab to the JEATH War Museum that was housed in a bamboo building. For the first time, the wives of the two POWs were able to see how their men lived during that war fifty years ago.

Early on the second day in Kanchangburi they visited the War Cemetery. From the guide they learned that 6,982 headstones were in the graveyard. The wives had purchased several plants to place by the headstones. The guide checked for names of comrades and found only one, Tex Shulmelda. He showed them the location on the map, which was quite a distance away. Arriving at the site, they saw a man and woman placing a plant alongside the grave next to Tex's. Dale noticed by the headstone he was an Aussie. The four knelt, and Alexander took out his pocket prayer book and read from it. When he was finished, the ladies, who had each brought along a small spade, began planting their plants. Dale then asked the Australian, "Are you paying respects to one of your comrades?"

The Aussie, putting out his hand, said, "One of many, mate. I noticed the mate you're visiting is a Yank. What section were you in?"

"Section Two," Dale answered. "And you?"

"We were in One. I remember the day you chaps arrived. I don't want to upset you, but I doubt your mate is really in that grave. It doesn't matter. What does matter is the thought and effort put into it."

"Why would you say that Tex is not buried in this grave?"

"When they put our friends in the body bags, they attached the name and branch of service. I once had the detail to bury them, and half the tags were missing. The Japs never gave a damn. So when the war was over, the headstones were furnished by our government and yours, and then placed on the graves. Doesn't matter, mate. Like I said, it's the thought."

Dale didn't mention to the Aussie that Tex had actually been cremated.

By the time they left the Kanchangburi it was mid-afternoon. They decided to wait until the following day to visit the graves of other *Stuart* shipmates. In the evening they visited the bridge and the railroad, which was all lit up. The tracks had been restored that were bombed out, better built now with better equipment. The guide at the gravesite in Kanchangburi told them the second cemetery had 8,732 headstones, and gave them a map with names of the buried servicemen, and advised them if they could not find the headstones they were looking for to try a third cemetery outside the city called the Chong Kai War Cemetery.

After breakfast they set out to locate shipmates' graves in the second cemetery. They found a few *Stuart* sailors, and like the day before, brought along plants to put in the ground. As they walked pass the gravestones, an eerie feeling came over them. Hughes then said in a low voice, "Tex and our other shipmates have been alone in this Godforsaken hole for a long time."

Dale shook his head in disagreement and said, "Not alone. Tex and the gang have had plenty of company."

They found several shipmates' graves: Tom Brown, Sal Castiano, and Bernie Zeeman. Like Tex's grave, all three needed weeding. Once that was accomplished, the wives put the flowers in the ground. Dale opened his prayer book and the foursome prayed for the shipmates. Dale said a few words in Hebrew for Zeeman.

Throughout the walks were benches to rest. About halfway back to the main entrance, Carol said, "Let's sit for a while. The heat is getting to me."

There were two benches. On one sat an old Japanese man who appeared to be their age, in the late seventies. He was short and slim and wore thick glasses. He overheard some of the conversation between the four and, understanding the English language, realized that the two men had been prisoners of war. He approached them shyly and bowed, then spoke slowly and softly, saying, "Please, may I introduce myself? My name is Kyoto Tsutsumi. You were both prisoners of war, yes?"

Both men nodded. Then Hughes, looking at the short man who stood no more than five feet, barked out, "You were a Jap guard, weren't you?"

Alexander kicked him gently and took over the conversation. "Yes, sir. We were prisoners here during the war. My name is Dale Alexander." Waving his hand toward the others, introduced the wives and Johnny. "We're pleased to meet you, Mr. Kyoto."

"Tsutsumi. Kyoto then stated, "I was a guard with the Japanese army. I have come to pay my respects to the men who are buried here.

Please let me apologize to both of you for our treatment of you during your captivity."

Hughes was about to interject again, but Dale stopped him with a look that said, let me do the talking.

"It was a long time ago, Mr. Tsutsumi. We have all made many mistakes that we regret in the later years of our life. As long as we have repented and have asked our God for forgiveness, that's what really matters."

"Today Japan is a democracy, and the ancient systems we had before the war are all but gone. We were brainwashed by out leaders and, as you know, the Japanese soldier had no say whatsoever. If he did not please his superior, he was beaten."

Alexander stood and towered over the little gray-haired man. He asked politely, "May I call you Kyoto?"

"I would be honored."

"Are you a Christian?"

"No, a Buddhist."

"No matter what your religion, it takes a man to know he was wrong at one point in his life and admit it." With that, Dale bowed, and the Japanese soldier returned the bow.

Later, Hughes, true to form, smiled and said, "Dale, sometimes I think your religious ideas get in the way of your brains. I wanted to kick the little bastard's ass, like he once did mine."

Putting his arm around the jovial Irishman and returning the smile, Dale remarked, "Johnny, you're all talk."